W9-BSI-111

Texas Celebrity Turkey Trot

By Peter Gent

TEXAS CELEBRITY TURKEY TROT

NORTH DALLAS FORTY

Texas Celebrity Turkey Trot

A NOVEL

by PETER GENT

WILLIAM MORROW AND COMPANY, INC.
NEW YORK 1978

Grateful acknowledgment is made for permission to reprint the following song lyrics:

"If heartaches were commercials, we'd all be on TV," from the song "Come Back to Us, Barbara Lewis Hare Krishna Beauregard" by John Prine, copyright © 1975 by Walden Music, Inc., and Sour Grapes Music, Inc.

". . . be careful what you're dreaming/soon your dreams will be dreaming you," from the song "It's Not Supposed to Be That Way" by Willie Nelson, copyright © 1974 by Willie Nelson.

Four lines from the song "Brahma Fear," quoted on page 117, written by Jimmy Buffett, copyright © 1974, ABC/Dunhill Music, Inc. Used by permission only. All rights reserved.

"He may be dead but he's still mean/I wrapped him in the white and green . . ." from the song "I Buried My Dog in My High School Sweater" by Larry L. King and Gary Cartwright, copyright © 1977 by Larry L. King and Gary Cartwright.

"I felt the watchman's nightstick go sticky on my mind," from the song "Reality So Long," written by M. D. Shafter. Copyright © 1974 by Dr. Livingston, I Presume, Inc.

"Whiskey and pain both taste the same during the time they go down," from the song "The Torch Singer" by John Prine, copyright © 1971 by Walden Music, Inc., and Sour Grapes Music, Inc.

Library of Congress Cataloging in Publication Data

Gent, Peter.
Texas celebrity turkey trot.

I. Title.
PZ4.G33Te [PS3557.E45] 813'.5'4 78-17286
ISBN 0-688-03334-2

BOOK DESIGN CARL WEISS

Printed in the United States of America.

First Edition

1 2 3 4 5 6 7 8 9 10

All the characters in this book are fictitious;
and any resemblance to actual persons, living or dead,
is purely coincidental.

For Jo Ellen, Holly, Carter,
and Charles and Elizabeth.
With thanks to Sterling and Hill
and remembering Billy Lee
and trips in the Texas twilight.

Texas Celebrity Turkey Trot

PART ONE

THE END OF SOUTHERN CALIFORNIA TWO-A-DAYS

If heartaches were commercials,

we'd all be on TV.

CHAPTER 1

I DON'T KNOW WHAT IT IS THAT WAKES ME AT THIS TIME every morning, but I have been doing it since I was a rookie. That's nine years of Southern California summers, waking just before the trainer makes his rounds.

The first thing I see is the white plaster ceiling. I always sleep on my back with my legs elevated. It gives me low-back pain but keeps my knee from swelling. Down the dormitory hall I hear the squeak of Dobie's crepe-soled Riddell trainer's shoes. I always wake before the squeaks. I don't know why.

I wake up completely, instantly, my mind alert and functioning at full speed. I begin to concentrate on the day's challenge. It's a good feeling, a slight rush. It's concentration that keeps me intact and in this business staying intact is what it's all about. I believe in the psychology of the victim. Alert is not only a good feeling, it's necessary. You have to make your breaks and never let down.

Dobie Rank, the trainer, rattled the door open.

"LD, Mabry, get up. Breakfast at seven, the taping schedule is posted." He left the door open and moved down the hall.

I stretched and listened to him continue his wake-up circuit. He would finish waking all the veterans on the first floor and then climb to the second floor and start rousing the rookies.

Today is the last of two-a-day practices. Two-a-days are

tough, with the humiliation and the heat of eighty-five-degree Southern California days. We train in California because Texas summers are brutal.

"There's always a cool breeze here," Coach Buck Binder says reassuringly. Only a Texas football coach would consider an eighty-five-degree breeze cool.

The hardest thing about two-a-days is getting out of bed, particularly from the nap before the afternoon workout. Today is also cut day. Some guys can't stand the anxiety of waiting out the cuts. But anxiety is the price of living in the future, and I'll pay it.

"Aaahh." LD Groover, my roommate, stirred on the other bed. The ice pack slid from his knee to the floor with a muted splash. "Goddamn. My bones have gone soft." He pushed his six foot seven inch, 275-pound frame upright in the small twin bed and dug a thick finger into the blond curls that framed his square face. Wiping his huge hand across his face, he rubbed the sleep granules from his eyes. His bushy eyebrows needed combing.

This would be LD's tenth season. It should have been his twelfth, but he lost two years when Titus Bean did a *Sport* Magazine piece on LD's privileged military status. The article appeared during the Tet battle for the American Embassy in Saigon. There was a great public outcry over LD's duty tour as a Fort Sill swimming pool guard while yellow Communists shot up the diplomatic corps on TV. LD got shipped to Vietnam for a full tour. It didn't matter that his knees were no good.

LD tried to sit up in bed. He failed and fell back heavily. "Jesus, what a dream." He shaded his eyes with a massive hairy forearm.

"Lhasa Apso reruns?" I asked. LD has recurring dreams about being attacked by feral herds of Lhasa Apso dogs that hunted post-Armageddon tennis courts in North Dallas. They pounced on their victims like fuzzy piranha and could operate electric can openers.

"Yeh." The big tackle dropped his arm to his side. "This time they hijacked the team plane and we crash landed in Uganda." LD kicked off his covers and looked at his naked crotch. "Ah, the legendary piss hard." He began to gently fondle himself. LD jacked off a lot. He read Wilhelm Reich and considered it a cancer preventative. In our Dallas apartment is an old Coldspot refrigerator LD lined with rabbit fur. He masturbates in it to recharge himself.

"Predators are the dreamers." LD turned loose of his still-rigid cock to punctuate the moment. "It's the prey who suffer dreamless sleep."

Doors started slamming up and down the hall. LD switched on his radio.

". . . and it's sixty-five degrees in Port Hueneme. The pollution index in Los Angeles is a big 105 . . . that's unacceptable . . . and now the CB song of the day, 'God's Got His Ears On.' "

A phone rang down the hall.

LD leaned over and quickly snatched the receiver off the hook, leaving our phone disconnected. On cut day Buck calls players in their rooms and has them bring their playbooks to the coaches' wing. We disconnect the phone on cut day. It won't keep us from getting cut, but it will make it more difficult for Buck.

This year I am not worried about cut days. I am having my best camp ever and after today the practice schedule eases off. We begin exhibition season Saturday against the Rams in the Coliseum. I have made it through the hard part. We still don't answer the phone. It is tradition and superstition and has worked so far.

LD and I share a connecting bathroom with Alex Hart and Ezra Lyttle. Ezra was bent over the sink brushing his teeth. He was wearing only blue net bikini undershorts. He had gotten $5,000 and a rainbow assortment of underwear for modeling the jockey shorts in magazine ads. Ezra gagged as he brushed his tongue. He is always freshly shaved and sweet-smelling. He has good teeth, a perfect tan, a well-proportioned six-foot body, boyish good looks, and thick sun-bleached hair. He was one of the most famous and popular players.

LD pushed himself stiffly to his feet, staggered into the bathroom, and plopped down on the commode behind Ezra.

I balanced myself against the dresser and pulled on Bermuda shorts. I was aching tired but felt good mentally. I did a few deep breathers, some stretching, then pulled on a T-shirt and headed for the dining hall. My thongs slapped out a comfortable rhythm on the tile as I made my way down the dormitory hall. I was ready.

The dining hall was across the common from the dormitory. I fell into a stream of players clad in shorts, T-shirts, and thongs, heading for breakfast. The uniform was a response to the amount of dressing and undressing during two-a-days. The parade of men with shaved legs wrapped in Ace bandages, gauze, and tape made me feel doubly healthy. I work at it.

Quarterback Sonny Jeeter hobbled ahead of me with the aid of a gold-handled cane. The quarterback's left leg was swathed from hip to ankle in elastic sponge wrap. He and LD had been jacking around in practice and LD fell on his leg. That's how things happen, goofing off, letting down and not being ready. Those two always gotta have a laugh. They never do the weight stations right. I always do them right. I get great joy from performing a task well, and good conditioning is a safety factor. I am coachable. It's one thing Buck Binder likes about me.

Alex Hart, Ezra Lyttle's roommate and our number two quarterback, walked undamaged alongside Sonny, commiserating and smiling big. Sonny would be out four to six weeks. It was a crucial time to be injured. I wouldn't be surprised if Buck went with Hart this year. Sonny hadn't looked that good in camp. He was getting old and had been hurt a lot.

Sonny didn't look worried this morning, laughing and jabbing with his cane. He knew how to handle anxiety, he'd been doing it for fourteen years. This morning Sonny was psyching Hart, working on *his* anxiety.

"Since the sixth grade, I always been the leader," Sonny said to Hart. I walked behind them and listened.

Hart was easy to psych. He thought Sonny Jeeter had no idea how bad he wanted the quarterback's job.

I never worry about psyching somebody. I just never let down. I cover twenty receivers a season. Pro football is a year-around occupation, the whole biomachine approach, and I just continue to cover those twenty receivers all year. When I see them at the Las Vegas players' conventions I am their best drinking buddy, but I'm covering them. I watch films. I get clippings. I see them on television. I watch for clues—an injury, a wife leaving, or a bad investment—anything that tips me they're spending emotions, depleting themselves.

Two years ago at the Rancho La Costa Celebrity Golf Tourney my partner was a rookie tackle from San Francisco. On the back nine he mentioned that their split end had caught his wife with a black teammate. That October we had the 49ers at Texas Stadium. The first play I moved up into a bump-and-run across from the wide receiver.

"I hear your wife fucks niggers," I said.

The poor bastard jumped offside swinging. They tossed him out. See what I mean? You can never let down. The old killer instinct.

Ezra Lyttle fell into step beside me. He had jumped out of the bathroom window, his shortcut to the dining hall. It saved him several hundred yards a day but "Jumping out of windows" was down for $100 on the fine schedule in the front of our playbooks. Already this year Buck had fined Ezra twice for jumping out of the bathroom window. Ezra has the team record for fines.

"Hey, fool." Ezra clapped me on the shoulder. "When you gonna brush your teeth?" Besides the underwear ads Ezra had done an Ultrabrite spot last off-season and now he thinks people really do discuss dirty teeth and bad breath.

"I'll brush them after breakfast." The club bought me a nice set of porcelain caps after Chris Hanburger's headgear crumpled my face during an onside kick.

"How do you stand the taste?" Ezra peered into my mouth. His pretty open face had brought him the modeling jobs. He was considering an acting career and had spent the last off-season in Hollywood with his girl friend, Stormy Claridge. You may have read about Stormy. She won the talent competition at the Miss Texas Pageant a few years back and this year at the East Texas Rose Festival she was crowned Miss Massey Ferguson. Ezra said it was great for contacts. Ezra's big on contacts. So is Stormy. They are pursuing careers together.

"I couldn't stand it if I didn't brush my teeth as soon as I got up," Ezra said. The early morning air was chill and damp.

"I don't really care about your teeth, Ezra." I held the dining-hall door for him.

I picked up a tray and got in line behind a red-faced rookie tackle from the University of Michigan who all during yesterday's pass-blocking drill screamed, "Root hog or die!" LD knocked the shit out of him but he kept on screaming. It set everybody on edge.

"Stormy's sure acting funny lately." Ezra turned plaintive. "She'll say she wants to meet me somewhere and then not show up, and now she's talking about moving to New York. She wants a shot at a network job. She says she definitely doesn't want to get married until she finishes her reign as Miss Massey Ferguson."

Ezra followed me through the line, getting whatever food I got. At the end of the line I got three bowls of prunes. Ezra did the same. "I can understand, though." Ezra always tried to understand. "She wants to find out who she is."

"How about let's skin-search her," I said. "That oughta tell us who she is."

Ezra frowned at me.

One of the owner's kids checked our names off the breakfast list. Everyone had to attend breakfast between seven and seven thirty A.M. Absent was fifty dollars. Tardy was twenty-five dollars. The owner's kid sat by the steam table and checked names off on his clipboard. He was nineteen and planned to have his own franchise by the time he was twenty-five.

"I don't know what to do, man. Stormy's coming out tonight." Ezra followed me to an empty table and we sat. "I'm trying to get her on the Carson Show. I got a friend over there. She's gonna be at Hondo's party tonight. You're invited." Ezra looked blankly at his three bowls of prunes. "Where the fuck did I get these?"

The clatter of breakfast dishes punctuated a college fight song. The University of Michigan rookie was standing on his chair, hand over his heart, singing "The Victors." Today was the last hazing day. After tonight's Rookie Show survivors would be allowed to eat and suffer in privacy and silence.

"You guys eat with niggers?" Black running back Smoking Jim Stewart banged his tray down at our table.

"Only if we can't get chopsticks." Ezra poked randomly at his prunes.

Smoking Jim grimaced as he eased down. He had a chronically bad back.

"The Turk was up with the dawn." Smoking Jim made a slashing motion across his throat. "Costa is gone." He glanced around the room as he squeezed lemon into his tea. "Buck woke him up to cut him." Setting his tea aside, Jim quickly drank down one of his three glasses of orange juice. His plate was mounded with eggs and ham. Three glasses of milk backed the orange juice.

LD Groover slid into a chair and pointed at Smoking Jim. "You guys eat with niggers?"

"Only if they can't get chopsticks." Smoking Jim didn't look up from his food.

LD's tray was heaped with food and a rainbow of pills. Besides the anabolic steroids he took to bulk up, LD had vitamins, protein pills for energy, salt pills for fluid retention and muscle cramps, calcium pills to prevent pulls and strains, and papase for swelling.

"They cut Costa."

"I know," LD nodded, "I saw him packing." He scanned the busy room. "Anybody else?"

We all shrugged. Ezra popped a prune into his mouth, grimaced, and quickly spit it out. A clattering drone filled the dining hall with energy.

Buck Binder and the other coaches walked in from their morning meeting. "They gotta cut ten more." LD touched the red running sore between his eyes where his headgear wore away the flesh during butt-blocking drills. He would have the ulcer until contact work tapered off. Until then he'd just bleed and scab up. Most linemen had years of scar tissue knotted up between their eyes.

LD eyed Smoking Jim's full tray. "Say, ain't today weight day?"

Smoking Jim pointed to a bottle of laxative on his tray. "As long as I can shit as much as I eat, I'll be okay, turkey."

Early in camp Buck had Smoking Jim on the Fat Man's table, restricting his calories. At every meal Dobie Rank sat with him and monitored his food intake. After one week Smoking Jim had gained three pounds. Buck and Dobie were baffled until the dormitory fuses blew while Smoking Jim was fixing a pot roast in the microwave oven hidden in his closet. Buck fined him two hundred dollars.

I glanced around the dining room and tried to figure who would be gone by nightfall. As camp progresses it gets harder to pick the likely cut victims. Today I can count several rookies who are being fed and paid ten dollars a day to hold dummies, but each cutdown day brings its own surprises. There are only twenty-five rookies left out of the original fifty-six who came to camp.

Cut day makes this business lonely. But the intensity counters the loneliness. I love the competition and the adrenaline highs—the high of living on the edge matched against equally intense men desperate to live on the edge, scratching and digging for your place right on the brink. You feel and taste more on one Sunday afternoon than most people do in a lifetime and you don't have to wait years to find out if you are doing a good job. The hitting gets me off—the strange mixture of pain and power, the shock in their eyes when opponents realize they are overmatched. I give it all I've got. I never walk off the playing field confused or uptight. Eventually all that adrenaline burns up your circuits, but like LD says, "Good football beats bad fucking."

It is my fifth straight season without missing a regular-season game. Confidence is the key.

"Negative thinking never got nobody nothin'," Coach Buck Binder always says. "Confidence and discipline. Without discipline talent is useless." Discipline enables a man to come back from humiliation. In professional football, every player is continually coming back from the last time he got knocked on his ass.

I prepare for games by studying the scouting reports on the specific situations and players I have to defend against. I create the plays, take my keys, imagine my opponents' actions, fantasize all the possibilities. If I do a good job preparing, nothing happens in the game that hasn't already happened in my imagination. You have to be able to imagine yourself before you become real. Imagination is the soul of an athlete.

I figure I have five more years in me. By then most guys will be into selling insurance or used cars. The average pro career covers about four years. I've already doubled that because I take care of myself. I never waste energy or emotions.

I left the dining hall and walked across campus to the field house to get taped. The sun had burned off the fog, revealing the blanket of split-level houses covering the sand hills. In nine years of training camps I have seen the brown desert hills disappear beneath a sprawling suitcase town living off Los Angeles. When I first came here there was only a bowling alley. Now there are three shopping centers. My eyes burned. Smog had become a problem this far out in the valley several years ago.

A rookie passed me, heading back toward the dormitory, his eyes down and his shoes in his hand. I never did learn his name. Two down. They had to cut nine more to get down to the roster limit. The sun warmed me. It was a nice day. I like California.

At the field house I took a quick run through the weight stations, enjoying the loud clang of metal against metal. I felt good. I never listen to weight-lifting theories—they change every year. I just like to do it. In the training room Dobie Rank taped my ankles.

"Buck's going to Los Angeles." Dobie was slapping Vaseline on my heels. "He's dealing for another quarterback." The training room was a prime source of rumor. "The doctor looks at Sonny this afternoon. They'll probably cut on him. He's all through for this year."

I can't say I am surprised. After nine years you get a feel for things. You pick up little signs.

Back at the dormitory I told the news.

"That so." Ezra Lyttle was throwing darts at the target on the back of our door. He was shooting poorly and punching holes in the woodwork.

"I saw a brother in the lobby." Smoking Jim sat crosslegged on my bed. "Had his bag with him." He closed his eyes and flexed his shoulders, working on a kink in his neck. He jammed it yesterday during gauntlet drill. "He was a big muthah." Smoking Jim had perfect elocution and fell into dialect for effect. "I didn't recognize him."

"An unidentified big muthahbruthah quarterback to be named later." Ezra bounced his last dart off the edge of the board. "I doubt it."

"Stranger things have happened than a black quarterback." I had one foot up on the desk and was stretching out my hamstrings hurdler style. I felt real good.

"I wouldn't be counting the Big Fella out so soon." Ezra was gathering up the darts. Everybody called Sonny Jeeter the Big Fella. Ezra looked at me and held out the darts. "To fifty for ten?"

I nodded.

"I'll go first." Ezra quickly stuck his first dart just outside the bull for eight. He dropped his hand, fingers slack, and rolled up on his toes in a smooth follow-through. He didn't pull the string like a lot of guys.

A phone rang down the hall. Smoking Jim checked to see if our phone was off the hook.

"Mail call." LD barged through the door just as Ezra let fly his second dart. The dart struck LD in the chest. "Gaww-damn," the tall man bellowed. He clutched at his wounded breast and fell back against the wall. The mail dropped to the floor.

"I get that shot over," Ezra said.

"I'll give you the goddamn shot over." LD jerked the point from his chest and hurled the dart at Ezra.

Ezra stepped back and snatched it neatly out of the air. He had great hands and reflexes. He was a fine defensive half-back. He shot again and got another eight. Smoking Jim was on the floor searching through the mail. LD lifted his T-shirt and inspected the tiny hole punched in his chest next to his red-eyed black panther tattoo, a Saigon whorehouse souvenir.

Bob Doyle, a second-year quarterback from Tulsa, passed by the open door heading toward the coaches' wing. He was carrying his playbook. Three down.

"Fifty and out," Ezra announced as his last dart dropped neatly into the bull's-eye. He was up on his toes, his hand flopped down in a perfect follow-through.

"Don't I even get a shot?"

"First one to fifty." Ezra recited the standing rules and held out his hand for payment.

"I owe you."

A phone rang, closer this time.

"I wonder what we're giving up?" Smoking Jim sat back carefully on my bed and opened a letter from his lawyer. "For a Negro quarterback, I mean. They're worth more since *Roots*." He unfolded his lawyer's letter and studied it. "Well, I see what I'm giving up for my roots." Jim kept his eyes on the letter. His wife was suing for divorce again. "All of my gardening tools." The letter informed him that his wife had taken possession of his new cranberry combo Eldorado convertible and was demanding a look at the incorporation papers on Smoking Jim Stewart's Wig Rental. "Ain't that a shame. A damn shame." Jim shook his head and then rotated his shoulders, trying to ease his chronic neck and back pain.

"They ain't getting no black quarterback." Ezra sounded positive.

"Hi, guys." Backup quarterback Alex Hart strolled out of the connecting bathroom. Since breakfast he had changed into a baby-blue jumpsuit with "Alex" monogrammed over the breast pocket. His fuzzy slippers were a matching blue. Hart changed clothes several times a day.

"I see they cut Costa and Bobby Doyle." Hart puffed on his briar pipe. Except for the rookie quarterback from Auburn, Doyle had been Hart's only competition for Sonny Jeeter's job.

"Hey, turkey," Smoking Jim said, "put that stove out. We don't want to be breathing your poisonous gas."

Hart grinned and nodded and kept puffing on his pipe.

He had started smoking a pipe right after he "accepted Jesus Christ" on the same Texas Stadium stage with Charles Colson, Billy Graham and Larry Flynt.

The Sunday after that when Andy Russell knocked Sonny Jeeter out for two weeks, Hart figured it as divine intervention. The rest of us put the blame on Andy Russell. Russell was a proven performer on artificial turf. Anyway, now Hart calls Jesus Christ "the Big Fella." I don't know how that sets with Sonny.

"Who's the colored guy in the lobby?" Hart smiled at Smoking Jim.

"Buck's dealing for a quarterback." Ezra Lyttle was sticking darts into the desk.

"And that's . . . him?" Hart wobbled slightly and his eyes narrowed. Nobody responded.

The darts thunked rhythmically into the soft wood of the desktop. Thunk. Thunk. They burrowed into the varnish.

"A colored guy?" Hart's face turned confused, dark. He looked at me.

I shrugged. "Use chopsticks myself."

CHAPTER

THE EAST TEXAS ROSE FESTIVAL WAS HELD LAST SPRING IN that part of East Texas where the oil derricks enfilade the pine trees and unpretentious millionaires sit on the sprawling porch of the East Texas House Hotel and talk allowables and football. I didn't mind being there.

LD Groover, Ezra Lyttle, and I were all celebrity guests. The Festival Committee paid us $300 apiece to lead the Rose Parade in full game uniform, with headgear, riding on a twenty-five-foot horse made of Pat Nixon roses and powered by a Volkswagen engine. Stormy Claridge, Ezra's girl, recently crowned Miss Massey Ferguson, followed us aboard a Model 1400 self-propelled manure spreader covered in American Beauties. She looked great with that long blond hair and her full, firm, legendary lower lip. I can see why Ezra fell for her and I can see what she wants from him.

I met Farah Everett that night at the East Texas House. She was sitting at the head table next to me. Her husband, Jace Everett Junior, was sitting, short and fat, on her other side. Her father-in-law, Jace Everett Senior, the parade grand marshal, was the honored guest at the East Texas Chamber of Commerce Rose Festival Dinner.

Ezra and Stormy sat together on the other side of Junior Everett. Stormy was resplendent in her purple cape and matching "Miss Massey Ferguson" sash. Junior and Ezra were engrossed in each other. They were close friends. Stormy was licking her lips and smiling at LD, who was the master of ceremonies and was telling war stories about Vietnam and the National Football League.

The dinner was to honor Jace Everett Senior and to drum up political support for renewal of his Everett Enterprises' $35-million government contract to assemble all-terrain vehicles at its East Texas plant. The contract was threatened by the end of the Vietnam War. They held the dinner in conjunction with the Rose Parade for better media exposure. A hand-illustrated poster was raised behind the podium. It showed two G.I.'s who looked like Willy and Joe driving an Everett Enterprises ATV over two very dismayed-looking Orientals. The poster read "The Everett ATV is everybody's friend."

Farah Everett has dark sad eyes and is an example of the two things I look for most in women. She's beautiful and she's married. I don't like the potential for involvement that single women present. In my business women can be problems.

I try to be a controlled and contained person. It's how I survive. I conserve emotions. It's a long game. But with women I don't do what I should but what I can. My relationships with women quickly get out of control. I'll do whatever is necessary. The old killer instinct.

"So you play with LD?" Farah spoke. LD was finishing up as master of ceremonies.

I nodded, figuring my odds with a rich young wife. I decided to try a few light moves. Nothing serious.

"Are you good?" she asked. "I've never been to a game. I don't like crowds."

"I'm real good." I nodded. "I draw crowds."

"How marvelous." She clapped. "Wonderful . . . humble but realistic acceptance of his God-given talent." She clasped her hands tightly. "I must possess you."

It was a very sarcastic scene.

After dinner a band played in the ballroom. Junior Everett

and Ezra Lyttle disappeared to discuss a possible partnership in a Dallas sports-motif bar while LD danced with Stormy. She rubbed her crotch against his thigh more than necessary for good dance rhythm—behavior frowned on by the Miss Massey Ferguson Selection Committee.

It was near midnight when LD and Stormy slipped out during the reprise of "Mothers, Don't Let Your Babies Grow Up to Be Cowboys." Farah went over to Jace Senior, who was in conversation with the president of the Chamber of Commerce. She pulled her father-in-law off to the side and they talked in low tones. Jace looked over at me and nodded. Farah kissed him on the cheek and walked back to where I stood.

"I want to go to the Gulf. Come on." Farah swept by and headed for the door. I followed a few steps behind. In the lobby she made a phone call and when we reached the airport a blue Cessna 410 was warming up. The pilot was a Cuban named Raul who used to fly for Batista. He flew us to Corpus Christi, where a Cadillac limousine was waiting. The driver, a South Korean, took us across Nueces Bay to Aransas Pass, where we caught the car ferry to Port Aransas. On the island the limo wound through the deserted streets, finally depositing us in the underground garage of a condominium fronting the Intercoastal Waterway. When we got into the apartment I remembered I hadn't collected my three-hundred-dollar fee and had left my uniform and headgear at the East Texas House.

"I'm not supposed to bring anyone else here." It was morning. Farah was speaking from the bedroom. "But Jace said it was okay this time. I think he likes you." I sat on the big print living-room couch that faced the glass walls, the Intercoastal Waterway, the outer island, and the Gulf of Mexico beyond. The sparkle of the sun off the Gulf was psychedelic. Little spots of light flashed off my brain. The morning haze made the sky a white blue. I was barefoot and wearing only my Levi's.

A rusty red-and-black Russian tanker churned up the murky Waterway toward Baytown. At the tanker's rail was a tall blond man with a ruddy face and a broad flat nose. The tanker passed twenty yards off the condominium's boat dock. The man was less than sixty feet from the fourth-floor couch where I sat. The deck was about fourth-floor level. He smiled and waved. I shifted my Bloody Mary and waved back. He seemed like a nice enough guy. It was like I could reach out and touch him.

"You know him?" Farah stepped into the bedroom doorway. She was in panties and a T-shirt.

I shook my head and kept waving.

"Jace would think the guy was a spy for the Russian Olympic Team." Farah smiled. Her legs were brown and thin but she filled her panties and the T-shirt hung from her full breasts. The boat disappeared from view. The gulls settled back onto the oily wake.

A red excursion boat sputtered across the Waterway to the outer island and discharged a load of beach-scavenging tourists carrying beach umbrellas and metal detectors. In the sixteenth century Spanish galleons smashed into the Texas Gulf Coast in vain attempts to get the Incas' and Aztecs' gold back to Iberia. Now the part-time treasure hunters spread out across the beach in their leisure-time search for the treasure of the conquistadores.

The excursion boat sputtered back. I sipped my Bloody Mary. Farah sat next to me on the couch. I put my hand on her naked thigh. A porpoise made a jump on the far side of the Waterway and the gulls swirled in front of the fourth-floor glass. I leaned over and kissed the inside of her legs. She tangled her fingers in my hair, pulling my face into her. The smooth silk of her panties felt cool on my face. I wanted to devour her. She lay back on the couch as I knelt between her legs and she guided me gently into her with her delicate fingers. My climax began to boil in my stomach. As I started to spasm, a ship's horn started blasting. Another tanker was sliding by and several men were standing at the rail applauding and waving wildly at us. We were putting on a live sex show for a bunch of Greek sailors.

Later Farah rubbed my back. "You're very tense . . . too tense." Her full breasts made her look heavy. "A Rubens quality," Stormy had called it. LD had said she didn't look Jewish.

"You're so tight . . . tense . . . you're holding back." Her strong fingers dug into the muscles along my spine, sending ripples through my belly.

"It was a tough day at the office." My face was buried in a perfumed pillow.

"High performance?"

"Yeah, high performance."

"You're so wound up." She rubbed harder. "You're crazy, you know."

Farah sat up in bed that night in Port Aransas, crying.

"Don't put him in there. Please . . . my baby . . . my baby . . ." she sobbed. The left side of her face was twisted into a grotesque scowl and her left arm and hand began drawing up, clawlike. She was going catatonic. "Please . . . please . . ."

I shook her gently. She stared, sightless, over my shoulder, her lips drawn back, baring her teeth. I shook her harder.

"Please . . . please . . ." She started to sag.

I slapped her hard across the face. She rocked back, startled, and then blinked.

"What the hell?" She swung at me. She battered my head and shoulders with her small fists.

"Wait a minute. Wait, wait." I grabbed her arms. "You were having a nightmare."

"Is that any reason to slug me?" She wrestled to free her arms. "You stupid . . ."

I tried to explain. "I'm sorry, but you were crying and acting crazy." I continued to hold her arms; she struggled to be free. "I'm sorry. I'm really sorry. All right?"

She calmed some, but her eyes still flared. "Okay, I remember the dream." She relaxed. "Jace was taking Trey away from me. He wouldn't even let me visit him. He kept him in a cage out at the ranch." Her eyes brimmed with tears and her face twitched. "Sometimes I'm so scared of him." She laid her head on my chest.

"Good old Grampa." I put my arm around her and we slept that way. In the morning my hand was asleep.

It was cold and foggy that morning. We walked the beach on the outer island. We were the only ones without metal detectors. Farah was wearing a green L. L. Bean goosedown vest. It hugged her, giving dim outlines of her body. She had her hands jammed in the pockets. Her head was down. She kicked at the smooth pebbles littering the sand. Several stones scurried off in front of us.

"I read once"—I started talking—"that when George Allen was coaching the Rams he would walk the beach picking up stones and if he bent to pick up a stone he wouldn't straighten up without it."

"What?"

"Well, you know, if he went to pick up a rock buried in the sand and found more rock under the sand, he would just keep digging until he got it out. He wouldn't let that rock defeat him. He didn't care if it was a boulder."

"Or the Rock of Gibraltar?" Farah laughed. It was the first time she had laughed all morning. I laughed at her laugh.

She turned to look at me. "*This* is the kind of information you have about life? How marvelous." Farah laughed harder. "You sure are nonfunctional. Can't you do anything but play football?"

"I played a little basketball," I said. We walked silently for a while.

"This has to be a one-night stand," Farah said finally. "I'm leaving in the morning."

I didn't know whether to fault her for metaphor or for addition, but I knew what she meant.

"Okay," I said flatly.

"I've got other responsibilities." She smiled. "This was a nice interlude and I enjoyed it, but let it end right here on these oily shores."

"Okay. It's all right with me," I said. "I'm not looking for a relationship anyway. Are you?"

She shook her head and kicked at the pebbles.

"Long-term relationships are difficult," I said. "I have to maintain a certain mental and emotional tightness to do my job. If I leave any loose threads in my life there's always the chance the whole thing will unravel. I can't waste emotions. I'm already wasting them talking about it."

"I didn't know emotions could be wasted." Farah stopped and looked up at me. "Isn't it pretty childish to get so wrapped up in a job of football?"

"No." I was irritated by her brusque dismissal of my life. "It's my craft. It's a way to live. It's the only freedom I know. As long as my skills stay sharp and I do my job for three hours on a Sunday afternoon, the rest of the time I can be myself. Who do you know who can do that?"

"You have to make room in your life to have people you care for," Farah said. "It's not magic. You have to create the space for someone else. Sure that takes energy and emotions, but it's your fault if you haven't got them to spare. You must be very lonely."

"I'm alone but not lonely," I said. Actually I was both. "Besides, I thought you were the one crying one-night stand."

"Well, I just wanted you to know there was no future in it. You haven't any power. It's power I need for me and the boy." She softened. "But that doesn't mean it's healthy to suppress your emotions. I should know." The wind whipped up off the ocean and we turned our backs to the water. "And that doesn't mean we can't be friends."

"I don't make friends very easy."

"Maybe it's because you expect too much."

"I've learned that you can't blame your friends for not being what you expect," I said. "Besides, I don't know how to be friends with rich people. My daddy worked nights in a foundry and days on a hundred fifty acres of poor ground. When I was a kid he told me that going to a job you hated for twenty years was being a man. At forty he had his first heart attack and started drinking because it depressed him. Now he's had three and lives in a house trailer outside Bob Wylie, Texas, with my momma, who's got Mamie Eisenhower bangs and hypertension. The heart attacks and booze got the farm. That's where I come from. I'm blue-collar poor people and I'm just trying to stay even as long as I can."

Never before had I seen my life so clearly.

"Well, you sure are testy." Farah stared back into the wind out at the water. "I'm not going to compare family trees with you, but my mama wanted me to be a beauty operator. She had a shop next to the ice house in Fabens."

"How many chairs?"

"I do like you, Mabry." She laughed. "But you're crazy, you know."

That was the second time she said I was crazy, but she said it so sweetly I took it as a compliment.

"You should open up more," she said, smiling at me. "You might find some peace."

"A peaceful man can't make a living forcing end runs or pushing hot metal."

"Well," she said, "I've got a son whom I must protect. I'd rather no one knew I brought you here."

A gull sailed by so close I could have jumped and knocked him down.

"Listen, I can be trusted." I was tired of discussions of

relationships and discretion. They have never been my strong suits. "That's one thing about me. I'm coachable."

It was getting colder.

I sprinted off about a hundred yards down the beach. It felt good with the wind rushing past. I'm pretty fast. I've always been good at physical things. I'm an athlete.

Another tanker was heading up the waterway. A swarthy man threw buckets of garbage overboard. The sea gulls zeroed in on the floating refuse.

That night in Port Aransas Farah didn't have a nightmare. When I woke in the morning she was gone. I had to walk back to the car ferry and hitchhike to the Corpus Christi Airport.

At our apartment in Dallas, LD was drinking beer on the couch with Stormy Claridge. Stormy's Lhasa Apso dog was between her legs, nuzzling her crotch. Stormy was writhing in some sort of ecstasy.

"See why I got nightmares about them things." LD pointed at the nuzzling Lhasa Apso. "They'll eat a person up."

We had stayed two days in Port Aransas, but it's not common knowledge. It gives me an edge over LD, who ended up with Ezra's girl. I don't know what Ezra and Junior did except that they are going into the bar business together.

It was all out of control.

CHAPTER

ALEX HART, EZRA, AND SMOKING JIM HAD GONE ON AHEAD. I waited for LD to wrap his knee for the walk to the practice field. We had to go through the lobby. It was a fifty-dollar fine for using the closer north corridor exit. Coach Buck Binder's sign on the door read:

"$50. There are no shortcuts in life."

In the lobby a gaggle of just-cut rookies stood awkwardly waiting for somebody to drive them to the airport. Their bags were piled by the door. They were embarrassed.

"I got a buddy with Pittsburgh," a defensive back from Grambling said to no one in particular. "I'm calling him."

"Hell, there's always Edmonton."

"The rosters are already set in Canada."

"They just don't know I'm available."

"You was always available. You just didn't know it."

They all laughed. There were six of them. Two more to go.

We walked across the dormitory parking lot. "I think I'm having a good camp," I said.

LD grunted and limped along beside me. His thongs slapped loudly on the asphalt with a rhythm different from mine. The day was starting to get hot.

"No kidding, I feel great." I did. I turned and backpedaled up the street and back. I made light tentative jabs to each side.

"You are obviously mistaking me for someone who gives a

shit." LD winced and stopped walking to rub his knee. "God-damn, I'm gonna get me some cortisones."

"No shit, man, I'm having my best camp ever."

"Famous last words." LD shook his head and resumed limping toward the field house. " 'I'm having my best camp ever.' 'The check is in the mail.' And, 'I promise I won't come in your mouth.' "

Bobby Doyle, the just-released Tulsa quarterback, came out the field-house door with his Adidas in his hand. His jaw was tight and his eyes were red. He waved at us but looked down. His lips were a tight line.

Inside, on a rubbing table, Alex Hart was holding a cold compress to his chin. The cloth was blood-spotted. Ezra Lyttle was climbing into the whirlpool. He grinned at us and pointed at Hart. "Bobby Doyle knocked his dick in the dirt."

"He suckerpunched me," Hart whined.

"They ain't no such thing as a suckerpunch," LD said. "Just the first and the last punch. In some fights they're the same." LD had stripped off his shorts and was fondling his genitals, assessing their size and shape.

"If a guy can't take getting cut, he shouldn't play the game." Hart inspected the compress and then touched his chin. The bleeding had slowed.

Dobie Rank walked in with a bandage for the quarter-back's split chin. Hart tilted his head back as the trainer applied the bandage.

"Bobby said Hart was a queer Christer." Ezra's head floated on the whirlpool's roaring white water. "A queer Christer quarterback." Ezra liked alliteration.

"Any man who won't fuck around on his wife is a queer to you guys." Hart shifted his jaw tentatively. "My woman's enough for me."

"Keep still, asshole." Dobie was struggling with the band-age. "I don't care if she picks nickels outta your hand with her snatch"—the trainer fastened a heavy gauze pad to the quarterback's chin—"you still might need stitches."

"I'm okay." Hart eased off the rubbing table and walked to his locker. He rubbed his jaw. "Goddamn chickenshit suckerpuncher."

Alex Hart hadn't fucked around on his wife since the party for the guy who went in the trade for Ezra Lyttle. That night Hart got drunk and let some groupie suck him off while the rest of us watched. By the time the porno films were running Hart was eaten up with remorse and apologized loudly, interrupting a great scene with a blond girl and a spotted hog. He finally got sick and passed out in the bathroom. Later, the whole offensive line went in and pissed on him.

I stripped and climbed on the scales. The rule was to weigh in before and after every workout and to enter it on the big chart. The fine for failure was fifty dollars. I had forgotten the day before, but LD had written it in for me. LD is last out of the locker room after practice because he soaks his knees in ice water to control swelling. He always checks the weight chart and fills in for anyone who forgot. LD saves a lot of fines.

Smoking Jim walked in from the training room with gauze and two rolls of elastic tape. He began to tape his ankles. It was a five-hundred-dollar fine if you sprained an ankle that you taped yourself. Smoking Jim had been taping his own ankles since high school.

"Full pads . . . full pads . . . full pads. . . ." Buck Binder marched through announcing the equipment of the day. "Full pads . . . full pads. . . ." His voice faded off as he disappeared through the training-room door.

"Shit." LD yanked his shoulder pads off the wall hook where he had hung them to dry last night. They were still damp from sweat. He shivered. "Goddamn, I'll bet we got pass rush." He slammed the pads to the floor, building emotions for drill.

I felt an anxious ripple through my stomach. Early in camp I like to hit to show the rookies who is boss and to remind any of the veterans who might have forgotten in the off-season.

But this late in camp there's no percentage in it. If you haven't convinced anybody by now it's too late.

LD filled a cup at the water cooler and washed down a pill. "Good morning, gentlemen." The deep, measured voice of Dr. Stanley Friedman filled the cement-block room. Dr. Friedman was a psychologist from Stanford. Buck hired him to administer psychological tests and to counsel us into more productive attitudes. It was like artificial respiration. Out go the bad neuroses, in go the good neuroses. Friedman was friendly, outgoing, and good for a few prescriptions.

"What do you think, pal?" Friedman put his hand on my shoulder. I was seated, trying to pull on a sock without having to bend over.

"You've got a lot of energy blocked that I could free up for you. I could make you All Pro if you pick a positive mode. I can help you control those emotions." He gave my shoulder a farewell pat and strolled into the training room.

Everybody wants to control my emotions.

Friedman and Buck both believed in the universal verities of positive thinking. I like Friedman well enough, but I can't wholly trust a man who makes my welfare his job. I know what a man will do to keep his job. Yesterday we had discussed my biorhythm. He said I was going critical.

I was suddenly tired. I could use that energy Friedman said he could free up. I hope we don't have full-speed force drill. It always gives me a headache. I took three aspirin and went out.

We walked to the practice field across the last undeveloped sand hill in the valley. "We'll get Jace Everett, his astronaut buddy George Billings, and Hondo Higgins all on the Celebrity Board of Directors." Ezra was explaining to LD his ideas for the sports-motif bar. He was trying to convince LD to join him and Junior Everett.

"Jace Junior is going to sign up his daddy and I'll take care of Hondo. We'll call it Ezra and LD's Celebrity Bar &

Grill. With those names on the letterhead we'll get all sorts of free publicity. I talked to Titus Bean and he says he'll do a story on the place for *Texas Monthly* if we get him drunk and laid. He's a good contact." Ezra felt good contacts were important in life.

The warm wind slapped sand in our faces. The sun was heating things up—I could feel it bouncing off the ground against my naked shins. Ezra stopped walking and knelt down, adjusting his new kangaroo Riddell game shoes.

"I hope I don't get blister from these." He was breaking them in before Saturday's game with the Rams. He adjusted the heel lock. "Junior's hired a guy from Disneyland to do the show bar. He designed the ride through the human endocrine system. It's a bee-u-tee-ful ride. You guys been to Disneyland?" Ezra snapped his chin strap and looked at LD and me.

We shook our heads.

"You guys never even went?" Ezra was dismayed.

Ezra went to Disneyland when we stayed in Anaheim before the Super Bowl. "It's an unbelievable place," he said. "You gotta see it . . . Mickey and Goofy just walking down the street . . . it's amazing. . . ." His tone turned serious. "You know, if we hadn't been in the Super Bowl I never would have seen it myself."

During Super Bowl week newspapers around the country carried a UPI photo of Ezra walking past the Matterhorn arm in arm with Mickey and Goofy.

"Why don't we just open a bar?" LD asked. "We don't need no designer."

"We need atmosphere, man, atmosphere." Ezra rubbed his hands together gleefully. He grinned, showing his perfect teeth. "We're gonna be dealing with a class crowd. With Hondo Higgins and Jace Everett on our letterhead we'll draw 'em in like flies."

"Like flies is right." LD growled and swung his pads over his head. They clattered onto his shoulders. I helped him pull on his jersey. As he seated the massive headgear, the gray rubber crossbars obscured his rugged face. "Listen, man, I don't want a buncha rich assholes hanging around, I jes' wanna drink and watch pussy."

"You won't care about pussy when you look at these." Ezra reached into his headgear and extracted a folded piece of paper from the suspension webbing.

"I always care about pussy." LD banged his helmet with his fist.

Ezra handed the paper to LD.

"What's this?" LD opened the paper and held it up to his face mask.

"The projections, man, the projections." Ezra pointed to the paper. "Look at that bottom line. That's the monthly net . . . projected."

"Fifteen thousand dollars," LD whispered. "You mean we'll net fifteen thousand dollars a month?" He was shocked. I was shocked.

"Sure will, man, and that's conservative." Ezra took the paper back and replaced it in his helmet. "Junior worked up these figures. We'll be paid off in no time." Ezra and Junior were borrowing $500,000 to start the Celebrity Bar & Grill. "We got Willy Roy Rogers and the Blackland Farmers for the opening."

The last time I had seen country singer Willy Roy Rogers was at a party at Sonny Jeeter's house. The evening ended when Sonny's wife threw Willy Roy out for pissing in the kitchen sink.

"Willie Nelson and Waylon Jennings may come up opening night." Ezra paused and scratched at his chin strap. "I'd sure like to get them on the Celebrity Board of Directors."

We topped the sand hill and started down toward the practice field. "Oh-oh," LD said. He pointed to the top of the coaching tower. Buck Binder was watching us through binoculars. We broke into a trot. Walking was a twenty-five-dollar fine. Buck kept the binoculars on us until we entered the practice field, ran the compulsory lap, and split up. LD went off to hit the blocking sled. Ezra and I ran the ropes, then picked up a ball, played catch, and stretched our legs.

Buck, still on the coaching tower, blew his whistle to start practice. He announced through his bullhorn that we would have a full scrimmage. Then he fined LD, Ezra, and me twenty-five dollars for walking to practice and fined LD an additional twenty-five for carrying his pads halfway. Even with his binoculars Buck hadn't seen my unfastened chin strap (a twenty-five-dollar fine).

Nobody was happy about the scrimmage. Guys got hurt in scrimmages. LD was furious about the fine. I accepted it all as dues. I can control *my own* emotions.

Buck put us through unusually long team exercises. He enjoyed giving grass drill and really ground us through the "ups and downs." We must have hit the ground fifty times. I stayed all the way.

We broke into offensive and defensive teams. Buck came down off his tower. Buck Binder had been cornerback in New York and being a target toy on Manhattan Island during the lean years had left its mark.

During our practices Buck would stand about twenty yards behind the secondary and never say a word unless we got beat deep. Buck couldn't stand to have his secondary get beat deep and if somebody did Buck would cuss him out in a whisper. Out-loud profanity was a twenty-five-dollar fine. It was eerie. Buck would walk back to the huddle, his arm hung loosely around the player's neck in a show of camaraderie, all the time whispering the vilest of insults. Yesterday he hissed that I was "a goddamn scum-sucking pus bag" because I let Billy Carr get behind me on a play action pass. Getting beat deep in Yankee Stadium must have been a horrible experience for Buck.

The offense took the ball on the twenty and Alex Hart was at quarterback. Sonny Jeeter was in the stands with his bandaged leg elevated. Hart ran an EGO sweep right at me. Billy Carr, the flanker, cracked back on the outside linebacker and I had the force. I charged up to meet the two rookie guards, looking over their mountainous bodies into Smoking Jim's bright eyes. The running back keyed himself for the results of the collision between me and five hundred pounds of crazed rookie. I took the outside away and planted to take the blow on my left shoulder. After contact I would spin to the inside and make the tackle. I took the lead guard's block on my shoulder and was making my spin when the second guard hit me just below the knee. I went down under both guards. Smoking Jim cut inside, but LD, pursuing from the tackle, hit him at the line. The crash could be heard out to the freeway.

Somewhere on the sidelines the rookie from U. of M. was screaming "Root hog or die."

"Now, that's good force action." Buck Binder was standing in the center of the huddle, a freshly lit Camel clenched between his teeth. He was grinning and had one eye closed against the smoke. In New York, before the league rule against it, Buck had been the national spokesman for Camel cigarettes. Buck's face adorned a Times Square mechanical billboard and every sixty seconds the whomperjawed rendering of Buck's lips would suck at a six-foot Camel and blow perfect nine-foot smoke rings out over Manhattan Island. It was the peak of Buck's career.

"Good force action." Buck repeated himself.

I rotated my arm and tried to work the soreness out of my left shoulder. Forcing end runs was dirty and dangerous. The willingness to crash was the difference between those who made it and those who didn't.

Buck Binder was the greatest force man of all time. In his twelve years he had dislocated both shoulders and had arthritic spurs on his cervical vertebrae the size of marbles. Once, in Cleveland, Buck hit Jimmy Brown head on. Both their helmets split down the middle. Brown bounced off and got six more yards. Buck got a headache for the whole month of October.

"The secret of a good force man," Buck said, "is not

minding that it hurts." Buck swiveled to look at the offense and then called a 31 strong-side zone. Since his neck went stiff Buck had to swivel his whole body to look to his left or right.

When Hart put the tight end and flanker to my side it made me the short man. At the snap I rolled up on the flanker and cut him at the line of scrimmage. I jumped back to my feet and was covering the flat.

Hart couldn't pick up his secondary receivers (he didn't have Sonny's cool) and tried to lay off on the opposite side to a rookie split end who was confused and drifting. Ezra was in a man-to-man with short help. He closed and snatched the ball out of the rookie's hands and ran thirty yards into the end zone, holding the ball over his head. The whole defense cheered.

As Ezra returned to the huddle Buck spoke in a soft voice. "Ezra," Buck said gently, "hotdogging is a twenty-five-dollar fine."

The remainder of the scrimmage was fruitless for the offense. They never got beyond midfield, while we intercepted three more of Hart's passes and LD Groover recovered two fumbles and made life miserable for the running backs and offensive linemen.

Near the end of the scrimmage Hart broke out of the pocket on a short run and I hit him at the sideline. He tried to spin free and I twisted his legs pulling him down.

"Goddamn you, Mabry," Hart yelled. "You're not supposed to tackle the quarterback."

I had wrenched his knee twisting him down. He was mad. I held tightly to his legs to keep him from kicking me. Finally he stopped moving and I released him and rolled away, getting quickly to my feet.

"Fuck the quarterback," I said.

Hart threw the ball at me and missed.

"Come on, you guys." Ezra got between me and Hart. They were roommates and friends. Ezra liked for everybody to get along.

Buck gave me a rest. I sat in the bleachers in front of Sonny and watched the remainder of the scrimmage. Sonny was enjoying Hart's inability to move the offense.

"I don't think Alex understands that football has become a game of centimeters," Sonny said.

Ezra Lyttle, working at my right corner spot, piled up the on-side guard and totally destroyed the running back on a power sweep.

"Goddamn," Sonny said, "that sonofabitch can hit. But not like you, Mabry . . . the old destroyer."

"What do you mean, old?"

Sonny laughed.

Buck ended the practice with twenty windsprints and five "Whoas and goes" the length of the field. Ezra threw up on the way back to the field house. The sweat inside his headgear had caused Junior's projections to run together.

The unidentified big black muthahbruthah quarterback never showed.

In the locker room Buck announced he would replace afternoon practice with a meeting and would extend curfew after the Rookie Show until one A.M. "as a reward for some good hitting."

On the way to the Pub for a few beers before lunch we passed the topless bar on San Bernardino. The marquee read:

NUDE COEDS WRESTLE IN THE MUD. WED. NO COVER
BIG SCREEN FOOTBALL. L.A. VS. DALLAS SAT. $1.

"Tell me television don't make or break a sport," LD said, lighting up a cigarette. Ezra was flicking the radio dial, trying to find the right station. He loved country and western music.

Sonny Jeeter's rented Cadillac convertible roared past us and pulled into the small stucco shopping strip that housed the Pub. Smoking Jim was at the wheel. Sonny and Smoking Jim were standing beside the car when we pulled up.

The Pub was dark and we banged through the furniture up to the bar.

"The studs are here early." Agnes, the owner-operator of the Pub, was behind the bar. It was eleven thirty A.M.

LD ordered two pitchers of beer and several glasses of ice. We pulled two tables together and set to drinking as much iced beer as possible before lunch.

"I sure hate cut day." Ezra sloshed beer into his ice-filled glass. "It depresses me." He took a long drink, wiped his lips, and frowned. "I'd sure like to do something for Costa."

"Costa who?" LD said.

"Costa who? That's good." Ezra smiled wryly and drank his beer.

"Nobody can do nothin' for nobody. Costa knows that. It don't make him any happier, but he knows it," LD continued.

The two pitchers were empty and Agnes brought replacements.

"Leave those two," LD instructed as Agnes set the full pitchers down. "Take these two." He handed her the empty pitchers. "And I'll hold these two until you get back." LD grabbed her large breasts. Agnes smiled wearily.

"Don't let your mouth overload your ass, LD." Agnes turned away from LD's groping hands.

LD and Agnes had a sexual relationship that extended over several training camps. During their first encounter LD reached orgasm while trying to put on his rubber. They were in the back seat of the Mercedes LD had borrowed from Dr. Friedman. Later LD told Friedman that the stains on the fabric were Rorschach tests. "It's a German car, ain't it, Doc?" LD said, like that explained everything.

Sonny and Smoking Jim challenged LD and Agnes to a game of bumper pool for shots of tequila. They left Ezra and me at the table.

"Did I tell you that Hondo wants Stormy in his next movie?" Ezra asked.

I nodded.

"She's coming out tonight. There's a party at Hondo's."

"You told me."

Ezra didn't say any more. He sipped at his iced beer and drew patterns on the wet tabletop. Ezra Lyttle looked sad. I don't know why, he had a great scrimmage.

Ezra Lyttle came to Dallas in a trade with New Orleans for our kicker Louie Rodriguez. It was at Louie's going-away party that the offensive line pissed on Alex Hart. The trade had worried me because Ezra was a right cornerback and a good one. But Buck moved Ezra to the left side and we became friends. Ezra had an uncanny clairvoyant ability and would often badger Buck Binder to put him in with me on kickoff or punt returns and then respond with a sensational runback. Last year he took a punt all the way in the final two minutes of the Redskin game when we trailed by three.

I yelled at him to let it go because it was inside the ten. You never field a punt inside the ten, there's no percentage in it. Besides, it's a hundred-dollar fine.

"Watch this," Ezra yelled back as the punt sailed toward us through the dirty Washington sky. He went ninety-five yards for a touchdown. It was an unbelievable run.

But Ezra is also cursed with colossal bad luck. Once, after eluding the entire Minnesota punt coverage team and heading in, Ezra turned to check pursuit at the five, twisted his ankle, fell down, and fumbled the ball out of the end zone. Minnesota got the ball on their twenty and won by three. Dr. Friedman had a field day with plays like that. Ezra and Friedman weren't on very good terms.

Friedman said that it wasn't bad luck but that the years playing for John Mecom Junior had damaged Ezra's mind. "After all," Friedman had said, "in football what is a fumble but a specific type of psychotic episode?"

Ezra disagreed. "I just want to win," he said. "I just get too uptight—it kills me when I let the team down. I love these guys. I can't sleep for nights afterward."

I thought *that* was psychotic.

"I just want a normal successful life," Ezra said.

"That's not possible, Ezra," Friedman said. "If you're successful you're not normal."

Ezra had been successful in everything. He was a Rhodes Scholar and an All-American.

"Play for things," Friedman told him. "Play for money, power, or women. Play for women, that's a good one. But don't play this game for success. The NFL is a place for misfits . . . evolutionary losers."

"What do I need things for?" Ezra's daddy was president of a gas and oil production company in Midland.

"I forgot you are a rich kid," Friedman said. "You shouldn't be playing at all. You're taking somebody else's place."

Ezra never liked being called a rich kid.

Sonny let out a whoop as Smoking Jim made a difficult bumper shot to beat LD and Agnes. LD paid for the round of tequila and aligned the balls for another game.

"Did I tell you Stormy's coming out tonight from Dallas?" Ezra sipped at his beer.

I nodded, watching Agnes drop her break shot. She had nice follow-through.

"Hondo's having a party." Ezra was still drawing patterns on the wet tabletop. He sketched a cock and balls.

"You told me."

Sonny and Smoking Jim beat LD and Agnes again. They all drank a shot of tequila and came and sat down with Ezra and me.

"Did I tell you guys about Stormy coming out?" Ezra asked.

"You told us twenty times," LD said. "And Mabry here has told us twenty times that he's having his best camp ever and I say who gives a shit?" LD grinned, pulled off his hat with "Farm Bureau" on the crown and ran his thick fingers through his blond curls. "Aggie, hon, brang us some more a that cactus juice."

We drank heavily until time to leave for lunch.

Ezra ran out of gas on the return to camp. He always does something like that. We piled into Sonny's car and arrived in time. The owner's kid was all set to mark us late. The little prick.

In the food line LD trapped the rookie from the University of Michigan against the milk cooler and filled the pockets of his Bermuda shorts with mashed potatoes and sliced carrots. Eyes glazed and reeking of Cuervo Gold, LD kept the rookie transfixed. "If you say 'Root hog or die' anymore, you dumb sonofabitch," LD growled, "I'll rip off your head and shit in your neck."

Buck Binder's wife had flown out from Dallas and was sitting in the front row at the Rookie Show when two hairy asses were thrust between the curtains and farts resounded through the auditorium. The acoustics were perfect. Buck's wife beat a hasty retreat.

"There's such a thing as good taste," Buck growled as his wife left.

There would be reprisals.

It was a standard Rookie Show, with all the jokes about jock straps, nigger cocks, and jacking off after lights out. A new generation of pro football.

As we were leaving the auditorium Buck called Smoking Jim Stewart off to one side.

"Oh-oh," LD said, looking back at the two men talking. "The Turk."

I glanced back. Smoking Jim's eyes were fixed on the floor. Buck put his hand on Jim's shoulder. The big running back was being cut. We were down to roster limit.

It was the end of Southern California two-a-days.

CHAPTER 4

THE PARTY WAS AT MOVIE STAR HONDO HIGGINS' SPRAWLING ranch-style house stuck on the side of Benedict Canyon a couple of miles off Sunset Boulevard.

We borrowed Sonny Jeeter's Cadillac because Ezra's car was still out of gas. LD was at the wheel. Ezra guided us to the Beverly Hills address. We pulled up to a high gate.

"Who is it?" A voice crackled out of a small black box attached to a tree near the fence.

"LD Groover here. The meanest muthah to ever come outta Muleshoe. I've got my friends with me and we're here to do some long toking and short stroking."

LD wasn't from Muleshoe.

There was a buzz and the gate swung open. A pack of giant Doberman pinschers chased us along the asphalt drive winding up the canyon wall. LD quickly rolled up his window.

The house sat on a ledge hewn out of the canyon wall, overlooking the road. LD guided the car through a second gate and pulled onto a parking apron lined with everything from motorcycles and Jap cars to painted vans and land yachts.

A pretty blond boy in a Hawaiian print shirt waited to park the car. We walked around the garage and onto the flagstone patio. People were scattered across the half-acre patio and around the pool.

After being around football players I'm always surprised by the size of regular people. They're tiny. We split up, having already learned that a herd of giants at a party often spawns unfair stereotypes. LD strolled toward the bikini-lined pool. I drifted aimlessly through the little groves of midgets. I was looking for Farah Everett.

I like Beverly Hills parties. The people aren't easily shocked and they like professional athletes. I guess it's because we bleed publicly and do our own stunts. They respect our style of theater. Sonny Jeeter calls himself "the real Burt Reynolds."

After the Ram game Saturday the locker room will be filled with celebrities. They're always fun to see on our turf.

Next to a thick planting of bird of paradise was a studio mockup of a Conestoga wagon. It served as a bar. A small Cuban dressed like Marlon Brando in *Viva Zapata* poured me half a tumbler of Sausa Commemorativo. I waved off his offer of lemon and salt. I don't like to get my fingers sticky early in the evening.

"Hello, Mabry." Sportswriter Titus Bean stepped alongside me. Titus was in California covering our training camp. "How you doing?"

"Fine, Titus. Fine. I'm having my best camp ever. How about yourself?"

"Still on the trail of truth." Titus smiled. He had dark circles under his eyes and his face looked puffy.

"You must have taken a wrong turn somewhere in New Mexico."

"LD still mad at me?" Titus was wearing bleach-faded jeans and a Levi jacket.

"What do you think?" I said. "You almost killed him for a good by-line."

"That was years ago. Somebody ought to tell him grudges are unhealthy."

"So was Vietnam. What have you heard from New York?" I asked. Titus and I had plans to collaborate on a book titled *So You Want to Be a Pro Football Star*.

"Nothing yet, but it looks good. Doubleday is hot to do it.

We just got to get the numbers right. Say, how are your contract negotiations coming?"

"Everything is great, couldn't be better. I'm having a great camp."

"Me too." Titus smiled and ordered a triple tequila. "I got a story so hot right now that if I break it first it means a Pulitzer. There's a cover-up of a massive food contamination in Texas. The Department of Agriculture, the Farm Bureau, and the FDA are all involved. Everybody in the state has been poisoned. It's in all the meat and dairy products." Titus drank his triple tequila like he was thirsty. He ordered a backup, then became quiet and seemed worried.

"This contamination thing is just like with LD," he said finally. "Do you think I want to know I'm contaminated and going to die of some horrendous cancer?"

"You sound like you're already poisoned," I said.

"Life is poisonous." Titus shook his head.

"What are you doing here at Hondo's?" I asked. "I thought you'd be at Buck's press briefing."

"Hondo wants to talk to me about writing a screenplay. A porno musical."

I like Titus. He's strangely plausible, but he makes me nervous. I guess it's because everything he raves about ultimately comes true. On the trail of truth, he got out ahead of it and hasn't noticed yet. I left Titus at the Conestoga-wagon bar for a closer look at the starlets by the pool.

Hondo Higgins stepped out of his house onto the patio. Stormy Claridge was with him. They circulated through the crowd. Hondo shook hands and hugged people in the classic Beverly Hills *abrazo,* making sure they weren't packing. Hondo looked big from a distance. He has a large head and it was easy to make out his facial features—the drooping moustache, cold blue eyes, and thin aquiline nose.

Every day, clothed in a Nudie's Western suit, movie star Hondo Higgins drove his Ranchero, with a bale of hay in the back and a Hereford Breeders sticker on the bumper, to the Twentieth-Century lot, where he administered his own production company. He was the perfect Beverly Hills cowboy.

Last year Hondo won two Emmys, one for producing a TV movie about a black rodeo cowboy with sickle-cell anemia and the other for his starring role in his long-running series *The Texas Ranger.*

In its five-year run *The Texas Ranger* held the record for on-camera pistol whippings. Hondo had dual roles in the series, portraying both the grandfather, a Texas Ranger at the turn of the century, and the grandson, a modern-day Texas Ranger. After the third commercial every Friday he would tire of "criminals freed on legal technicalities" and resort to the proven technique of pistol-whipping. The series traveled through Texas Ranger history, the common threads being Hondo's dual roles and affinity for pistol-whipping the shit out of thieves, murderers, Mexicans, and carpetbagging Yankees. It must have been a genetic thing.

"Hondo's gonna be on our Celebrity Board of Directors." Ezra and LD stepped up beside me. We watched Ezra's girl and the movie cowboy circulate through the crowd. "Stormy's already asked him."

Stormy and Hondo walked up to us. The soft wet flesh of Stormy's full, pouting lower lip quivered slightly with each step.

"This is Hondo's estrangement party," Stormy said. "His wife took the kids and left. We're celebrating tonight."

Hondo nodded.

"We went to Esalen for a whole fucking weekend to try and save the marriage," he said. "It cost a bundle but we got into this fantastic all-night group . . . young executive types, hippie types, housewife types, all there to let go and confront the truth." Hondo smirked and smoothed his moustache. "About four in the morning I fall out, start crying, and confess the other women, the lies, the whole bit. It felt great.

Everybody's hugging me and talking about breakthroughs and cosmic consciousness." Hondo looked at each of us. "Why not? I paid my money, right?"

We all nodded.

Hondo shook his head. "My wife was *so fucking mad* she filed for divorce as soon as we got back to L.A. She expected the truth to be better news."

"Hon, that's too bad," Stormy said, "but put it all out of your mind. Tonight's your night. I want to make sure you have a good time. Right, Ezra hon?"

Ezra nodded and smiled.

Stormy stripped off her wraparound skirt and tossed it aside. She wore a leotard and tights underneath. "Let me show you the dance number that won me the Miss Texas talent competition." Stormy began cavorting *a cappella* about the ridge. Her moves were a combination of the Fort Worth Junior Ballet and amateur night at the Spot 77. Bounding through the flowers, Stormy alternated between dainty pirouettes and humping the citrus trees. She finished with a running leap over some bags of potting soil and landed on one knee at Hondo's feet.

Hondo was enthralled. I was enthralled.

She pulled a card from the bodice of the leotard and handed it to Hondo. "File this for when you're casting that porno musical."

LD and I applauded.

Ezra began talking to Hondo about joining his Celebrity Board of Directors. Stormy gathered up her wraparound skirt and she and LD wandered off to look at the garden.

I sipped at my tequila and watched the party, looking for Farah Everett.

She was near the pool, talking to a small man in Levi's and a western shirt. Farah looked great in a red-and-white striped boat-neck sweater and white pants. Her feet were bare and her eyes were still sad. I was glad to see her.

She smiled as she saw me approach across the crowded patio.

"Even though I promised I wouldn't, I missed you," I said. "Especially on the walk to the car ferry."

Farah laughed softly and glanced around.

I noticed a couple of additional lines around her eyes. The skin beneath seemed darker.

"Well, how have you been?" Farah gripped my hand.

"Fine," I said. "I'm solid. How about yourself?"

"The same old things. I've got to get Trey ready for fourth grade. Spend the rest of my time buying diamonds by the yard down at Neiman's." She grinned. "We're coming to the game Saturday. It's the first professional football game I've ever seen. Do something exciting, will you?"

"Sure, I'll take a lot of bennies."

The slight man in Levi's and western shirt laughed. His bowlegged stance could best be described as cocky. He looked familiar.

"Mabry"—Farah pointed toward the small man—"Billy Bentson here says he knows you."

"Shore do." Billy Bentson stuck his hand out. "Hidy, Mabry boy, hidy, hidy." We shook hands.

I met Billy Bentson when LD was off in Vietnam and I was hanging out in Forth Worth pinball bars with a couple of Seventh Street car dealers and an overweight insurance salesman called Big 'Un. Billy Bentson was a small-time Fort Worth hustler, gambler, and part-time heist man who was trying to graduate to big-time gambling and a good string of whores. I had played a lot of pinball with Billy.

"Billy and Junior met at the sailboat races on Eagle Mountain Lake," Farah said.

"My powerboat broke down." Billy was a Fort Worth speedboat cowboy. "Lucky for me Junior was there." Billy knew a mark when it sailed by.

Billy grinned at me and winked. He had moved up a couple of gambling notches. I didn't ask about the whores.

"Junior's looking for you." Billy hooked his thumb toward the greenhouses at the top of the hill.

"All right." Farah turned and headed up the ridge toward the greenhouses.

"Follow at a safe distance," Billy said to me, smiling. "You don't tell on me, I don't tell on you."

A small stone staircase led from the back of the house up through the terraced garden dotted with citrus trees to four large greenhouses set on the high ground.

I watched Farah and Billy Bentson climb up the flowered canyon wall and absently rubbed my neck. Tightness from my shoulder had moved into my neck and given me a slight headache. I must have bruised my shoulder during the scrimmage. I rolled my head from side to side, grinding the spurs on my cervical vertebrae. My neck popped loudly and the tightness eased momentarily.

I drank down my tequila and got a refill before attempting the climb. I seldom drink, but when I do I drink heavily. "Binge drinking," Dr. Friedman calls it.

It was a steep climb and my knee was sore when I reached the top. Billy Bentson was talking to Junior Everett. Farah nodded in time to Billy's gesticulations.

"Mabry," Billy hailed me, "come here and say hello to Jace Everett Junior and his wife."

Jace Everett Junior had a flat, wide face framed by tight, curly black hair. He was thick bodied, about average height, and had unusually short limbs with thick, stubby fingers. LD said that Junior married Farah because his arms were too short to jack off. LD knew him from the University of Texas before Junior transferred to Princeton.

I shook hands with Junior. His fingers were too short to grip. He inserted his hand in my palm and I pumped his arm a couple of times.

Junior was wearing a flowered body shirt, unbuttoned to reveal a white, hairy chest. He had a lot of gold chains and medallions around his neck and he jingled when he moved.

"I believe you know my wife."

"We met at the East Texas Rose Parade." Farah took my hand.

Junior held what looked like a Bic disposable lighter up to his nose. He pressed on the side and snorted, repeating the process with the other nostril. "Try this." He passed the gadget to Billy, who did the same. They both stood around grinning and snuffling. It was a cocaine machine that delivered premeasured snorts. Junior offered the machine to Farah, who declined. I followed her lead.

Junior put the machine in the front pocket of his tailored hip huggers. A small chain and solid gold fob in the shape of a clenched fist dangled from the pocket. Billy and Junior snuffled and grinned at each other.

The two men nodded and smiled. Farah moved between Junior and me and leaned back against me, pressing into my crotch.

"Like I was saying . . ." Junior spoke to Billy. His tiny Gucci shoes peeked from under his flared cuffs. "We buy this lease and we get the rights all the way down to 10,000 feet. I can steal it from this old boy."

"It sounds like a good deal, but I'd rather have my money bet on cards," Billy said.

Billy slipped me a sly wink.

"You help me get some people in on this oil deal and I'll play you some gin," Junior said, "only this time I'll win."

Farah started to rock against me ever so gently.

Farah was slowly grinding into my crotch. Junior continued to talk oil deals. Billy Bentson grinned at me. I was slack-jawed.

"What you all doin'?" Ezra Lyttle topped the stairs.

Farah moved away from me quickly and I almost fell forward. Ezra went directly to shake Junior's hand.

"Just talking, old buddy," Junior said. "Daddy's agreed to be on our Celebrity Board of Directors."

"That's great, Junior." Ezra was excited and pleased. "I think I got Hondo lined up."

My knees were about to buckle. Farah had her compact out and was touching up her eyes and watching me in the mirror. My underwear felt sticky.

Ezra turned to me. "Junior owns Rock On Productions in Dallas. They're setting up the show bar. We're getting everything at cost."

"Anything for my buddies." Junior smiled. "Say, don't call me Junior, okay?" Ezra nodded.

Farah smiled at me. Billy Bentson was rolling a Bicentennial half dollar over his knuckles.

"You all seen Stormy?" Ezra asked.

"She and LD went inside," Junior replied. "He needed a button sewed on."

We all fell silent on that one and gazed down at the party in progress. The famous and near-famous swirled around. It was a powerful sight from the ridgetop—beautiful young men and women laughing and drinking. A warm breeze ruffled the citrus trees and an orange thumped to the ground. Ezra stared, openmouthed, his breathing audible. Stepping back from the edge, he turned to me. There was wonder in his eyes.

"Damn," he said. "This must be what it's like to know Sylvester Stallone."

I nodded and Farah laughed.

It was time to go back to camp.

Missing curfew was a thousand dollars for the first fifteen minutes and five hundred dollars per hour thereafter. Buck considered it a preventative rather than punitive fine. Ezra was the only player ever to miss curfew and get caught. When he reported the next morning he handed Buck his Master Charge card.

Ezra drove. He was mad at LD and Stormy. They had disappeared for over an hour and when they returned Stormy had her leotard on inside out and LD's shirttail was sticking out of his fly. Ezra showed his anger by driving Sonny's Cadillac through Hondo's gate. He crumpled the right front fender and turned all the Dobermans loose. We drove down Sunset at ninety miles an hour.

I lay down in the back seat. LD sat up in the front and began hooting and yelling.

I closed my eyes and tried to rest. If we crashed, we crashed. Tomorrow was getting close. I wished I hadn't drunk so much tequila.

LD lit a cigarette and began assuring Ezra that he and Stormy had only been swimming and that's why their clothes were in disarray. Ezra said he believed and trusted both Stormy and LD. They made up and decided not to tell Sonny what happened to his car.

"Deny everything," LD advised. "Ask him who he believes, you or his lying eyes." They both laughed.

LD sighed and locked his hands behind his head and started tapping his foot. Nobody spoke the rest of the drive. LD tapped his foot the whole way.

Five minutes to curfew we pulled into the parking lot. Ezra got out and walked quickly to the dormitory.

"I like that boy." LD watched Ezra. "People can say what they want about dumb jocks, but there ain't no better people than athletes." We crossed the asphalt parking lot. "At least we all believe the same fantasy. Those other assholes, I don't know what they believe"—he shook his head—"but they're all failed athletes and that makes them dangerous."

I stopped to rub my knee, which had gotten sore during the evening. It felt tight.

"Man," LD said, "we got a job to get done."

I don't know what he meant by that.

Inside the dormitory was the usual night-off chaos. In the lobby somebody had written "Buck Binder Sucks" on the blackboard and pinned a huge pair of women's panties on the bulletin board. "Tuesday" was scrawled in pink across the crotch.

There had been a water fight. Overturned wastebaskets littered the hall and the floor was covered with water.

Ezra Lyttle stepped into the hall, pressed a finger to his lips, and signaled us into his room. "You guys ain't gonna believe this," he said. Ezra's roommate, Alex Hart, was passed out in bed with the sheet drawn up to his chin. Beer bottles littered the room. Sonny Jeeter was sitting on the other bed, grinning.

"Alex was unhappy about the scrimmage," Sonny said, "so he got drunk and picked up this old whore and brought her back here through the window." He pointed to the bathroom window, Ezra's shortcut to the dining hall. "He screwed her while a bunch of us watched from the bathroom. When she wanted to go home Hart told her to go fuck herself and passed smooth out." Sonny smiled. Ezra looked at his roommate and shook his head. "Smooth-talking sonofabitch."

"What happened to her?" LD asked.

"I don't know." Sonny shrugged. "I went down to say goodbye to Smoking Jim. She was gone when I got back. But look at this." Sonny held up the sheet with two fingers. In the center of Hart's tan, muscular chest was a huge turd. "She shit on him." Hart stirred slightly and whined in his sleep, then he smiled.

"That's the biggest turd I ever saw." Ezra whistled softly.

"Well, now Alex is a man," LD said. "He's been pissed on, shit on, and punched out. Who says this ain't a tough game?" LD turned and walked through the bathroom to our room.

LD lay on his bed with his hand in the front of his shorts. The television was making warming-up noises.

"Ain't that a bitch?" He pointed toward the next room.

"It's the coast, man." I sat on the bed and pulled off my boots. "The coast is the most."

"Fuck the coast," LD growled and reached beside his bed

for his copy of *The Sexual Revolution: The Function of the Orgasm.* Before LD went to Vietnam I never saw him read a book.

I pulled off my Levi's. My knee was swollen to about twice its normal size.

"Sonofabitch," I said. "Look at this." I worked the knee and could feel the fluid squishing through the joint. There was a dull ache.

"Better get some ice on it." LD peered over the top of his his book. "Get me some, too."

I was in a panic. Injury is very disorienting to me. I limped into the bathroom, where we keep a styrofoam chest filled with ice and beer and Dr. Pepper. I grabbed a couple of plastic bags off the floor and filled them with ice. I tossed one bag to LD, then lay down and put the other bag on my swollen right knee.

"Do you feel any chips?" LD asked, watching me massage and probe the knee with my thumb.

"I dunno, it's too swollen." I grimaced, fighting panic more than pain.

A Hondo Higgins rerun flickered onto the television screen. Hondo was pistol-whipping a Mexican who looked just like the bartender at tonight's party.

"I'm not letting them cut on me again." I lay back and tried to relax.

"Don't worry, man," LD said, "Dr. Badd try and cut you, I'll turn the fucking mongoose loose."

CHAPTER

I HAD HURT MY KNEE LAST SEASON, RIGHT AFTER WE HAD broken camp and returned to Dallas for the Baltimore exhibition game.

It was the third quarter. Short yardage. We had a pistol force, which put me close to the line. The Colts flanker was in a short split and I could tell he was getting ready to cut-block me. At the snap I knifed inside and got to the running back just as he took the pitch. The flanker chased me and all three of us collided in the backfield. We went down in a tangle and I felt something pop in my knee. I tried to stand and couldn't straighten my leg.

On the sideline, team doctor Felix Badd stressed the joint, checking for stability. It popped again and I could straighten it.

"I don't think it's too serious, not much pain." Dr. Badd was probing the knee with his thumb and forefinger. "There's no ligament damage . . . ah . . . there it is." He trapped a bean-sized chip of cartilage in the lower left front of the joint. "A joint mouse—probably broke off the articular surface. As long as it's in the front we'll just block it, make a little incision right there"—he traced a short line on the side of my knee—"and slip the little bastard out. We won't have to open up the whole joint and you'll be back in a couple of weeks."

That sounded good to me. The club had drafted a defensive back from UCLA number two that year. I couldn't afford to miss much time.

"If the chip stays in the front we can do it tomorrow." Dr. Badd started toward the tunnel. "I'll go call now and schedule you for surgery." He usually scheduled his surgery according to his golf calendar and mortgage schedule.

By the time I had showered the game was over. We won and Buck walked into the locker room with his arm around the number two draft choice from UCLA.

I was dressing, trying to step into my pants leg, when the knee locked again. I stumbled forward and in reflex tried to step with my bad leg. The joint ground and snapped and I felt the chip slide into the back. I told the doctor.

"Well, no sense checking into the hospital, but come in in the morning anyway. It may slip to the front again. We can't get it out if it's in back."

LD drove from the stadium to the team party at the Holiday Inn. I worked my knee viciously, trying to pop the piece to the front of the joint. Several times the joint locked, but each time I freed it the mouse slid to the back.

By the time the Western band started playing I was totally depressed. The season, potentially my greatest, was going down the drain. I began drinking Champale with Smoking Jim and dancing with Sonny Jeeter's wife, Susie.

When I tried to get my face down into Susie's full breasts, Sonny grabbed me by the scruff of the neck and tossed me into the drum set. I twisted my knee as I crashed to the floor, and with a loud snap the joint mouse slipped to the front of my knee. I don't remember the rest of the evening, but the next morning LD pulled me out of bed and took me to the hospital. The sun hurt my eyes. My knee throbbed and I had a terrific hangover. My ass hurt where I had fallen on the drummer's cowbell. I felt my knee and found the chip floating next to my kneecap.

I offended the hospital parking lot attendant by vomiting out the passenger side while he was giving LD the parking stub. "Very sick man," LD said as he looked over at me hanging on the door. "Ate a bad pussy." We drove to the back of the lot and parked.

"I think I'll take my mongoose with me." LD leered at me. "People in hospitals hardly ever get to see wild creatures."

LD dug the mongoose cage out of the back seat. It was a box divided in half by a wooden partition. One half of the box top was enclosed with wire mesh, the other half with wood. Through the wire mesh you could see the animal's tail sticking through a hole in the partition. The rest of the animal was in the enclosed half of the box. Warnings were painted in LD's scrawl.

Keep fingers away—dangerous varmint.
Do not feed. Watch it. Look out. Stay away.

I thought he overstated it.

It looked like an animal in a cage. What it was actually was a squirrel tail attached to a spring-loaded trapdoor on the box top. After a suitable buildup about the dangerous "mongoose" and its man-killing abilities, LD would pull the latch and the spring-loaded door would snap the squirrel tail into the intended victim's face. Usually all hell would break loose.

On the surgical floor LD stayed at the nurses' station, warning the nurses not to get too close to the little varmint, while a frowning surgical nurse escorted me into a small dressing room. I put on a gown that let my ass hang out and went to the operating theater.

"Sit up," Dr. Badd instructed. "We may need your help to locate the chip."

I was on the operating table, surrounded by people in surgical gowns and masks. The light was bright and hurt my eyes. Dr. Badd was probing my knee with his thumb and forefinger. He caught the joint mouse and pushed it to the inside of my knee.

"Okay, I've got it." He held his hand out and the nurse

laid a four-inch needle in his palm. "Okay, I'll secure it now." He drove the needle through my skin and into the cartilage chip, pinning it securely. His forehead wrinkled with the strain of pushing the needle through the cartilage. It hurt like hell. I moaned and broke into a sweat.

Dr. Badd proceeded to inject the skin around the pinned chip. The skin ballooned with Xylocaine. The Champale from the night before began to seep through my skin. I noticed the smell. A nurse laid a sheet over my leg. She wrinkled her nose and frowned at me as she rewashed the area with alcohol. Dr. Badd made his incision. When the nurse reached over to sponge the blood, she knocked the needle loose and the cartilage chip slipped into the recesses of my knee.

"What the goddamn hell are you doing?" Dr. Badd screamed. "You stupid cunt. Get the hell out of here." The nurse broke into tears and ran from the room.

"Now what the fuck are we gonna do?" Dr. Badd stared at my bleeding knee. His face was obscured by the mask. His eyes were wild. "You'll be out all season if I open this thing all the way up."

My gown was beginning to soak with sweat. The doctor probed around the inside of my knee, looking for the elusive chip.

"Try the rakes." He nodded to a nurse who hooked each side of the incision with two instruments that looked like miniature garden rakes. She pulled and the cut stretched open. The doctor inserted one of his thick fingers. Big hands. Big scars. He wiggled the finger around inside the joint, trying to catch the chip. No luck. A nurse wiped the sweat from his brow. *I* was sweating more than he was. The smell off my body was overpowering. Champale does not travel well.

"Shit, I can't find it." He stuck a pair of forceps into the incision and dug around. The pain shot dully up and down my leg as he scraped around the inside of my knee. No luck. "Can you feel where it is?" He shook his head. "A knee like this is no damn good." He was blaming my knee.

I groaned. The Xylocaine had only deadened the skin, but the swelling it caused had obscured the small chip. My back was aching and sharp pains shot up my neck into my head.

"Get me an anesthesiologist. We got to put him under."

"I hope you mean the anesthesiologist," I said, " 'cause you're not putting me under. Ether and Champale don't mix. Lemme try and find it myself."

The nurses looked at Dr. Badd. He shrugged.

They scrubbed my hands and I slipped into a pair of surgical gloves. I was faint and nauseous. I dug into the recesses of my own knee joint and after what seemed like hours I extracted the lima-bean-sized chip and dropped it into the doctor's hand. Then I leaned over and threw up for the second time that morning. A nurse wiped off my face, frowning at the smell of my body. I lay down and watched the spots swim across my eyeballs. My whole leg throbbed.

"Watch out!" LD's voice bellowed from the hall. "The varmint is loose!"

The surgical nurse screamed and came flying backward through the door. She crashed to the floor, struggling desperately with a squirrel tail that had her by the throat.

I worked out again in five days and started in the opener. I just didn't let down. The rookie from UCLA went in the last cut. New Orleans picked him up and kept him about three weeks. I had a good year and never had another bit of trouble with the knee. Until now.

CHAPTER

"HOW'S IT FEEL?" LD WAS STANDING NAKED BY THE TELE-vision, scratching his ass with one hand and stuffing a chew of tobacco into his mouth with the other.

LD pointed at my leg. "The knee, how does it feel?"

"Okay." It didn't really feel okay but LD didn't really want to hear. He flopped back on the bed after changing the channel.

"You know"—LD sat up and began picking at his toes—"when I was over fighting your ugly Asian war, old Hondo Higgins came through. The USO sent fucking celebrities to tell us how they appreciate the way we're wasting all the little yellow people. The day Hondo showed up we had been out on a sweep and a couple of guys got lit up and I'm scared and pissed and sitting beside an APC in the compound drinking warm beer and smoking joints with these two crazy LURPs from Houston. You know? The guys that sneak out with knives and bicycle chains and come back with bags full of yellow ears. Well, the three of us are stone crazy when Hondo comes through the compound gates standing up in the back of a jeep, holding onto the mounted machine gun, all dressed in his cowboy drag. When the jeep stops he pulls out a pair of pearl-handled .45's and starts yelling that Hondo Higgins isn't afraid of Charlie. The MPs hustled his ass right off. He coulda killed someone." LD paused. "Like the goddamn VC gave a good shit about the Texas Ranger. I had to grab one of them LURPs, they wanted to shoot his ass."

LD tore off a portion of his big toenail, smelled it, then dropped it into the wastebasket. "Celebrity war." He shook his head. "Jee-sus."

"Did you know Junior Everett?" I asked.

LD grinned and scratched himself. "I met Junior in Austin before he went off to Princeton."

"Don't call him Junior."

"Yeah, I know." LD frowned and spit a brown stream into the trash can. The housekeeper always complained about LD's tobacco juice. "Old man Everett is a big alumnus . . . used to get us cars and clothes. He was a U.T. football manager years ago."

It surprised me to think of Jace Everett Senior, the head of Everett Enterprises International, as merely the ex-manager of the Texas Longhorns. That's what LD considered him.

"He's not a bad ol' boy," LD said.

"Junior?"

"No, the old man," LD replied. "Junior's a prick."

"Then why are you going into the bar business with him?"

"He's Ezra's buddy. They were fraternity brothers. Fucking Phi Delts." Ezra and LD were two years apart at the University of Texas. "Ezra says we need him for contacts." LD spit again, missing slightly. The brown juice ran down the side of the waste can.

"Junior's sure got a good-looking wife." I shifted the ice pack on my leg.

"Say, Farah asked me about you." Brown juice coated LD's teeth.

"Yeah?"

"Yep, she wanted to know if you always looked like a dog-ass." LD laughed and slapped his naked thigh. He choked and swallowed some tobacco juice. "Haah, shit." He coughed and hawked and spat. "Gaw damn . . . that's tasty."

LD got up and shuffled into the bathroom. He looked like

a giant little old man. He shuffled back with two Coors. We drank the beers and then I tried to sleep.

LD was wired and stayed up watching a movie about a CIA motorcycle gang in the Angolan Civil War. They killed an assful of Angolans. I drifted in and out of sleep. At two thirty Buck Binder opened the door.

"Hey, you guys are supposed to be sleeping." Buck smelled of Scotch.

"C'mon, man," LD yelled. "We're watchin' a movie."

"Okay. Okay." Buck backed out. "But don't be talking . . ."

Talking after lights out was a twenty-five-dollar fine.

Around six LD got up and took a shower. The sound of the running water woke me. The television was still on. Steam billowed out of the bathroom, making the whole room damp. The big lineman materialized out of the steam cloud and toweled himself by the foot of my bed. I eased upright. My knee felt better and the swelling seemed to have gone down. The ice pack had helped.

LD walked to his dresser and began his morning pill ritual.

"You know, Mabry," he said thoughtfully, "some of us are meant to dominate. It's just the way it is with all animals. I'm strong enough to get what I want. Why should I feel guilty?"

"I dunno, man, but apparently you do." I wondered if he thought he dominated me and if there was something I could do to show him he didn't.

"I mean, if I can screw Stormy, why shouldn't I?"

"Friendship?" I offered. "I know you like Ezra."

LD frowned and shook his head. "Not as much as I like screwing Stormy."

"I think he likes *you more.*"

"I was afraid of that." LD shook his head. "I think she tells him everything she does."

"Terrific."

"She says he doesn't believe her."

"How can he afford to?"

"I ain't afraid of him."

"He ain't afraid of you either, LD. He was pretty pissed last night."

"He gets over it," LD said.

"He has so far," I said.

Dobie Rank pushed open the door. He was startled to find us up.

"Oh . . . ah . . . are you guys awake?"

"No, asshole."

"Your nose up my ass, LD. Put your phone back on the hook. You got a long-distance call. Breakfast in fifteen minutes."

LD returned the phone to its cradle. Cut day was over. He smiled. "I wonder if Hart got the shit off his chest."

The phone rang. LD answered and talked for several minutes. I walked into the bathroom and pissed. My back ached. It hurt my neck to look down. I pissed by ear.

"That was Smoking Jim." LD put down the phone. "He's filing a grievance. He says his back needs surgery. Dr. Badd says he doesn't. I gotta call Garvey." LD picked up the phone again.

LD was our NFLPA representative. The union was a constant source of friction between LD and Buck.

I stepped into the bathroom and rinsed my face and combed my hair. LD was finishing his call when I returned.

"Garvey says for Smoking Jim to get himself a couple more medical opinions." LD replaced the receiver and furrowed his brow. "God, I hate this. I know it's gonna get ugly." LD pursed his lips. "I guess I better talk to Buck."

Buck hated Executive Director Ed Garvey and the NFLPA.

LD stepped into his red-and-white plaid Bermudas and pulled on a clean practice T-shirt. "See you at breakfast." The big man shuffled off, his sandals rasping and slapping down the hall.

* * *

"Buck says Jim is trying to rip off the insurance company." LD had come to breakfast directly from his meeting with Buck Binder. "Those were his exact words—'rip off the insurance company.' What a giant asshole." LD lit up a cigarette. "He says he's gonna fight Garvey on this one. Like it's Garvey's idea Jim's back hurts." LD's hand shook as he held the cigarette to his lips.

"What does Buck care?" I asked.

"He says it's the premiums," LD said. "I never thought I'd be worrying about insurance premiums."

"Do you think he's hurt?"

"How do I know?" LD stubbed out his cigarette and rose to leave. "I don't know if *I'm* hurt." He shuffled off.

I drank the rest of LD's orange juice and limped down to the training room.

The league sure has gotten strange in the last few years. Maybe I've just begun to pay attention. Go along to get along. It was fine with me. When I get signed I'll be knocking down eighty thousand this year with a contract that pays ninety thousand next year and one hundred thousand the year after. A couple more days bluffing on my option and I'll finally be able to put some real money away.

"Two minutes in the hot. One minute in the cold." Dobie Rank was explaining the contrast treatment to me. I had done it many times before. Soak my knee two minutes in a 115-degree whirlpool and then immerse the leg to the hip for one minute in 33-degree ice water. It felt like my leg was being alternately scalded and frozen. I got used to the hot but never to the ice water. It was bone-crushingly cold.

"Buck was in this morning already," Dobie said. "He was checking asses to find the Rookie Show openers."

"What happened to Smoking Jim's back?" I asked, trying to put the pain out of my mind.

"I think he ruptured a disc." Rank was rolling gauze and

stacking it on his taping table, getting ready for the workout. "He's had trouble with it for several years. I put a lotta hot packs on that boy's back." Dobie sounded weary from all the hot packs.

"I'll bet you did."

I changed from cold water to hot. The skin stung, but the deep ache ceased. Sonny Jeeter limped into the training room to get his calluses cut off. Outside, the weight machines were clanging; someone was going through the exercise stations.

"Did you see what your buddy Ezra did to my car last night?" Sonny was unwrapping his injured leg.

"I deny everything."

"And what's the matter with LD?" Sonny watched Dobie pare the dead skin off his feet.

"He's preoccupied." I changed from hot to cold. "Jim Stewart is suing the club for surgery and his salary." The pain washed up into my stomach. "LD's gotta get involved."

Dobie had stopped whittling on Sonny's foot and was listening.

"Is Jim hurt bad?" Sonny asked.

"Dobie says it's a ruptured disc." I was bobbing up and down to distract myself from the cold ache.

"Hey, asshole." Dobie still held Sonny's foot. "I didn't tell you that for publication. You didn't tell me he was suing the club." Dobie wiped his hands in the towel he kept around his waist. "I didn't know you were collecting evidence."

"I ain't collecting evidence, for Christ's sake. I was just asking." My foot had begun to throb. I moved it around in the water. It throbbed more. "Besides, if he *is* hurt . . ."

"Who knows if he's hurt." Dobie began rolling gauze again. He picked up speed. "The back's a funny thing. I ain't seen no X rays." He rolled faster. "He could be trying to rip us off."

"Oughta shoot the fucking chiseler," Sonny mocked.

"You guys can laugh"—Dobie began stacking rolls of tape—"but it happens all the time."

Dobie taped Sonny's little finger, as he had for every practice since Diron Talbert stepped on it and ground the knuckle joint to dust.

"Goddamn, Sonny," Dobie said, "I'm sick of taping this finger every day."

"Me too."

"Hell, son"—Dobie smiled—"let's save us both some trouble and cut the sonofabitch off."

Back at the room there was a message to call Buck. He invited me to his room and we discussed my contract. It was friendly. We were only fifteen hundred dollars apart and just had to get the wording right on a couple of bonus clauses and deferred payment schedules. I'm a good negotiator.

The swelling went down rapidly in my knee and by Friday I felt better and worked out with the first team during short-pass skeleton. I wasn't 100 percent, but I was close. Discipline and confidence. I would be ready Saturday. I ran ten extra windsprints and Bob Lee Washington stayed out and worked on timing with Hart so I got some extra man-to-man work.

In the locker room after Friday's workout Buck Binder came through checking rookie asses, still trying to find the two that opened the Rookie Show.

LD and I went to the Pub. We borrowed Sonny's car. The steering wheel shook the whole way. Inside, Agnes was washing and waxing the floor. I limped to the bar and sat next to LD—two big strong men watching a one-hundred-pound woman work her ass off. We were there for sympathy.

"It don't matter, LD." Agnes looked up, breathing hard. "It's just goddamn football." She bent back to the floor. LD walked around the bar and drew himself a beer. The bar smelled of disinfectant.

"That's like me telling you it's *just* the bar business." LD sipped his beer.

"Well, that's all it is." Agnes bore down on the mop, working on a splash of vomit. "One of your teammates puked all over the floor and the bumper pool table last night." She rubbed at the stain. "You meet such wonderful people. I keep the lights down so it don't come in so clear." She sloshed the mop into the bucket. The water changed color.

"The guy's got a wife and kids and he can't work with a bad back." LD walked to the jukebox across the just-washed floor. Agnes watched disgustedly, then washed out his sandal prints.

"I didn't mean you shouldn't demand Smoking Jim's back get fixed," she said. "I meant you shouldn't worry about getting fired for doing it."

"Oh, great. That's terrific advice." LD looked at me.

"It doesn't sound like something I would do." I shrugged.

"They got films of him working out. Buck said they took 'em just in case something like this happened. Dr. Badd says he's fine. Dr. Friedman says it's psychosomatic."

"What happened to your leg?" Agnes noticed my bandage.

"Nothing," I said automatically.

"Nothing?" Agnes sneered. "Jesus, you're just like my thirteen-year-old. Nothing. Ha." She looked at my leg encased in the elastic wrap. "What's that? Panty hose for a one-legged fat woman?"

"I twisted my knee." I don't like talking about injuries. "It'll be okay."

"Because you say so?" Agnes eyed me skeptically.

I nodded. "That's discipline."

"Ha." She went back to wiping up the stains. "That's stupidity. You're as hooked on confidence as some people are on drugs."

The beer tasted bitter and stale.

LD punched up Bill Boyd and his Cowboy Ramblers on the jukebox. A scratchy fiddle led them through the weird Western sentiments of "Going Back to My Good Old Texas Home."

LD began stomping his foot and clapping his hands and singing along. Agnes stopped mopping and watched as LD danced and howled.

Suddenly LD stopped dancing and looked at Agnes. "Say, honey, would you give me a blow job?" LD's voice was uncharacteristically gentle and plaintive.

Agnes sighed and dropped the mop. She took LD's hand and led him to the back room.

CHAPTER

SATURDAY AFTERNOON THE TWO BUSES THAT WOULD TAKE us to the L.A. Coliseum to play the Rams were idling in the dormitory parking lot. We would leave in half an hour, but first Buck had scheduled a team meeting with the Everett Chemco artificial turf salesman. The coach felt we needed to renew our knowledge of the advantages of artificial turf versus the real ground. Besides, Everett Chemco was trying to sell the league on insisting on Everett Chemco artificial turf on all NFL Fields. Jace Everett and the commissioner are old buddies. This was the only day the salesman could meet with us. We all hate artificial turf. It's like playing on carpeted concrete.

After a pitch designed to convince us that increased injuries on artificial turf were a "statistical quirk," the salesman in his red-and-yellow checked sport coat and white pants led us to the parking lot for a demonstration. He removed his coat and knelt down. He laid a foot-square swatch of "new, improved" Everett Chemco turf on the asphalt.

"Okay." He pressed the artificial turf down. "Somebody run up and cut on this and see how good it is. I'll hold it."

We all looked at each other.

"In our street shoes?" somebody asked.

"Doesn't anybody have game shoes around here?" Buck was angry. He liked artificial turf and felt a good sales demonstration would stop any complaining.

A rookie ran to the bus and returned with a pair of Adidas.

"LD," Buck said, "you try it."

"You kidding?" LD looked shocked. "I'll bust my ass cuttin' on that.

Buck turned pink and glared at the big tackle. The rookie was pulling on his Adidas.

The salesman was beginning to sweat through his shirt.

"I'm ready, Coach." The rookie bounced to his feet.

Buck nodded and the young man dashed at the tiny green swatch of plastic. He hit it with his right foot and cut hard. The plastic square ripped out of the salesman's fat hands and shot halfway across the lot. The rookie smashed to the asphalt with a sickening thud. He just moaned and lay still. He was hurt bad. Dobie Rank walked over to tend him.

The salesman looked sheepishly at Buck. "It must of slipped," he said. "Wanna try again?"

"That's okay." Buck looked at his watch. "Thanks anyway, but we got to get going. Saddle up, boys."

The players began drifting to the buses. Several stared back at the rookie writhing in the parking lot. Buck leaned over and patted the man's shoulder.

"Tough luck, son," Buck said and turned to the bus.

The rookie grimaced bravely.

Dobie moved the injured man into the shade of Sonny's damaged Cadillac to await the ambulance.

The bus wound out of the tail end of the mountain range, ran a few miles along the coast, and then cut into Los Angeles County. The sun was low and orange when we pulled up to the Coliseum.

Hondo Higgins and Stormy, along with Farah and Jace Everett Junior, were waiting as the bus unloaded at the tunnel. Ezra Lyttle had tickets for them. As she took the tickets from her fiancé Stormy whispered something to Ezra. He jerked back, glared at LD, shook his head and walked quickly down the tunnel to the locker room. Stormy smiled and waved at LD, who looked at me and rolled his eyes in exasperation.

"She's taking the heat off Hondo by putting it on me."

"You've buttered your bread," I said, "now you have to sleep in it."

While getting taped I noticed Ezra pop a couple of Dexadrine hearts.

I hated to see my friends unhappy, but I had my own problems. The goddamn knee, my shoulder was sore and had kept me from sleeping well, and the last couple of days my little finger had gone numb.

"That collarbone is loose." Dobie Rank grabbed my clavicle and jerked. Pain shot through my shoulder and neck. "See. You oughta think about getting it fixed in the off-season. It'll be okay for now if we pad it."

I nodded. Nobody was cutting on me.

I went out with the kickers and practiced catching punts. Ezra and I were the return men. He was a flashier runner but I was smarter. Buck Binder wanted Ezra to field everything possible. I had had a twelve-yard average a couple of years ago. I was still good but I contented myself with good blocks and an occasional fielding opportunity on short kicks. I'm a team man.

I liked pregame warm-up in the Coliseum. Between punts I could scan the stands for movie stars and knockout chicks. No wonder the Rams don't play well at home. Who can pay attention?

Skybuster Eaton, our punter, thumped a perfect spiral up above the lights. The ball hung in the twilight sky, then nosed over, came spinning down and smacked into my shoulder pads. It weighed a ton. Skybuster kicked a tall, heavy ball. He was a great kicker, although he cost us a game against the 49ers when a Kezar Stadium headwind got one of his towering boomers. Skybuster had looked forlorn standing there watching the football hang motionless high in the San

Francisco sky. Then, as the Kezar wind took over, Skybuster had cried in horror, "My God—it's *coming back*."

I saw Hondo Higgins, Stormy, Farah, and Jace Everett Junior in the stands. James Garner and John Wayne were sitting several rows behind them. Sonny Jeeter was behind our bench, leaning on his cane and talking to Burt Reynolds.

The Coliseum was slowly filling. The stadium lights came on as Alex Hart led the rest of the team out of the tunnel to join the kickers and receivers for pregame warm-ups. It would be the last time all night that the backup quarterback would smile.

We lost the toss and kicked off. I was second man on the right and was closing in on the L.A. return man when a yellow-and-blue flash knocked me out of bounds and into the photographers. Ezra helped me to my feet. He had a distant, angry look. His eyes were bright as we walked to the defensive huddle.

The Rams had the ball on their 28. We were in a flex 4-3 man-to-man. The Rams tried a draw-delay trap. LD slipped his block, filled the seam, and hit the ballcarrier a yard deep in the backfield.

Second and eleven. We were in a 4-3 roll strong. The tight end and flanker set to my side. I inched up to cover the short side. At the snap I tried to bump the flanker. The pain in my knee made me stagger and I lost recovery. I left too big a zone and the Ram quarterback dropped the ball behind me to the flanker, who had hooked up. I was a step too slow. I dragged the flanker down from behind, but they had their first down.

Buck Binder shook his fist at me. I can imagine what he was whispering. My knee ached as I leaned into the huddle.

The next play they swept right at me, leading with the on-side guard. I tried to protect my knee, but the guard ducked under my outstretched hands. His helmet smashed into my kneecap. The pain burned up the front and back of my leg. I was hurt and went down like I had been shot. The runner cut inside, but LD closed fast along the line and cut him down. The L.A. guard lay next to me as I writhed on the ground. "Sorry, man," he said. "Didn't mean to hurt you."

As Dobie Rank helped me off the field, Buck sent a rookie from Arizona State in at my corner spot.

I sat on the bench with my knee packed in ice. A couple of plays later I got up and jogged. The pain was minimal and I was ready to return. Buck told me to take a rest. Sonny came and sat with me and we watched the Ram defense totally intimidate Hart. He threw three interceptions in the first half. But our defense played well, particularly Ezra, who played with a vengeance, making several unassisted tackles and a key interception in the end zone, and it was only 7–0 Rams at the half.

"I'm going to rest you," Buck told me in the locker room. "No sense getting really hurt this early in exhibition season."

I didn't mind. My knee was beginning to stiffen.

Hart couldn't generate any offense in the second half, but neither could the Rams. Our defense held them scoreless. Ezra was all over the field, making tackles and knocking down passes. The job was doubly tough because they had to call the zones to the rookie at my corner, leaving Ezra man-to-man most of the night.

In the last two minutes, with the score 7–7, Ezra fielded a punt on the six and took it back ninety-four yards for the winning touchdown.

In the locker room after the game Buck awarded Ezra the game ball and fined him a hundred dollars for fielding a punt inside the ten-yard line.

I was getting my knee wrapped when Ezra walked up, his face streaked with dirt. He was smiling and wired.

"You'd a won this if you hadn't gotten hurt." He tossed me the ball. "They did everything we were expecting. I knew everything that was coming."

"I sure didn't think you'd field that one on the six." I tossed back the ball.

"No guts, no glory." Ezra's eyes flashed.

LD Groover, still wet from the shower, stopped. He toweled off his chest. His tattoo of a black panther with red eyes scratched at his right nipple. The hole Ezra had punched in his chest with the dart was almost healed.

"How is he, Dobie?" LD asked the trainer, who was scowling as he swathed the damaged joint in sponge wrap.

"It ain't bad—a couple of days," Dobie said.

I immediately began to plan my rehabilitation and comeback. The rookie hadn't looked too good, but then he hadn't looked too bad. The films on Monday would tell.

Ezra started to head for the showers, then turned back and shook the game ball in LD's face. "What do you think about this? Sonofabitch." The defensive back laughed at LD and then disappeared in the steam of the shower room.

The Coliseum dressing area was broken up into individual stalls. As I passed the stall closest to the training room I heard Ezra's high-pitched giggle. I pushed open the door to investigate.

"Shut the door, turkey." Bobbyday Burke, the L.A. cornerback, decked out in suedes and platform shoes, was sitting next to Ezra. Ezra was snorting cocaine off the nail-file attachment to his fingernail clippers. I stepped in and quickly shut the door. The resulting breeze blew the cocaine off the nail file onto the floor.

"Oh, *man*," Ezra cried. "You lame motherfucker."

Bobbyday Burke laughed. "I can afford it." He threw some more coke on the floor.

Ezra finally snorted and offered the cocaine bottle and fingernail clippers to me. I waved them off. Cocaine can make you bleed. Bobbyday slipped the bottle into his leather belt bag. Ezra put his fingernail clippers on the bench.

"This is sumthin', man." Bobbyday leaned back and put his feet up on Ezra's equipment bag. "This is some life. I mean, look at this fine shit." Bobbyday held his arms as if to embrace the confines of the dressing stall. He picked up a towel and held it up. "I mean, this is some fine shit, man." He smiled and shook his head.

"Mabry, do you know what we used for shower towels in high school? Do you know?"

I indicated I didn't know.

"Our jockeys, man. That's right, our goddamn jockeys." Bobbyday got up and eased to the door. "But we didn't care, man. We was the niggers. Hell, when I went to SMU the freshman coach wanted me to get him a color TV. I was the only nigger he knew. And niggers know where to get hot TV's, right?" Bobbyday laughed. "I bought a used one in the want ads and charged the motherfucker twice what it cost. Everytime he sees me he winks and grins. Stupid sonofabitch."

The Ram defensive halfback laughed and pushed out of the dressing stall, heading for the tunnel. He stopped to hug Ryan O'Neal and Doug McClure, who were sitting and grinning on an equipment trunk. Their feet didn't reach the ground.

The tunnel was crowded with clusters of fans and family. Each group surrounded its player like piglets sucking a sow.

Los Angeles has the best-looking postgame tunnel show in the league—young men and women, tanned and beautiful. Pittsburgh and Cleveland always have the worst—everybody wears too many clothes and has a terminal head cold.

Ezra Lyttle moved quickly from one cluster to another, shaking hands and laughing, the game ball tucked under his arm.

I walked stiff-legged over to the crowd around LD, who was standing next to the giant motorized Ram helmet. LD had his arm around Farah Everett and was talking to her husband, Jace Junior. Hondo Higgins stood grinning in his cowboy drag. Farah formed the words "Are you all right?" silently on her soft red lips. I nodded.

"Listen, Junior," LD said, "I vote we go to the Luau and meet up with Sonny and Burt Reynolds."

"Well, I don't really care," Jace Junior responded, "but Ezra wanted to drop by the Daisy. He says Sinatra will be there. He wants him for our Celebrity Board of Directors."

Jace Junior paused. "Listen, man, don't call me Junior."

"Right." LD nodded, his mind on the benefits of the Luau's toy drinks versus the Daisy's chicks.

Farah Everett smiled and said something to LD, who looked at me and laughed. LD hugged her to him. Her black hair was tied back under a paisley scarf that knotted behind her right ear and flowed over her shoulders. Her breasts filled a fitted Neiman's glitter T-shirt. She wore tight white jeans and deck shoes. A thick gold chain circled her neck.

Ezra walked up. "I think I got Merlin Olson and Bobbyday Burke on the Celebrity Board of Directors." He grinned and shifted the game ball from hand to hand. Then he spotted someone else in the crowd. "Klosterman. Hey, Don." The manic defensive back yelled at a man who had just left the Ram dressing room. "I wanna talk to you." Ezra strode toward the startled man.

LD watched Ezra go. "He still spends half his time coming and the other half going."

"Yeah," I said, my eyes on Farah Everett's face. "Let's hope he never gets there."

"Well, let's decide where *we're* going."

I wanted to go to every place in town and end up with Farah Everett in a bungalow at the Beverly Hills Hotel, but instead I found myself alone on the bus heading back to camp. I had to elevate my leg and get some ice on it. Being injured is lonely business.

"How's it feel?" Buck Binder slid into the bus seat next to me and grabbed my thigh, giving it a hard squeeze. He smelled of Scotch. "You could always get good Scotch in New York," Binder often said wistfully. My coach was definitely sentimental about the Big Apple. It was a strange emotion to regard.

Buck patted my knee. "I'm sorry you got hurt."

"Thanks." I was embarrassed. He *was* sorry. I liked old, beat-up Buck Binder.

"I just want you to know you're still number one with me. We need older guys like you."

"What do you mean by that?" I asked.

"My God, Mabry." His Scotch breath reminded me Buck was a sentimental drinker. "I was just trying to cheer you up. What's gonna happen in this world when everybody's as paranoid as you?" He got up and staggered back to the front of the bus. The lights glared off the freeway.

The dormitory was strangely quiet. Those who hadn't stayed in Los Angeles were loose out in the Valley. A lot of them would be over at the Pub trying to screw Agnes while LD was in L.A. Curfew wasn't until two A.M.

"The lame and the strange, that's all that's here tonight." Jerome Beecher, the "root hog or die" rookie from the University of Michigan, talked to me from the doorway. I was on my bed, damaged leg elevated and packed in ice.

"The lame and the strange is all there is anywhere." I picked the ice bag off my knee and applied it to my head.

Jerome had an ugly gouge under his eye and both his knees were wrapped in Ace bandages. He was shaking slightly at the bottom end of thirty milligrams of Dexadrine. His eyes were big and dark. Jerome was an example of "the new young players" that the club was acquiring in what LD called "the android versus the animal dilemma."

"I'm just trying to get used to an organization," Jerome said. Jerome was an android.

LD and I were animals. We weren't trying to get used to anything.

"I hate this." Beecher lay down on LD's bed and clasped his hands behind his head, staring at the ceiling. "The coming down. It's really miserable. They tell me it has something to do with the going up but I can't keep it straight." There was no anger in his voice.

Jerome had spent the previous winter snowbound in the Bitterroot Mountains, doing yoga and reading Baba Ram Dass. Training camp in Southern California gave him cabin fever.

I returned the ice pack to my knee. "Jesus, I get lonely." Beecher shuddered and wrapped himself in LD's blanket. "I miss my kids."

Another *Texas Ranger* rerun flickered soundlessly on the television. Hondo Higgins was pistol-whipping another Mexican. I think Beecher started crying, but I didn't look to see. You'd think he'd take enough goddamn amphetamines to get him through the night.

CHAPTER

THE NEXT AFTERNOON BUCK BINDER WAS NAILING THE POST-erboard performance charts on the lobby wall. In blue and red ink the chart graded each player against the Rams. There were spaces remaining for the rest of the exhibition games. Good performances were recorded in blue ink, poor performances in red. A player was graded on every play: a zero if he did his job, a plus if he did more than his job, a minus if he failed. The charts were shot through with red lettering and players bunched around to learn the judgment on their last night's performance.

"Goddamn," someone growled. "How can they give me a minus? I pushed him all over the fucking field." Other players were making similar claims in the face of the red ink. Ezra Lyttle had gotten a plus 42, an unheard-of score. I looked for my name. It was followed with a red-ink −2 and the small notation "injured due to bad basic position." Because I was injured I had figured on getting a pass, not blame.

Buck Binder walked up. "Say, can I talk to you?" He clapped me on my sore shoulder.

I followed Buck to his room in the coaches' wing of the dormitory. The flapping of my sandals echoed down the empty hall. I figured he wanted to discuss some of the final details on my new contract. I wanted to get it signed this week. I needed the $15,000 front money. I had some paper due back in Dallas on a bad investment in a Willy Roy Rogers outdoor concert. Willy Roy got drunk and never showed.

"Listen, Mabry, we hate to do this . . ." Buck started talking as soon as I entered his room. ". . . it's just the way things worked out . . . I mean we have some real problems setting the roster, what with Sonny's injury and now your knee"—Buck dug in his pocket for his Camels—"and today Bobbyday Burke was available. We traded for him." Bobbyday Burke was the Ram cornerback.

"You traded me?" I was shocked.

"No." Buck frowned.

That was a relief. I could beat out Bobbyday Burke.

"We couldn't make a deal for you . . . nobody was interested." Buck put his hand on my shoulder. "We're putting you on waivers. I'm sorry, you're a hell of a guy."

I lost my breath and my heart started pounding. Confusion, fear, and embarrassment crashed together in the back of my head. I lost my balance and quickly shifted my eyes to stare at a spot on the wall behind Buck's head. I concentrated hard to keep from coming apart. Discipline. Discipline. What the fuck was happening here?

"What do you mean nobody was interested?" I was suddenly mad.

"Nobody was interested," he repeated calmly, lighting up a Camel.

I was afraid that was what he meant. "Not even goddamn Tampa Bay?"

He shook his head. "Still . . . somebody might pick you up on waivers . . ." He tried to sound hopeful.

"Not even goddamn Tampa Bay . . ." I couldn't believe this was happening. It's not the kind of thing you think about a lot. "Those assholes . . . I'm better than anybody in that whole fucking secondary."

"I know you are, Mabry." Buck patted my shoulder. "Listen . . . I was wondering . . . we gotta make this move today." He looked at his watch. Smoke wafted off the cigarette in his hand. My mind raced, looking for a place to rest. I knew this would happen sometime, but not now. I was having my best camp ever. "Mabry, why don't you retire . . . you're thirty years old . . . it'll save the embarrassment of having to put you on waivers . . . you've had a great career . . . go out with your head up."

I had my head down, staring at the gray asphalt tile. One of the squares had been placed wrong and the pattern ran opposite to the rest of the tiles.

A long time passed.

"C'mon, buddy," Buck urged, checking his watch. "Make a decision."

"Me? Retire? I'm only thirty years old . . . I feel great. I'm having my best camp ever." My speeding brain searched for some explanation, some calming circumstance.

Buck shrugged. "It's up to you."

I needed to rest my mind; it was racing too fast. "Okay," I said suddenly. "You make the announcement . . ." I turned and walked away. It was like a dream . . . a nightmare.

"Okay, Mabry," Buck yelled and called after me, "I'll tell them you retired to spend more time with your business interests."

My business interests?

I had my bags packed when LD returned to the room.

"Traded? Cut?" He looked at my luggage.

"Cut." I nodded, embarrassed to the point of tears. My mind still searched for someone to blame . . . some soothing thought. This had to be a mistake. "Officially I'm retired."

"What about the knee?"

"The doc's looking at it in a little while—it ain't that bad." My voice creaked. "Jesus, what a fuck-up."

"Why today? I thought we were under the limit."

"They just traded for Bobbyday Burke, they had to make room." I walked into the bathroom and rinsed my face.

"Bobbyday Burke," LD said. "He's one hittin' sonofabitch."

"Goddamnit," I yelled from the bathroom. "*I'm* one hittin' sonofabitch."

"Yeah, but you ain't gonna be around."

"Asshole." I limped over to my bed. "Jesus, am I embarrassed. I don't know if I can stand this."

"Hell, man." LD stared at the floor. "It's just football."

"Shit." I lay back and stared at the white plastered ceiling. "I was going to have a great season. I was having my best camp ever."

"Famous last words."

I knew he was going to say that.

Ezra Lyttle came into the room and saw my packed bags. "No shit!?" His eyes were wide. "Those fuckers . . ." Tears came into his eyes. "Those dirty fuckers." His voice turned to a whine. "I told you not to go on your option. I told you."

He was right, he told me.

"C'mon, Ezra," LD said, "everybody told him. He don't wanna hear that."

"Nobody picked you up?"

"Not yet. Buck says nobody was interested. They tried to deal me first."

"Not even Tampa Bay?" Ezra couldn't believe it. "Not even goddamn fucking Tampa Bay. . . . Those assholes."

"That's what I said."

"Everybody says their front office is fucked," Ezra said.

"I'm getting out of here." LD opened the door. "This might be catching. I'll see you back in Dallas in a few weeks." He was gone down the hall.

"You just can't stand to see Mabry cry," Ezra yelled.

"Mabry who?" LD yelled back.

Ezra tossed some darts while I lay on the bed. My life flashed by. All that fucking work come to this. All those miserable hours, the lumps, the scars, the hours spent feeling bad. All that fucking work and it's over so quick it's like it never happened. I began to feel old. I never thought I'd feel old at thirty. Jesus, was I sad.

"I'll shoot you to fifty for that ten dollars you already owe me." Ezra retrieved the darts from the target.

"I'll shoot first," he said. Ezra's first five darts all hit in the eight-point zone. He dropped his last dart in the bull. I still hadn't gotten off the bed.

"That's twenty dollars. I'd like it before you leave. Damn," he said, looking at the dartboard. "No wonder they cut you."

I walked over to the campus medical clinic to have my release physical. First they X-rayed my knee and shoulder. Then I sat on the brown leather table in the small examining room and played with the stainless steel stirrups.

Dr. Felix Badd came into the room holding my still-wet X rays. He clipped them against the light box. His upper lip was sweating. He nodded and grunted at the X rays of my knee and then nodded and grunted at the X rays of my shoulder. He wrote something on his clipboard.

"Okay, up on your feet."

I stood. I was in my shorts.

"Bend over and touch your toes." He checked the alignment of my spine. "Okay, up." He grabbed my clavicles and pulled. I flinched at the pain.

"That doesn't hurt," he said.

"I know it doesn't hurt *you*."

"Okay, up on the table." He began probing my knee with his thumb and forefinger. He twisted and straightened the leg. I flinched again at the pain. Dr. Badd frowned.

"Boy, you sure are tender." He wrote something on his clipboard.

"Dobie said it could be torn."

"Dobie isn't the doctor," he responded, "and it isn't torn. Maybe a little hyperextension." He looked at me wryly. "But not enough to get your contract, so don't you go trying to rip off the club like Smoking Jim."

"Hey, I just want to get well. I want to play again."

The doctor looked puzzled. "They already cut you, boy.

You aren't playing anymore and it isn't because of that knee."

"I'll play again."

"You've got fluid in there." He pointed at the knee. "You want me to drain it?"

I shrugged.

"Well, it's no skin off my ass. Make up your mind. It won't be as stiff."

I frowned and nodded. It hurt to have a knee drained.

He got out his syringes and needles and went to work, placing the point of the needle at the top of my knee, pushing and twisting simultaneously, trying to screw the needle in under my kneecap. The needle was large to allow the passage of the bloody, thick joint fluid, and it took pressure to punch through my skin.

"I know this was your only chance at being something." The doctor talked while he struggled with the needle. "I wanted you to make it."

Finally, with a sharp sting, the needle popped through and slid in behind my kneecap. Drawing the plunger back, he filled the syringe with bloody pink fluid. Then, leaving the needle imbedded in my knee, he unscrewed the syringe and emptied it into a stainless steel pan.

"You'll suffer later with arthritis, but you'll suffer later anyway. Getting old is a crime. You may hurt more than it was worth, but at least you've got your memories."

He filled and emptied the syringe four times before he injected cortisone into the joint and withdrew the needle. He was tense and sweating heavily when he finished. He slapped a band-aid on the hole, then ran his thumb over the old scar on the inside of the knee.

"You remember the time we took that out?"

"What do you mean, we?" I said. "I took it out. All you did was cuss and sweat."

The doctor laughed. "That was some surgery." He wrote something on his clipboard. "Okay, Mabry, that's it. It was nice knowing you." He clapped me on the shoulder. I pulled on my clothes and started out the door. He called after me.

"Say, what ever happened to LD's mongoose?"

I kept on going and pretended I didn't hear.

"You have to recognize the real trauma here, deal with it and get it behind you." Dr. Friedman dropped by the room after I returned from my separation physical. He had a book for me, *Looking Out for Number One*. "I was just looking at your biorhythm chart . . . today's critical for you. Tough luck."

"I'll be back." I looked through the drawers, making sure I hadn't left anything. I limped into the bathroom and checked the medicine cabinet for the second time.

"Is your knee that bad?" He sounded like he didn't think it was.

I didn't respond. I stared out the bathroom window. There was a brown path worn through the grass to the sidewalk leading to the dining hall.

"You know," Friedman continued, "setting your goals too high can be worse than setting them too low. You're being too hard on yourself. Now, Smoking Jim, for instance . . ."

"Fuck Smoking Jim." I jerked open the closet door and checked inside again.

Friedman went on, "Smoking Jim won't accept it that his career is over, so he's created this bad back to compensate for the failure. It's going to be tough, but like the guy said about his hunchback brother, I'll get him straightened out."

I looked through the desk drawer, then sat on my bed. "How about some pills instead of this advice."

"Don't you see?" Friedman held out his hands. "You don't have to do that anymore. You're free to work out other solutions to your life."

"I'll be back." I smiled and glared into his eyes. "I'll be back and you'll still be here passing out free advice."

"Look at you, just spitting and snarling, you'll haul this around with you like so much excess baggage until you learn you can just set it down and walk off that much lighter." Friedman shook his head. "I know it's tough, man. Hell, I remember when they cut me off the seventh grade basketball team in Indianapolis, they said it was because I wasn't any good. It was because I was Jewish. Do you know what it's like *not* to play basketball in Indiana?" Friedman frowned. "It isn't fun, but I didn't let it ruin my life. I picked up and went on. You can do that. Whatever you do I'll still love you as a human being." Friedman loved everybody as human beings.

"You know what you are?" I said, staring at the bottom of an empty dresser drawer that I had checked twice before. "You're just another groupie. You want to be the Howard Cosell of psychology. I liked the old-school groupies—they just fucked us and left our illusions alone. We have sex groupies and press groupies and now we got a psychology groupie."

Friedman rubbed his chin and squinted at me.

"What do you mean, we?"

PART TWO

RUNNING IN PLACE

. . . be careful what you're dreaming
soon your dreams will be dreaming you.

CHAPTER 1

My first days back in Dallas I fought the panic of disconnection by cruising the bars and working the telephone. I followed the news from camp and interpreted everything as indication that they were getting ready to call me back. I knew it was only a matter of time before the team—no, the whole league—collapsed of its own weight without the necessary ingredient of Mabry Jenkins and his amazing discipline.

I called a scout I knew with the Falcons.

"Yeah, man, we'd love to have you," he said. "I'll get back to you."

When my knee felt better I began workouts again and went to the recreation center, where I got into pickup basketball games with total strangers. I felt like the housewife that hooked on the side. I would terrorize poor fat junior-high-school teachers with ferocious drives and savagely blocked shots. Growling and snorting, I would end up alone, shooting baskets until they closed the center.

Saturday night I sat in the apartment and watched Dallas wipe up the field with San Francisco. I paced from LD's bedroom to the living room, watching both televisions, drinking beer, and being anxious. Bobbyday Burke's play at my corner spot upset me, but when I saw they had given my jersey to the new Yugoslavian kicker, I was out of control. I didn't belong on this side of the screen and I began to feel disoriented. In the third quarter I saw someone who looked like me wandering across the field in street clothes. The police arrested him.

When the game ended I was afraid to turn off the set for fear the whole world would disappear. I turned to Channel 11 and watched all the syndicated Country shows. Whispering Bill Anderson sang about cowboys and rich girls not living in the same world. I was neither. I don't know if I can take not being anybody.

Sunday I drove around all day, never able to decide whether to go to a movie or drive home to Bob Wylie and see Luther Watt. I couldn't sit still but there was nothing I wanted to do. Time was the enemy. I was bored.

Monday I phoned around the league, trying to connect with a club. The scout from Atlanta never called back. Finally I called the semipro team in Fort Worth. What the hell, I thought. What the hell.

I had met the owner once at Texas Stadium. He owned a Fort Worth trucking company. He told me to come see him if I ever wanted to play in Fort Worth. He didn't seem happy to see me, but sent me down to meet the coach.

"Well, boy." Jumbo Pantagruel, the coach, scowled at me. Jumbo had played at Texas A & M in the early sixties. I was leaning against some crates in the shipping department where Jumbo worked during the week. "We don't play no fancy-pants finesse football. We just go out there and knock their cocks off." Jumbo looked like he ate furniture. He rubbed his A & M ring. "I know about your pro football. I went in the last fucking cut in Miami the year they won the Super Bowl." To Jumbo there was only one year Miami won the Super Bowl. "They said I was the toughest and meanest they ever saw. Shit, I was better 'n Larry Little, but them niggers get all the breaks. I'm still a mean sonofabitch."

Jumbo hadn't learned the skill of masking his craziness. You never give anything away. If they want to find out how nuts you are they have to pay for it.

"When did you get cut?" Jumbo asked.

"Last week."

"No, I mean what cut?"

"I dunno what cut, it was last week."

"I went on the last cut," Jumbo said. "You didn't go in the last cut—this is still August. The last cut ain't till September."

"Big fucking deal."

"You're goddamn right, big fucking deal." Jumbo began clenching and unclenching his fists. His eyes flared under his prominent brow ridge. "If we decide we want you it's seventy-five dollars a game and you buy your own shoes, socks, jock, and T-shirts, but I gotta tell you we got a couple a niggers from North Texas that you probably can't replace. But if Mr. Bill says to I'll give you a tryout."

It was all too familiar, reminiscent of all the bullshit I had ever endured on the way up, and now I was heading down. I didn't have the prospects or the energy to deal with somebody as crazy as a Fort Worth semipro football coach. There was no light at the end of this tunnel and probably no end to the tunnel.

"I tell you what, Jumbo." I moved to put a packing crate between us. "You keep the seventy-five dollars, the two niggers from North Texas, and Mr. Bill, and when you get a little time off from your executive job here in the shipping department you shove them all up your ass."

Jumbo's head snapped up. He growled, gathering himself to charge. His basic position was too high; I kicked the packing crate into his knee and he crashed to the floor. I was out the door and into the business office before Jumbo could regain his feet. He was too domesticated to start trouble among the civilized folks in the trucking business.

"I'll find you, peckerhead," he yelled at me as I climbed into my car in the parking lot, "and when I do I'll beat you like an old rug."

"Better bring your lunch and twelve of your best friends, Fatso."

I laughed and drove out of the lot and steered the car toward the Town Pump. The Pump was my old Fort Worth pinball hangout.

Inside the Pump was cool and dark. I could see the pinball lights flashing and hear the porcine snorts and squeals of my old pal Big 'Un as he wrestled the machine for free games.

I stood inside the door and let my pupils recover from the Texas sun. The room slowly materialized out of the yellow and red spots. The bar was at the back, surrounded by tables, and against one wall was the pinball machine. I could make out the huge shape of Big 'Un and smaller shapes around him. The front wall was lined with green leather booths.

"Mabry, come sit down." Titus Bean was signaling me from the recesses of a booth.

My bootheels clunking heavily on the dance floor, I walked over and slid onto the cool leather.

"What brings you to cowtown?" Titus waved at the bartender.

"Pursuing a rapidly retreating horizon," I said, still scanning the room. Junior Everett's sailing and gambling pal, Billy Bentson, was at the pinball machine with Big 'Un. "And me with a bad leg." I glanced at the door. "What's your excuse for getting this close to Comanche country?"

"It's my hometown. I come here for reality when I can't stand the truth anymore." He drank a martini. Titus was one of the few people I knew in Texas who drank martinis. I think most of them live in Houston.

"Doubleday just canceled our book contract," Titus said. "They called this morning. We don't have to return the advance."

"What advance?" I hadn't known about any advance.

"It wasn't much. Say, do you think LD would be interested in doing a book? He's got a great story. Vietnam and the NFL."

The bartender walked over and I ordered tequila with lemon and salt.

"I'll bet you get a lot of questions about what you're going to do now that you aren't playing football," Titus said. "Maybe we can sell them a book about that."

"Maybe so," I said. "The jock stereotype has been replaced by the ex-jock stereotype and people get irritated if I don't play my part well."

"Don't worry," Titus said. "You'll learn it."

"Well"—Titus looked at me expectantly—"what are you going to do?"

"First I'm going to knock the shit out of the next guy that asks me that, then I'm going to try and get on with my life. Maybe something like your job. I could do your job."

"Feel free to use my name in job interviews." Titus laughed.

Somebody punched up the jukebox and Jerry Lee Lewis's "Middle-Aged Crazy" filled the bar.

"I started out here at the old *Fort Worth Press*," Titus said. "My first assignment was to cover a rape-murder. They found a pretty little sixteen-year-old girl chopped up and stuffed in a well in Ridglea. A city reporter named Coody and I took about five big pulls on his half pint of Wild Turkey and went to interview 'the victim's mother.' She just stared at us through the screen door. On the television set behind her was a picture of the girl. One of those high-school pictures, hand-tinted, in a cardboard frame. Coody just jerked open the screen, pushed the woman aside, and snatched the picture off the TV. It was one of those blond Danish-modern consoles with the metal legs. We were in the car and gone before she knew what happened. The picture ran in the next edition. It was the only picture anybody had of the girl. Coody got credit for the whole thing." Titus laughed. "That's when I learned it don't *make* a shit and I don't *give* a shit. I moved to sports the first chance I got. The toy department of life."

In the back of the bar Big 'Un snorted and slammed the pinball machine against the wall.

Billy Bentson left Big 'Un and the pinball machine and slid into the booth next to Titus. "You telling war stories, Titus?

How you doin', Mabry?" He hooked his thumb toward the pinball machine. "Big 'Un's beating the shit outta that machine, just like the old days."

The last time I had seen Billy Bentson he was with Farah and Junior Everett at Hondo's party in Beverly Hills.

"Why aren't you out sailing Eagle Mountain Lake trying to get into Junior Everett's pocket?" I asked Billy.

"He's off in South America shooting pigeons with a couple of his Cuban friends," Billy replied. "That family knows more goddamn Cubans and South American greasers . . ."

I didn't hear the rest. I headed for the booth in the corner and placed a long-distance call to Farah Everett in Dallas.

Farah answered and asked who placed the call. I told the operator and the operator told her. She told the operator she wasn't there and hung up. The operator told me and hung up. I hung up.

And then Jumbo Pantagruel walked in out of the glare. He had two of Mr. Bill's drivers with him. They stood inside the door, peering into the darkness, looking for me. I was just pissed enough not to care.

I rejoined Billy and Titus. Shortly Jumbo stood over our table. I had my hand around the heavy cut-glass ashtray.

"Well, peckerhead." He grinned. He had big teeth. "I brought a couple of friends—we'll get the other ten if we need them. You wanna settle this . . ."

I think he was going to say "outside" but I'm not sure because I jumped up and hit Jumbo above the ear as hard as I could with the cut-glass ashtray. Blood splattered onto the table. I hit him again on the way down to his hands and knees. I hit him once more in the back of the head. The ashtray shattered and Jumbo collapsed on his face in a pool of blood. I turned to face the other two. They weren't coming. Billy had one up against the wall with a short-barreled pistol stuck in his neck while Titus hammered the other guy all over the dance floor. Titus fought Golden Gloves before he began looking for truth. The battered truck driver retreated into a corner and held up his hands in surrender. The two drivers dragged the bleeding Jumbo out the door.

"I thought you were giving that up for a good string of whores." I pointed at Billy's gun.

"Lucky for you I still got some old-time thug habits." Billy smiled and shoved his gun back in his belt. "Those fellas didn't know there was five of us—you, me, Titus, Mr. Smith, and Mr. Wesson."

"Lucky for you both, you sonsabitches," Titus interrupted, "that I still got the fastest hands in North Texas." He rubbed his knuckles. "We better move on, somebody's liable to piss here."

We headed north in Billy's gold Cadillac convertible, towing a red-and-black flame-painted Chris-Craft powerboat. Billy was a real speedboat cowboy.

"Mabry, I think you wanted to kill that old boy." Titus started talking just out of Fort Worth. "I know how you feel now that you're all through. When I was boxing and had my glimmer of glory, I loved it. God, what I did to people. They called me 'The Psycho.' The more they said it the more I tried to be The Psycho. Well, I succeeded. One guy I held up with my knee just so I could hit him. He was already out. Whew. I cringe. You can't go back and apologize. That's what makes it tough getting old." He grinned. "I'm glad I didn't kill anybody. I used to think being The Psycho was at least being somebody. Being my own man." Titus looked out the window. "Nobody's his own man," he said softly. "Nothing works out . . . nobody's nothing."

I watched out the rear window and wondered if I did try to kill Jumbo. The fire-painted Chris-Craft cruised along behind, leaving Fort Worth in its wake.

We headed up 35W, rolling over the green North Texas hills, and turned east on a farm-to-market road and through a gate marked private. The private road wound through pastures and occasional patches of Angus cattle. We pulled up to the stockade entrance of the ranch main house. There were cars and trucks of every condition, including two Cadillac pickups and a Cadillac station wagon with mink seat covers. Just past the entrance was the roping pen.

It was a high-stakes matched roping, National Champion All-Around Cowboy Luther Watt against Ernie Taylor, the 1973 Calf Roping Champion. Five thousand dollars, winner-take-all, on ten calves. Billy hurried over to the scorers' table, where the gambling was the heaviest. He was looking for the owners of the Cadillac pickups. Titus and I stayed at the far end of the arena, away from the chutes. I didn't want to distract Luther Watt while he was competing. I would see him afterwards.

Luther Watt and I had been friends since seventh grade when the Bob Wylie school system consolidated the old Coal Corners school.

Lately I didn't get back to Bob Wylie much. Luther and his wife Nadine still live there.

Luther won the roping with a 7.5 on the last calf. Billy had bet against him.

Billy and Titus wanted to get back to Fort Worth. I told them I would find a ride and waved good-bye in the noise and confusion of the cow people heading home. The sun was low over the western hills. The dust hung gold in the air.

I found Luther Watt sitting in the trunk of his Eldorado sorting his gear. He had his white grizzly-style hat pushed back on his head and was pulling off his boots. He replaced them with blue-and-white Adidas flats.

"Howdy, Mabry." He spoke without looking up as he tied his laces. "I thought that was you." He stepped out of the trunk, threw his saddle in, and slammed the lid. "It's been a while. Let's go get a steak."

Luther responded to every situation with a steak. It's a cowboy's way. We drove to Fort Worth and ate at Cattleman's.

"Still in love with my wife?" We had finished our steaks and were picking our teeth and drinking beer.

I nodded. I had pursued Nadine Mercer Watt in high school.

"Me too, except she keeps after me to get off the road," Luther said. Luther was still wearing his grizzly hat. "You know how that is. Hanna's in junior high now. The time sure has flown. I remember Nadine washing diapers in more motel sinks . . ." His voice faded off. He stared down. Luther Watt had been rodeoing twelve years.

From his back pocket Luther pulled a can of snuff. He flashed the sterling silver custom-made top. "We gotta face getting old, Mabry. We're looking at our forties an' fifties next, good buddy." He took a pinch of snuff and stuffed it into his lower lip.

"We got our thirties yet."

"Hell, boy, we're in our thirties." Luther grinned, his teeth brown. "Think about all the versions of 'El Paso' Marty Robbins has sung since you fucked ol' Virgilene Mead."

"You're older than me," I said.

"One goddamn year." Luther had been held back his first year in the Bob Wylie school. "You know, that's funny. I was just thinking the other night about getting left back. Boy, it scared me." He laughed a short bark. "I hated the kids in that class, but I didn't want to be left back. It's what they did to wounded guys in Hondo Higgins movies. They don't come back to get you." He stared at his dirty scarred knuckles. "I guess it all worked out for the best." Luther smiled and the left side of his face closed down in a squint.

"Well, at least you got your degree," Luther said as we drove away from Cattleman's. "All I ever did was rodeo." Luther went one year to Sul Ross on a rodeo scholarship. "Of course, that's all I ever planned to do. Everybody at college was crazy. I already had my degree in craziness." He steered his Eldorado through the dark Fort Worth streets. "You gotta adjust, Mabry, you're in the part of life where nothing is really ever solved. It just goes on and on. Boredom is gonna be your enemy. Try and relax. One thing you got now is plenty of time."

He rummaged through the glove compartment and extracted a fresh can of snuff. A 35-m.m. contact sheet fluttered to the plush carpet. It was a series of photos showing a bull killing rodeo clown Porter Hobbs.

In the first picture the 230-m.m. F4 telephoto had stopped the action the moment Porter turned the bull off Luther. Dust was frozen in billows, framing Luther's frightened eyes as Porter's broom hung forever over the bull's head. The clown had just bounced it off the big animal's nose to distract him from Luther, who was down. With greasepaint grin and baggy pants, Porter Hobbs succeeded beyond his wildest expectations.

The high-speed photos showed the bull turning and smashing the clown to pulp against the arena wall after he missed his grab for the top of the fence.

Luther said that just before the bull hit Porter, the feisty clown held up two crossed fingers and yelled, "King's X motherfucker."

"Let's just stop in here a minute." Luther guided his big Eldorado into an apartment parking lot. "I need me one of them hot beef energy injections."

The cowboy had a Fort Worth model stashed away. A diminutive blonde opened the apartment door.

"This little heifer reminds me of an ice cream cone." Luther hugged the tiny girl to his dusty Levi's and they retired to the back of the one-bedroom apartment. They left me in the living room, staring out at the nighttime Fort Worth freeway traffic. In a while Luther hollered from the bedroom, "Mabry, c'mon in here . . . gimme a hand." He was naked, on his knees at the foot of the bed. The blonde ice cream cone was on her back with her legs splayed. She watched me with indifference.

"Help him," she said.

"Yippie Ki O, an orgy with a cowboy and a model." I started to unbutton my shirt.

"No, no, you asshole," the blonde said. "He's hurt his back."

"Muscle spasm," Luther groaned, his face buried in the mattress. "Help me into the saddle."

"What?"

"In the saddle. Goddamn, don't you speak English. I can't move, but I ain't stoppin' now."

I picked Luther up by the hips—he was amazingly light—and settled his wiry body between the starlet's upraised legs.

"That's great, Mabry," Luther groaned. The blonde sighed and spurred Luther's bony ass with her heels pulling him in tight. She looked over Luther's shoulder and smiled at me.

"Okay, pal, get out."

Later, walking back to the car, Luther said, "You know, Mabry, women are like dogs. Just when you get to liking one, she either gets hit by a car or runs off with the pack."

The wind was coming from the Panhandle. It had a chilled edge.

CHAPTER 2

I AWOKE TUESDAY WITH A GROWING SENSE OF PANIC.

"A re-re attack," Titus Bean said. Titus had just returned from West Texas with autopsy photos of a four-month-old child. It was for his food contamination story. "Reruns and regrets, you'll get over it." We were driving up to the Texas International Speedway for the Willy Roy Rogers Annual Texas Music Festival.

"I never have re-re attacks," Titus said. "I refuse to be responsible for anything that happens after nine P.M. Janie never understood that about me." Titus's wife Janie died two years ago of a rare disease that caused her epidermal cells to shrink. She was squeezed to death.

"She actually died, man," Titus said. I didn't know if he was talking about his wife or the four-month-old.

Titus used his press pass to get us into the speedway and we parked next to Willy Roy's bus in the pit area. A deputy with a pump shotgun guarded the bus. The wide stretches of concrete baked in the August Texas sun. Hippies and rednecks milled in front of the infield stage, drinking beer, smoking joints, and parboiling their brains.

Titus was doing a story on Willy Roy for *Rolling Stone* and soon we were sitting in Willy Roy's bus, drinking tequila and snorting cocaine. The Blackland Farmers, Willy Roy's backup group, left to go warm up the crowd.

"I'm changing my image." Willy Roy said after the band

left. "I'm getting rid of those fucking Blackland Farmers and changing this old alky cowboy look-at-me-feel-bad act. I'm going straight outlaw." He passed around his cocaine bottle. "We got twenty million dopers in this country. The liberal pricks trying to ban guns will give us another forty million outlaws. Then there's the outlaws that were against the war and now Calley and all them outlaws that were for the war. And nobody drives fifty-five. It's a goddamn growth industry." Willy Roy stuck a spoonful of coke up his nose. "In a country where thirty million people go to bed hungry every night and it's against the law to be poor or to kill yourself on purpose, I can't miss."

Just before Willy Roy went on stage I got in an argument with his bus driver over whose turn it was to sniff Willy Roy's cocaine.

Titus and I tried to follow Willy Roy backstage, but we didn't have backstage passes and the guard waved us away with the shotgun. We sat out in front with the beer-drinking hippie groundlings and redneck stinkards.

Willy Roy did a short set. During the reprise of his Grammy-winning "I Buried My Dog in My High-School Sweater" he passed out flat on his back. He had done a little too much cocaine and tequila for an afternoon in the Texas sun.

"He's quite a showman." Titus pointed at the unconscious country singer. "Until he trained himself to fall over backwards, he used to go through two or three guitars a tour. Fall face down and smash his Gibson to smithereens."

The Blackland Farmers finished out the set, gathered up Willy Roy, and made way for Waylon Jennings and Willie Nelson. During Waylon and Willie's set I pictured myself up there singing. I could do it. I could do anything. It just took discipline. Country singers never get too old. The crowd loved them. I needed a crowd to love me.

After Willie and Waylon's set a girl from McKinney walked up without her blouse. Her titties stuck out straight and glowed red from the sun. During the rest of the program

Titus and I sat on either side with a tittie. It was pleasant and made me feel calm. At nine o'clock the promoter read a county ordinance prohibiting public gatherings after nine P.M. and closed the show. A few people didn't want to leave and threw beer cans at the stage. Police with telescopic rifles appeared atop the speedway press box and horseback sheriff's deputies enfiladed the crowd, herding them toward the exits. It was an eerie scene—the fading Texas twilight shining through clouds of dust as the riders worked the mixed herd of rednecks and hippies.

I woke the next morning at home with the girl from McKinney, her sunburned titties, and what was becoming an ever-present panic.

"You didn't seem to enjoy it. If you know what I mean," she said. I knew what she meant. Reruns and regrets.

I showered and dressed. Titus and the topless girl from McKinney sat in the apartment kitchen, drinking vodka and apple juice.

The girl had cleaned up the kitchen and washed the sinkful of dishes. It was a pleasant surprise and I felt guilty that I had decided to toss her out at noon. There was a phone call for Titus.

"I gave a few people this number," he said, closing himself off in LD's room.

"You want to try again?" She sat on the kitchen table, her brown legs dangling. Her toenails were painted bright red. Her cutoffs hugged her crotch. Her titties glowed.

"Naw," I said. "I'm content to objectify this whole relationship."

She rolled her eyes and then smiled. "You sure aren't very tough." She hopped off the table. "Oh, while you were dressing two sheriff's deputies came by. The bank wants its car. I told them you moved."

Titus came out of LD's bedroom. He was wearing LD's College All-Star Game jersey and his Vietnam fatigue hat.

"That was the office of the Commissioner of Agriculture." Titus opened the refrigerator door and stared inside. "I'm not very popular. He says I have a combative attitude about the food contamination story. They heard about the autopsy photos. Dead babies really frighten politicians. He says my attitude could hurt Texas agriculture, quoted me a lot of figures about cattle and vegetables, and reminded me that his great granddaddy's Uncle Bill died at the Alamo and that I'm just second-generation white trash from Tennessee."

I didn't know Titus's parents were from Tennessee.

"He said he already talked to my publisher." He closed the refrigerator door. "All that shit in there is poison."

"C'mon, Titus," I said. "It's paranoid thinking all your food is poison."

"That and wanting to be a politician are two sure signs of craziness," Titus agreed.

The phone rang again. It was Luther Watt calling from Bob Wylie.

"Let's go to Mexico," he said. "Mr. Jace Everett hisself gave me orders to bring you with me to the Annual Baja Celebrity Fish Tourney. I'll pick you up at Love Field in an hour." Luther hung up. Communication with Luther was often a one-way affair.

I went to pack a bag. I made a note to check the phone bill.

As I was leaving Titus held up his glass. "Mabry, while you search for your identity with your old high-school chum, remember you have to forgive *us* before you can forgive yourself."

They sure looked funny. That old gal's red titties and Titus barefoot and red-eyed in LD's spangled jersey with a little smear of blood on the blue just below the white field of red stars.

CHAPTER 3

IF ANY ONE POINT IN MY LIFE MARKED THE HARD SWERVE into insanity, it was the Annual Baja Celebrity Fish Tourney.

I flew to Baja with Luther and Nadine Watt in Luther's new Cessna 410. As Rodeo Cowboys Association All-Around Champion, Luther qualified as a celebrity, and some rich sportsman would pay heavy to fish for marlin with the five-foot-ten-inch calf roper, bull and bronc rider.

We flew from Fort Worth to Tucson, then south to La Paz, capital of Baja California, Sur Territory, where we went through customs. Luther grimaced as he brought the plane down. The previous night roping a calf he had hooked his foot in the hogwire fence and tore up the ankle ligaments. He packed the ankle all night in ice. Sore ankle included, I was envious of Luther. I was becoming envious of anyone with apparent purpose, no matter how bizarre. I was envious of the Mexican customs man in his leisure suit and dark glasses. I was superfluous and it made me crazy.

Returning to the plane from the customs search, Luther limped noticeably and sweat beaded up on his forehead. As we took off I read the graffiti outside the terminal—"Viva Echeverria" in blue foot-tall letters above a "Viva Revolución" in red. My favorite was scrawled on the wall outside customs: "Suck Me, Marcia."

I tried to relax at 2,000 feet, unemployed and in the hands

of a rodeo star. I needed this trip. It was like being on base in tag. Except maybe I was already It.

Below, impaled on the rocky shoreline, the hulk of a Japanese freighter rusted red in the tropical sun. It had been lured aground by false lights and stripped by Mexican pirates.

Luther banked the red-and-white 410 out over the ocean. Through the starboard window I could see clear blue sky, the port window filled with the freighter, the cockeyed thrust of the brown peninsula, and the lines of green-white breakers slapping against the volcanic rock. The plane wobbled violently.

"Oops." Luther corrected and leveled out. People were camped on the beach near the wreckage of the Jap freighter. A purple-and-white van sat at the water's edge.

"Heepies," I shouted over the engines and pointed to the small knot of people on the beach near the van. "Probably passing around a joint and listening to Paul McCartney and his wife. God, I love the concept of young hippie chicks."

"Please, Mabry." Nadine, Luther's wife, turned her dark angular face to me. She was one eighth Cherokee on her daddy's side. "Small black dots on a thin ribbon of sand and you're having sexual fantasies about them. Your giddiness has reached insane proportions." She frowned at me. "Besides, if there are any hippie chicks left in the world they won't truck with a man who thinks of Wings as Paul McCartney and his wife. Hanna'll tell you that." She smiled with her wide-set blue eyes. They made a nice combination with her dark skin. For a woman married thirteen years she was a knockout.

Nadine turned to the front. My eyes traced the fine line of hair on the back of her neck. Her pigtail grew thick from beneath a red scarf and fell heavily over the back of the white leather seat.

I met Luther Watt in the seventh grade. His daddy was a bootlegger in the old coal-mine country. He made it big when they brought in the Ranger oil field. He had Luther late in life and stayed on near Coal Corners after the boom. Nobody knew anything about Luther's mother. Luther grew up on a vegetable farm. He trained to be a rodeo cowboy just like I trained to play football. I was a better athlete than Luther and that's why I always thought Nadine would choose me. It's funny what you think.

Nadine moved to Bob Wylie from Fort Worth in the ninth grade after her daddy caught her in the back seat of a shaved and decked '52 Ford with a sprinter from Paschal who set the state 440 record. It was during the Cowtown Relays. Big Bob Mercer closed his Fort Worth house and moved Nadine and her momma to the family ranch outside Bob Wylie. Luther bought that place after he started winning steady.

Nadine Mercer was the most sophisticated woman Luther and I had ever known. She was the first person we knew who had ever eaten pizza. Nadine thought Bob Wylie was Devil's Island. She had wanted out and a lot of the competition between me and Luther was over who was the best qualified to accomplish that. I sure thought proficiency in a television-intensive sport like football had it over rodeo. Fucking rodeo. Most folks thought rodeo cowboys were wild and shiftless. Hell, Luther dipped snuff in the seventh grade.

It was with me Nadine would do the wild things. She wouldn't do anything with Luther because she didn't want him thinking bad about her.

I thought I had a chance with her when I made All State and got the scholarship offer from Texas Tech. Luther was in Fort Worth for the Fat Stock Show. Nadine got her daddy's pickup, I stole a quart of my daddy's dandelion wine, and we headed to Fort Worth. We stopped at Lake Benbrook, finished the wine, and started making out. She only allowed Luther above the waist and no sucking, but she let me get my hand in her panties and suck like crazy on her right tittie. She wouldn't let me unfasten her bra and it made a burn mark on my chin, but I could always take pain. Then she jacked me off into my blue handkerchief. Her young hands were smooth and soft. I was overwhelmed.

"That's better than that dirtyleg Virgilene Mead can do." Nadine threw my handkerchief out the window. It was a new handkerchief.

Virgilene Mead and her momma sold rocks from their house trailer beside the Thurber road. Virgilene was reputed to "go down." It infuriated Nadine that I went out with her. I never mentioned that if old Virgilene went down she did it with somebody else.

"You better not tell Luther about this, and maybe next time we'll do something better." Nadine leaned against the passenger door and watched me drive. She snaked her tongue around the neck of the wine bottle. "He knows I'm not like Virgilene." Nadine giggled. "And now you know I'm better."

I thought she had just become mine. It's funny what you think.

We were strolling the midway at the Fat Stock Show when she met her Paschal sprinter from the Cowtown Relays. "Don't you tell Luther now," she sang back at me as she walked away with the tall blond fellow with TCU across the back of his purple jacket. He had turned into a college boy.

I never knew how she got back to Bob Wylie, but her daddy sure gave me a dirty look when I returned the truck. Two months later Nadine and Luther got married in Ciudad Acuna. That summer they moved to Alpine, where Luther had his rodeo scholarship. In the late fall Hanna was born. I never told Luther, and we never had our next time but Nadine was right. It *was* better than old Virgilene could do.

Luther banked the tiny plane out over the Gulf and brought me back to the sky over Baja. It was not a reassuring feeling. I have ridden in cars with Luther Watt.

"Gol dang it, Mabry, it's nice to have you along." Luther patted Nadine's thigh and with the other hand leveled the plane.

I turned loose of the seat back. The color returned to my knuckles.

"When you said a celebrity fish tourney I figured I'd get to meet Charlie Tuna." I laughed at my own joke.

Nadine smiled and clutched Luther's hand. "We've sure been lucky." Nadine sighed. "Luther's doing so well."

I didn't give a rat's ass how well Luther was doing.

"It's sure nice to be on top for a change." Luther was currently $3200 ahead in his defense of the All-Around Cowboy title and Larry Mahan, his closest competition, had broken his arm at the Cheyenne Frontier Days.

"We all prefer the top to the bottom," I said.

"Well, the bottom had begun to look like the top to me," Luther drawled. "Some folks say they're both the same."

"People can't piss on you when you're on the top."

Luther laughed. "I guess you better be gettin' yerself a good hat."

"Now Luther," Nadine cautioned, "don't get ugly just because we've been lucky."

"Mabry don't mind." Luther chuckled.

"I don't mind. I was looking for a job when I found my last one." I had a vast store of cliché responses to failure. They were good at postgame parties.

"What are you going to do now?" Nadine Watt asked.

"I'm purposeless," I said. "I'm like everybody else and I can't stand it. I didn't realize I would have to come to terms with total failure at thirty."

"You're not a failure," Nadine said. "Everybody in Bob Wylie is real proud of you."

"Try and relax," Luther said. "Enjoy this trip."

"Well, tell me, does the panic turn to boredom or is the panic *because* of the boredom?" I leaned back in my seat. "All the things I looked forward to are memories and I can't calm down enough to remember anything. I can't adjust to it being over."

"You ain't going to get to do it over again," Luther said.

"Better face that. You have passed the marker from experienced to old." Luther looked out at the starboard engine.

"A lot of guys play after thirty," I argued. "I'm in good shape and I can play Buck's defenses, not many guys in the NFL understand Buck's defenses. I'm waiting on a call from Atlanta right now. I can't believe Tampa didn't snatch me right up. Stupid fuckers, that's why they're last place. They don't know football. It's management that wins championships."

"What are you worried about?" Luther said. "You're one of the smart ones. You had yourself an off-season job."

To Luther the rest of my life was to be an unending series of off-season jobs. I wanted to cry.

"I'm an athlete," I said. "*Coming back* is my job. It's what I am. Ain't no hill for a stepper."

Luther shook his head.

"I'll be back." I could already see the headlines:

JENKINS SENSATIONAL IN COMEBACK. FANS SWOON

"I just have to get screwed down a little tighter. Make a few sacrifices and don't let down. I can overcome a little adversity."

ADVERSITY MAKES JENKINS STRONGER . . .
50,000 TEXAS STADIUM FANS GIVE
COURAGIOUS CORNERMAN STANDING OVATION

"I can make it happen. I have made tougher things happen. It just takes discipline and pride."

"Pride's a dangerous thing," Luther said. "I've seen bulls hook a lot of proud men."

"I'm sure you will do it, Mabry," Nadine said. "You've always been lucky."

"I think we just crossed the Tropic of Cancer." Luther held up a chart and compared the dead brown landscape and deep blue of the Sea of Cortez. If anybody knew about confidence and pride it was Luther Watt. His path to special celebrity status in the Annual Baja Celebrity Fish Tourney had been long and tortuous. He worked stock to earn entry money while Nadine washed diapers in sleazy motel sinks. They spent lifetimes on long, lonely all-night drives in battered trucks, to some shitbox rodeo where Luther would get tossed, sprain his wrist and miss the roping. Finally they got the house trailer in Bob Wylie and Luther went on alone.

The hours spent standing, sitting on fences, squatting behind the chutes, staring off into space, trying to decide whether to go on or quit. It took its toll: the exalting successes, the bone-breaking failures; the fear and the joy. He burned up his circuits and left pieces of Luther Watt from coast to coast in the arena dust, pickup cabs, and motel rooms.

Luther competed in all the riding events and calf roping. Sometimes he did a little bulldogging. His best events were bulls and roping. They're what got him to the Finals.

Luther often entered three rodeos a week, using the telephone, fast cars, and planes in a mad dash to amass enough total winnings to be declared the World's Champion All-Around Cowboy. The first year Luther qualified for the National Finals Rodeo his winnings were over $32,000. He had qualified in the bullriding and calf roping, won an additional $2,600 at the Finals, finished third in the all-around standings, and still ended up broke at the end of the year.

Finally, last December in Oklahoma City, in the last go-round on a bull named 00, in front of ten thousand screaming rodeo fans, Luther Watt won the World's Champion All-Around Cowboy buckle. I cried watching it on TV in the motel before the Eagles game. It seemed a long time ago.

"Say," I yelled above the drone, "how you gonna pay for this airplane?"

"Let the accountants worry about it," Luther replied. He touched Nadine's neck. She flinched and then smiled distantly.

"That's what LD and Ezra say about their bar and grill."

"I think we got the same accountants," Luther laughed.

"Say, hand me that instruction manual. I gotta read about landing this thing."

The Cessna was a new tool in Luther's chase. It was supposed to give him a bigger edge, making it possible to enter even more rodeos. He hired another cowboy to haul his roping horse. It all seemed pretty risky to me. In his years of rodeoing Luther walked away from a large number of car wrecks and breakdowns. That kind of luck required both feet or at least one foot on the ground. Hell, even in football they tell you stay on the ground. But Luther had a frenzied confidence in his ability to fly. The law of gravity didn't put no fleas on this cowboy. His confidence was what Nadine had loved about him. He was definitely there and it didn't matter to him why or how long. He was in a hurry in his life. He wanted to see how he finished. It mattered to Nadine not how he finished, but when, and her panic to leave Bob Wylie had been replaced by a panic to stay. Hanna was growing up and would be leaving soon. I'm sure glad I don't have any kids. Today's world is just too weird for kids.

"Gol dang it, Mabry, it's sure nice to have you along." Luther repeated himself.

"We've been so lucky," Nadine said.

"Rodeo's becoming a big sport and we're gonna go with it. I got endorsements and television appearances lined up."

"Luther's gonna be on Dinah," Nadine said.

"It ain't set yet," Luther interrupted. "It looks solid, though. Hell, I even got a guy from American Tobacco wants to put me up against ol' Walt Garrison and there's a fella in Dallas that wants to give me my own line of Western clothes."

"Did Luther tell you about the offer to do a television series?" Nadine asked. "Hondo Higgins wants Luther to help develop a series about rodeo starring Stephen Ford." Nadine was excited. Luther's ears turned red. It meant he was embarrassed. "Hondo says Luther will add authenticity to the show."

"That shows you what Jews know about the rodeo."

"Oh, come on, Mabry." Nadine didn't like my attitude.

"I don't know if I can take the coast." Luther said. "Buncha freaks. I think it fell into the ocean, but with all the smog and bullshit out there ain't nobody noticed." Luther laughed. He made the same joke on the *Tonight* show last month.

"Well, we've sure been lucky," Nadine repeated. "Since Luther's been winning we've . . ." She seemed to lose the words.

"Added two hundred acres to the homeplace," Luther picked up. "Me 'n' the boys at the Ranchers and Merchants Bank."

"Daddy's a director there," Nadine said. "He's been advisin' Luther."

One of the first things Big Bob Mercer did upon moving to Bob Wylie was to buy a big chunk of the bank. "It makes it feel more like home," Big Bob had said.

"Luther and Daddy are adding on to the indoor arena and opening a rodeo school. Then Luther can spend more time at home."

"Well now, honey," Luther said, "I still gotta git out and down the road. I can't be hanging around the house." He seemed uncomfortable.

"I know. I know." Nadine waved a hand. "But you can spend more time at home."

"Sure, sure, hon." Luther was quick to reassure. "Sure I wanna be home."

I don't believe him, but I'm cynical and bitter. And I can't believe Nadine doesn't know about athletes on the road. Hell, she knew a sprinter with a '52 Ford. The sonofabitch still holds the state 440 record.

"You're sure one busy man. Where do you get your time?" I asked.

"Borrow it." Luther laughed and coughed. "Just like everything else. I got me one of them A-1 credit ratings."

"We've been so lucky." Nadine gazed into the Gulf. "It almost scares me."

"That's rich people's paranoia, Nadine," I said. "Worrying about getting something because then someone can take it away. Look at me. I'm worried about getting things back."

"Well, good buddy, if anybody in this here sky is paranoid it ain't Nadine." Luther grimaced. His leg was hurting. I touched my knee out of reflex.

Luther leaned forward to rub his twisted ankle and accidentally pushed the stick forward. The plane went into a steep dive and we dropped toward the rocky shoreline. Nadine screamed. My stomach banged off the roof of my mouth and I braced for the crash. Adrenaline hummed through my extremities. Luther pulled back and the plane leveled off. We had dropped about two hundred feet. The cowboy smiled sheepishly and went back to digging at his sore ankle.

"Say, pal." I tried to regulate my breathing. "I wish you'd pay more attention to the driving. This here ain't the Amarillo highway."

"You're just paranoid, Mabry." Luther laughed and banged the heel of his hand against the instrument panel.

The cowboy leaned back and banked the Cessna casually away from the peninsula. From the custom hat carrier above the windshield Luther retrieved his crushed panama cowboy hat with the Luther Watt special crease and placed it on his head. Then, swinging the plane gently from side to side as we droned above the Gulf of California, Luther studied the instruction manual and sang in a thin raspy voice:

I'd like to ride the rodeo
but I got Brahma fear
So I'll jes' stick to aeroplanes
that gently pop my ears . . .

"That must be the hotel." Luther banked for a better look. It was Cabo San Lucas, the southern tip of the Baja Peninsula, where the Gulf of California met the Pacific Ocean. Here was some of the best sport fishing in the world.

At land's end the massive white stone hotel sprawled on

the cliffs. White water lashed at the rock below. In the cove west of the hotel brightly colored fishing boats bobbed in the blue-green surf.

Luther swung the plane low over the massive A-frame red-tiled roof. People were sitting in big wicker empress chairs in the bar overlooking the water. We flew so close I could see the flowers in their drinks.

The Cessna sailed above the beach, then Luther banked a sloppy one-handed turn to the north and headed for the dirt airfield above the cliffs behind the hotel. The plane shuddered slightly and I went tense. I had been going tense a lot lately.

We passed over the stick hovels that served as home and community for the hotel's Mexican help. Ragged brown children stared up at us. This was barren, isolated country, miles from any real town. The plane slowed, wobbled, and lost altitude.

"Goddamn." Luther frowned in pain and confusion. "I can't move my foot. I don't think I can work the rudder pedals." Luther was pale and sweating. "I can't land the plane."

"You were just working the goddamn pedals with your goddamn fancy dan turns." I was angry. My heart began to pound. I didn't want to die in an airplane crash in the ass end of nowhere. I was on a comeback.

JENKINS COMEBACK ABORTED IN AIR TRAGEDY

"You wanna argue about it or do something?" Luther growled.

"I just knew we'd been too lucky," Nadine whined, burying her face in her hands. "I just knew it."

Nadine was beginning to bug me.

"Hon, now calm down." Luther took a deep breath and patted his wife. "You're gonna have to work the pedals."

"I can't. I can't. I just can't." Tears filled her eyes.

"Christ, Nadine." I said. "This is no time to be modest."

"Fuck you, Mabry," Nadine snarled. "You don't know. You just don't know."

"Fuck me is right." I sat back and covered my face.

The airstrip occupied a high hogback behind the hotel. We had to approach it over the water. The dirt surface began at the cliffs, was uneven and ran uphill, ending abruptly in a mass of boulders tossed there by a long-extinct volcano.

"Okay, hon, easy now." Luther aimed the plane toward the runway. "Easy . . . *easy* . . ."

We were dropping fast and rocking from side to side. The plane listed and leveled.

"Easy, hon . . . easy . . . No, *no*, the other one . . ." The plane shuddered and the ground rushed up to meet us. We barely cleared the rock face of the cliff. Luther was soaked with sweat. "Damn . . . too steep . . . too hot . . . sorry. My fault, my fault . . ."

We hit with a resounding thump, bounced back into the air and then settled back down in a series of progressively smaller rebounds. The plane held together and with a struggle Luther brought it to a halt at the end of the runway. A billowing wake of white dust was strung out behind us.

"Goddamn." Luther stared at the boulders marking the runway end.

We sat silent, unbelieving, frightened. Then Luther snorted a laugh and banged the instrument panel with the heel of his hand.

"Smooth as silk . . . ol' rocking chair." He tried manipulating his ankle.

Nadine began to cry softly. "We were so lucky . . . so lucky."

I couldn't stand it. I scrambled out past Nadine. My knee hurt when I jumped to the ground.

CHAPTER 4

A WHITE CLOUD OF DUST FOLLOWED A BATTERED RED FORD pickup up the hogback from the hotel. The truck rattled alongside the plane and a small, wiry man in a campbusting shirt, his Levis stuffed into the tops of his dusty boots, stepped down from the cab. He had a red calico bandanna around his neck.

"Howdy . . . I'm . . . Red." The man gulped air and burped out the words in a strange staccato. "I'm . . . foreman . . . here . . ." He forced the air with his diaphragm to belch the words. His vocal cords were gone.

He dug into his shirt pocket, extracting a pack of Camels and his lighter. He lifted his calico neckerchief and inserted the cigarette into a small hole in his throat where his Adam's apple should have been. He lit up and dragged deeply. "You alone?" he burped.

"No," I said, watching the smoke trail from the hole in his throat. "There's two more fools inside throwing up."

He laughed. Air whistled through the hole.

"Nice . . . landing." Red took another drag on the cigarette and let the neckerchief drop.

"Wait'll you see us take off." The blue smoke wafted from beneath the red calico.

"Hello." Nadine stood, clear-eyed and beautiful, in the hatchway. She had done some face work and erased the strain of the landing.

"Red," I said, "this here's Nadine Watt, wife of celebrity

angler Luther Watt. Nadine, this here's Red, he's the foreman here . . . whatever that means at a hotel."

Red took Nadine's hand and helped her to the ground. She squinted in the tropical sun. The foreman belched out a "Howdy . . . m'am." Nadine flinched but kept her poise. Red opened the luggage compartment and began hauling the bags to his truck. A starter ground in the distance and another truck started out from the hotel.

"What's wrong with him?" Nadine said, watching Red tossing our suitcases into the bed of his pickup.

"Cancer, I guess."

Red lit another Camel, leaned against the tailgate and watched a green fishing boat sputter out of the cove near the hotel, heading for open water. The sun was brutal. It bounced ferociously off the rock and surrounding water.

"We just don't know how lucky we are." Nadine's lower lip quivered and her chin cauliflowered.

"I don't feel all that lucky. Just because your asshole husband didn't kill us and I ain't got cancer. You watch too many insurance company commercials."

The second truck pulled up. Dust billowed around and past us. A tiny man in a white panama suit and a duck-billed fishing hat stepped from the truck and grinned his way up to Nadine and me.

"Hidy. Hidy." He extended his hand to me. "I'm George Billings, your official host and celebrity coordinator, and on behalf of Everett Sports Enterprises welcome to the Annual Baja Celebrity Fish Tourney." He pumped my arm vigorously and then did the same to Nadine. "Are y'all guests or celebrities?"

"Uh . . . celebrities." I said. "We're celebrities. I'm Chuck Tuna and this here is Nadine Watt, wife of rodeo star Luther Watt."

"He's a celebrity angler," Nadine said proudly.

"Hidy. Hidy." George Billings shook our hands again. "Nice to meet y'all."

Luther emerged from the plane. He limped slightly. Pushing his tall-crowned straw hat back on his head, he gazed through his light blue aviators at the sunburnt rocky landscape. He looked the perfect modern rodeo cowboy. I felt like I was in a beer commercial. Luther looked at Billings last and nodded.

"Hidy. I'm George Billings, your official host, and on behalf of Everett Sports Enterprises welcome to the Annual Baja Celebrity Fish Tourney."

"Are you *the* George Billings?" Luther asked. Billings nodded.

"The George Billings *who*?" Nadine was puzzled.

"George Billings, the astronaut," Luther said. "You've heard of him."

Nadine looked more confused and slight frenzy clawed at her eyes. Confusion was not Nadine's favorite place.

I had never heard of George Billings the astronaut, but Luther read more than I did. It had to do with spending most of his nights the last twelve years in motel rooms. Luther possessed some rather bizarre esoteric knowledge.

"He did the experiments underground." Luther pressed Nadine. "I know you've heard of him. He stayed in a cave for three weeks."

"If you say so, darlin'," Nadine replied, trying. "But I just . . ."

"I know an acid head who did that once," I said.

"Let's tie down your plane," Billings interrupted. "Then we'll go join the others for lunch. Most of the celebrities and guests have arrived." Billings took off his hat, which had marlin leaping toward the crown, and wiped his forehead. "Your fishing partner is Mr. Jace Everett himself," he said to Luther. "He requested you." Billings beamed at the apparent compliment.

"Oh, Luther," Nadine gushed. "How lucky."

Luther smiled and his ears turned red.

I watched Red stick another Camel in his throat. He watched another boat, this one blue, sputter out of the cove. God, it was hot.

"What's Everett Sports Enterprises?" Nadine asked. We had tied down the plane and were heading for the hotel. We were sitting on wooden benches bolted to the bed of Billings' pickup. Red led the way with our luggage.

"I think they make sports equipment and clothes," Luther replied. "They own some ski mountains in Colorado, stuff like that."

I looked back at Luther's red-and-white plane disappearing in a wake of hot dust. I was on the southern tip of nowhere. I had gone about as far as I could go. I couldn't run anymore. I just had to stop, lick my ass, and collect myself for another assault on reality.

I stared at the hotel thrust out, white and pristine, over the deep blue ocean. Not until this moment did I ever consider the possibility I wasn't fated to be rich. It was going to be a big disappointment to me. I had to come back. I hadn't finished dreaming.

We rattled down off the hogback onto a narrow neck of rock leading to the hotel. The ocean smashed noisily a hundred feet below. The XLT coasted through the stone-arched courtyard entrance and banged to a stop against the battered tailgate of Red's pickup. Red burped out a "God . . . damn . . . it."

In the whitewashed courtyard a covey of Honda dirt bikes gleamed in the sun. Lizards scurried along the walls and into the rocks. Two barefoot Mexican women in white blouses and black skirts were scrubbing the red-tiled stairs leading into the hotel lobby.

The lobby was small and cool, roughly hewn from native stone and heavy timbers. Nadine's wooden clogs clattered on the uneven tile floors. Big paintings of famous Mexicans hung in heavy wood frames. Off to one side of the small reception area was a gift shop specializing in full-carat diamonds and twenty-two-carat gold. Opposite the shop, an old man wrapped in a yellow-and-blue serape was doing portraits in Day-Glos on velvet. Billings told two Mexican men in black slacks and white shirts where to deposit our luggage.

"You won't need keys to your room," Billings said. "We don't lock up anything. Everyone can be trusted here."

I wondered if Billings believed that. I guess a man who dedicates his life for a chance to ride strapped to the nose of a rocket has a high faith threshold.

"Mr. Jace likes a relaxed atmosphere," Billings explained. "No barriers between people. He likes to say that we're all human beings under the skin."

That seemed like a strange place to start.

"How wonderful," Nadine said. "Boy, around our place in Bob Wylie you have to lock up everything. Last year Luther had three tons of oats stolen."

"No." Billings seemed genuinely shocked.

"The law didn't do diddly shit," Luther added.

Luther didn't mention that he and Billy Bentson got the oats back. They just checked the grain elevators in the county until they found the guy that sold three tons of oats. He turned out to be a neighbor of Luther's, a guy named Hurley, living in a house trailer down by the river. Billy and Luther went to the house trailer. Billy introduced Mr. Smith and Mr. Wesson to Hurley while Luther shoved a blasting cap up Hurley's ass. He named his accomplices before they got it lit. Hurley and his pals paid Luther in cash for the whole load at ten cents a bushel over market. Even Nadine didn't know that.

"Let's have some lunch," Billings suggested. "The pompano is delicious today."

"How lucky," Nadine squealed. "I love pompano."

I think I mentioned she was the first girl I ever knew who had eaten pizza.

Two hallways led off the lobby. One led down to a red tile courtyard surrounded by whitewashed guest bungalows. Billings took the other hallway, into the sunlit dining room. The A-style red-tile roof towered two stories. Clerestory walls allowed a panoramic view of glittering blue ocean and white sand beach. The airport and the Mexican stick village were out of sight back to the north. An open stone staircase led off the dining room to the terraced Aztec Bar.

In the cove, the brightly colored fishing boats rode the swells that broke white on the beach. Their outriggers whipped as the boats rolled. Small thatch-roofed palapas dotted the beach. They would serve each night as bars where the wives, lovers, and affiliates gathered to drink and await the return of the celebrity fishing fleet.

In the Aztec Bar, slender young women were perched on the stone bas-relief barstools. Each stool was a carving of an Aztec god. A photographer scurried around the bar, composing panoramic shots of sky, water, rock, and flesh—the basic elements of life. Down on the patio, a slender brunette was stepping from a pool and tugging at her string bikini. Several other women lounged in the sun. I gasped aloud at the sight of that many nearly naked women.

Maybe the struggle is for the women. The power, money, and prestige are useful only for that end.

"Fashion stuff," Billings said. "You interested in fashion photography?"

"They're going to be shooting around the tourney," Billings continued. "Celebrities make a nice backdrop." Billings made the southern tip of Baja sound like stage flats.

"There's your table." Billings headed toward the far side of the room.

We moved across the dining room crowded with the rich and famous. They all looked tan and healthy.

There were oil men and land developers, computer tycoons and bankers, models and movie stars, a tennis champion and an all-pro hockey goalie, the NBA MVP and the PGA leading money-winner. The wealthy and the successful filled the sunlit room.

While Luther exchanged greetings with fellow celebs, I was watching Farah Everett.

She was sitting hunched over a round table, eating shrimp cocktail with her fingers. Her legs were folded under her, yoga style.

Farah licked red sauce off her fingers as she watched us approach.

Jace Everett, dressed in white slacks and a seersucker coat, sat stiffly with his back to the ocean's glitter, forfeiting the view to have the light behind him. Ora Bell Everett, Jace's second wife, sat on his right. She was in a soft brown floor-length dress. Farah was purposely ragged in cutoff wheat-colored jeans and a navy blue sweatshirt stenciled "The Third World Sucks." I found out later it was a gift from Jace.

Jace was up and greeting Luther and Nadine. "I'm proud to be fishing with you." Jace pumped Luther's hand vigorously. "People like you are an inspiration."

"Aww . . ." Luther's ears went red. Nadine beamed. Ora Bell grinned wide. I stared at the Olmec pictographs carved into the tabletop. Farah and Nadine shook hands, leaving Nadine with red sauce on her hand. Nadine acted like it was donkey semen.

Junior Everett and Billy Bentson walked up from the bar. A small man wearing a black glove-leather suit, pancake makeup, and a full-blown, red natural hairstyle was with them.

"Junior, introduce your friends." Ora Bell smiled. Her even teeth were flecked with gold.

I knew Billy Bentson. The redhead turned out to be Ora Bell's hairdresser, Stephano Valentine.

"Was that y'all in that red-and-white 410?" Ora Bell asked. "Such a cute little plane. Raul couldn't land our Lear on that teensy strip, so we're using our 410, too. Isn't that nice?"

We all nodded. I waited for Nadine to say it was lucky, too, but she studied her fingernails and stole glances at Farah.

"There just isn't enough room in a little ol' 410 for a person's clothes," Ora Bell continued, "so Jace sent Raul back to Dallas for the rest of my things. I told him not to bring everything so he only has to make two trips."

They were kind to their pilot. Raul had flown Farah and me to Port Aransas.

"Raul's a good man. Damn good man," Jace interjected. "He used to fly for Batista before that goddamn Castro got in there."

"I tell you, Daddy, that dude can handle a light plane," Junior interrupted.

The small gray man looked quizzically at his son.

After the pompano Luther and Nadine left to take a nap and George Billings left "to check on Mr. Tuna's fishing partner." He was sure a far cry from my fantasies about Tom Corbett, Space Cadet.

"What's the matter with him, anyway, Junior?" Jace watched Billings leave. "He's been acting strange lately."

"I'll check into it, Daddy."

"You do that." Jace turned to me. "First military man I hired since Hondo Higgins got out. At least Hondo followed football. George is a soccer man." Jace sipped his rum drink. The orchid tickled his nose. "Soccer fans are the goddamn Puerto Ricans of the sports world. Where did he get 'Mr. Tuna'?"

I shrugged.

"Well," Jace said to me, "what are your plans now that you are out of football?"

"Try again." I didn't know what else to say, or do.

"Fine. Fine. That's the spirit. I'm sure you'll make it." Jace wasn't convinced. He held up his thin finger. "One of our divisions is Everett Sports Enterprises. We own this hotel through our Mexican partners. We believe that sports, spectator and participatory, is the coming thing. The leisure time expenditures will be astronomical. As soon as the government turns amateur athletics over to the corporations we will be kicking the holy bejesus out of the East Germans." Jace leaned back. The light behind him made me squint. I couldn't see him clearly.

"Athletes are the next folk heroes. They'll be bigger than the biggest movie stars. In this world of personalities they are international heroes. They will cultivate worldwide markets, worldwide allegiances." Jace pointed at me. "Everett Sports Enterprises is in the international sports business. If you're ever interested, talk to George Billings. We think ex-athletes are good, disciplined technicians. Confidence and discipline, that's what counts today."

I didn't like being called an ex-athlete.

Stephano excused himself to go check Ora Bell's star charts. Stephano did hair astrologically. He touched Junior lightly on the back of the neck as he left. Junior pulled back and scowled.

The waiter cleared the dishes and everybody ordered margaritas. Jace demonstrated how he wanted his glass rimmed with salt. "Beaners never get anything right." Jace watched the waiter retreat to the bar. "We should have taken this whole country over when Cardenas nationalized the oil companies. My daddy lost forty million in that deal. Should have taken the whole son of a bitch over down to the Panama Canal."

Ora Bell smiled. Junior nodded.

"Jace, Mexico doesn't control the Panama Canal," Farah interrupted, "and our waiter isn't responsible for foreign policy."

"Ha! Farah, honey"—Jace smiled—"don't mock an old man. You know what I mean. It took the Mexicans forty years to find all that oil around Vera Cruz."

"That's because your daddy and all the oil people took their geologists' logs when they left."

"People shouldn't be allowed to ignore resources like that," Jace said, ignoring Farah's argument. "Every nation has responsibilities to support the world market system. They wanted to hold out. I mean, come on, it's the deal. They aren't living up to it. Goddamn Ejitos taking people's land and the government not doing diddly shit."

Ora Bell smiled and Junior nodded.

"Oh, come on, Jace," Farah interrupted again. "You're just mad about the ranch in Torreon."

"Six hundred and eighty thousand acres." Jace turned and held out his hands. He seemed to be pleading to me. "Six hundred and eighty goddamn thousand acres, they just walked in and ran my foreman and hands right out. The law didn't do diddly shit."

"They claim you don't use the land," Farah said. "Besides, only Mexican nationals can own land—it's a law."

"Who the hell's side are you on?" Jace whined. "Who ever heard of a law that says only Mexicans can own land? That's ridiculous. I paid cash for that land and it's mine. A man has the right to do whatever he wants with his property. By God, in my daddy's day he didn't wait around for the courts. He'd be out there shooting beaner asses right off that place."

"This is too much." Farah was exasperated. "Your daddy was an East Texas lush banker who used depositors' money to back his own crooked oil deals. He did only two decent things in his life. He had the unbelievable luck to actually strike oil and the thoughtfulness to get himself burned up in a Longview whorehouse fire shortly afterward."

Ora Bell nodded. Junior looked like somebody had just shit in his lap.

Jace began laughing. The waiter arrived with the margaritas and Jace scooped one up. "Here's to Daddy."

Ora Bell still smiled. Junior looked relieved. We all drank. Rich people celebrate the strangest things. I would make a good rich person.

Farah and Jace obviously enjoyed the verbal confrontation. The little gray man took relish in Farah's impertinence and the discomfort it caused his son. I watched the glint in Farah's eye and the slight curve of her mouth as she constructed another attack on the fortress of the small man's ego. He took punishment well. He was a sticker.

"You know what your problem is?" Farah had her bare feet up on the table. Her sweatshirt had pulled up, exposing her brown stomach, "You are so rich and well connected that you're in conflict with yourself. You need an old ideology, a commitment—something besides dedication to the world market."

"The world market is all there is," Jace replied. "Anything less is Nazis and the Japs and World War Two. One world of producers and consumers. That's peace."

"But you have opposing interests," Farah replied. "First you're against détente because of all your Pentagon business, but then you're in favor of it because you want to go after the Siberian oil and gas."

"It's what is known as balance," Jace interrupted, smiling. "There are two true principles in life, balance and beauty. A man needs both to survive. That's why we make such a good team. You're beautiful and I'm balanced."

"Just ten minutes ago," Farah interjected, "you and your long-dead daddy were going to go shoot a bunch of Mexicans over a few hundred thousand acres of desert. You call that balance?"

"A few hundred thousand acres!" Jace turned to plead to me. "Do you hear that? A few hundred thousand acres, like it was so much dirt under your feet."

I thought it was, but kept my response to a nod and a knowing smile.

"You people are too young to remember that the Second World War started over a few measly acres. Property rights. Dedication to the rule of law. That's what holds the world together. Somebody doesn't obey the law, you blow their ass off. People have to live up to their agreements.

"Why do you think terrorism is so big today? We were the original terrorist after the war. We had the A bomb and had just hijacked the world. But we got scared, we quit blowing their asses off. We were the classic bully who forgot how he got that way. We believed our own foreign aid stories and decided everybody liked us." Jace sighed and shook his head. "Now we have a bunch of college kids and professors who don't know or care how they got to be rich, fat, and educated. They think it had to do with college entrance exams and the essay they wrote on democracy for the Jaycees. We keep building weapons we won't use and every four years forty-five percent of the voters elect somebody to sit in the White House with his finger on the trigger and make threats about human rights and how free America is." Jace leaned foward. "Well, America is becoming a bad place to do business. A twenty-billion-dollar trade deficit. The big banks have bad paper spread all over the third world. The less developed countries aren't about to pay because they know we won't blow their asses off." Jace sipped his margarita, then licked the salt on the glass rim. "One day the big corporations will take their top executives, their Swiss bank accounts, pack up their computer tapes and New York will be a ghost town." Jace took another drink. "The question is, what will Texas do?"

I didn't know that was the question.

"My choice would be secession." Jace sat back.

Funny, I knew that was going to be the answer.

"Horseshit," Farah said.

"It can be done," Jace argued. "It's legal."

"I've heard that before," Farah replied.

"Look at this country." Jace pointed back up the peninsula. "This is America in one hundred years. A few rich and the rest poor. That's your communism and your democracy. The right to be as poor as these bastards. No middle class."

Farah laughed and clapped her hands. "Wonderful." She pointed at Jace. "A simple man who wants to make the world safe for insurance salesmen."

"The insurance business built America," Jace said. "Everybody wants to sleep with their hand in the other guy's pocket. Nobody works anymore."

"Righto, Daddy." Junior spoke for the first time since

agreeing with Jace that the stock market would crash in '79 if the price of natural gas wasn't deregulated. Jace made it sound like a promise.

"We could join OPEC and if them Yankee peckerheads don't like it," Jace said, "let the bastards freeze in the dark. Texas is the frontier and the frontier is for the strong individual. He stands or falls on his own. There isn't any substitute for work. Mabry here knows that." Jace pointed at me. "Athletes have frontier mentalities, it's what makes them a valuable resource. You have to be tough. You have to take responsibility and you have to work hard. It's the individual who advances civilization. Renee Richards is an athlete designed by committee, like them goddamn East Germans." Jace hit the table with his fist. "But, by God, we'll beat them Commie bastards because we got great individuals. You know it's independents like me that find eighty percent of all the oil and natural gas in the world, not the major oil companies." Jace looked around the table. "You got that? *In-Dee-Pendents.* If you want to survive you depend on the individual, not on a committee."

"I don't want to just survive," Farah said. "I want life to be better."

"That's dreaming with one hand and shitting in the other." Jace smiled benignly. "You won't find out if life gets better until the end. It's the *total* that counts."

Jace and Ora Bell excused themselves to go take "la siesta," as Ora Bell called it.

"He's a grand old man." Junior watched them cross the dining room. "I just want to make him proud of me."

"I'm sure you will, Jason." Farah patted her husband's arm. It was the first time I had heard anybody call him anything but Junior. It seemed to startle him. Farah smiled. Her face was radiant. The extra flesh of her thirties softened the thin straight nose and high cheekbones.

Jace and Ora Bell stopped halfway across the room to talk

to a Dallas man who made a fortune teaching silicone chips to remember things. His guest celebrity was the retired National League batting champion. Baseball players are the weirdest of all. I think it's all that organ music.

"Daddy was 'horn manager, you know." Junior turned to me. 'Horn manager was the guy who got towels and water for the University of Texas football team. "And I was a pretty good football player at Saint Mark's, but I couldn't see any future in it. The coach was a real prick." He looked around the room and then back at me.

"Say, are you interested in some gas leases?" Junior asked me. "I'll cut you in on proven fields just waiting for deregulation. There's already a lot of famous people involved. It's a gold mine."

"Is that a mixed metaphor?" Farah asked.

"They're ignored reserves," Junior pressed. "It's a great investment. Just sit back and wait for the Congress to deregulate. You should see the numbers . . . great numbers." Junior stood. "Well, I've got to run. Billy and I are going to play some gin." He bent down and kissed Farah. "Be a sweetheart and don't tell Jace. Ta-ta."

Billy Bentson winked at me and followed Junior out of the dining room. Billy was the best gin cheater in Fort Worth.

"I wouldn't invest too heavily in anything with Junior," Farah warned. "He has no idea about business, he's just trying to get Jace to like him by making the big score. He thinks he's gonna win big in the Celebrity Pigeon Shoot. Billy Bentson keeps cleaning him out. There's your ignored reserves."

Farah reached across the table and touched my arm. "Welcome to the elite international event for winners. I asked Jace to invite you."

"Why the change? I figured I wasn't successful enough for you."

"I got lonely for someone dependable," Farah said. "You don't have to be successful, just be dependable."

"What does Junior think about this?"

"I have a duty to my son to stay with Junior," she said. "As long as he doesn't publicly embarrass me, I won't publicly embarrass him."

"You like that power, don't you?"

She stiffened.

"I'm looking for a relationship," she said, "and I think you are, too. But I want promises and guarantees that you won't cause trouble."

"No guarantees," I said, "but I might just get me some of that power."

"Fat chance," Farah said. "You used to be a crazy football star, now you're just crazy." She smiled and scratched lightly on my wrist. "But I guess I'll settle for you. You want some help repairing your damaged ego?"

"I already fixed it myself with plastic wood," I said. "You'll have to run your fingers over my naked body to find the rough edges."

A fifty-foot Chris-Craft glided into the cove from the Pacific. It was Hondo Higgins' boat, the *Gorilla Woman*. Hondo stood on the bow with his arm around Stormy Claridge. The last of the celebrities had arrived. Tomorrow the competition would begin.

"You'll need to get a job. I'll talk to Jace," Farah said.

"Who wants a goddamn job?"

"You'll adjust, if you want that power. Learn to take instead of want," Farah said. "I had a job once. That's how I met Junior." She rubbed my wrist with her soft fingers. "I worked at the New York World's Fair, selling corny dogs and Dr. Peppers in the Texas Pavilion. The New Yorkers called them 'Gorny dogs and Mistah Peppah.' " She fell into a Brooklynese. "I was eighteen and just out of El Paso County. New York City was so glamorous. Junior had one of those little Alfas and he was so intense at Princeton, studying and writing poetry and talking about joining the Peace Corps. He said he was never going to work for Jace. I thought Junior was a shy, sensitive boy from North Dallas who would make it in spite of his daddy's money." Farah gazed out at the sparkling cove. Hondo and Stormy were being rowed ashore from the *Gorilla Woman*. "In New York I saw my first Afro."

"When did you first eat pizza?"

Farah smiled. "One day Sonny Jeeter lost his watch and one shoe on the Log Flume Ride. I think he'd been drinking."

"It's guys like Sonny that give the rest of us bad names," I said.

"I got pregnant about that time, and Junior and I went to Dallas and got married," Farah added. "He's no Jace, but he's always been good to Trey and me." Farah stopped to watch Hondo and Stormy step ashore. "Junior just hasn't been the same since his mother drowned herself at our wedding reception. Nobody missed her until we started opening the gifts."

The sun was sinking behind the high rocks that protected the west side of the cove. The fishing fleet bobbed at the end of the long shadows, crawling across the water toward the hotel. Torches were lighted in the dining room and the Aztec Bar. Hondo and Stormy joined us. Both of them were sunburned. We ordered another round of drinks.

Hondo was a celebrity angler. Stormy had a modeling job. Ezra had set it up.

"They're shooting swimwear and beachwear stuff around the Celebrity Fishing Tourney," she said.

"I know," I said. "Celebrities make a nice backdrop."

"Yeh, well Hondo offered me a ride down on his boat and I heard about that dinky little airstrip. I saved my plane fare and got a little sun on the way down." She turned to Farah. "Ezra set up an appointment with your father-in-law about a television job."

"You still trying to be a sportscaster?" Farah asked.

"Yeh." Stormy's eyes lit up. "I'm a natural. I'm going to marry one of the premier players and I know as much about sports as Phyllis George. The rest is just remembering numbers and looking cute." She licked her lips. "And I can do that standing on my head. Especially standing on my head. Did you see me on the Carson Show?"

Farah shook her head.

She frowned. "Johnny wasn't there. I got Joan Rivers instead." She was disappointed. "I've got some great ideas for televising women's sports. I'm going to tell them to Jace."

"Honey," Farah said, "he doesn't want to hear *your* good idea, he only wants to hear his good idea."

"Women's sports is booming," Stormy enthused. "After the last Olympics the interest in women's gymnastics skyrocketed. Television sports is very positive."

"Television will make all those little girls want to be Nadia Comaneci," Farah said. "All the neuroses of pro athletes without the skills or the income."

"Sports teaches successful technique, a certain mentality," Stormy said. "My tennis coach says actors have the minds of natural athletes. He says acting expands the imagination—that's why I'm such a good tennis player after only one year."

Stormy couldn't play tennis for shit.

"Can I tell them about the movie?" Stormy asked Hondo. Her eyes were big and expectant.

Hondo nodded.

"Hondo liked my dance so well the other night he wants me in this big-budget porno musical." Stormy was enthusiastic. "My experience in the Miss Texas Pageant sure has paid off."

In the Miss Texas Pageant Stormy danced to "Ragtime Cowboy Joe" in a gold lamé cowboy suit. She was chosen to hold the Roman candle during the "I Love Thee, Lone Star" finale. On the extemporaneous questions she said she wanted her own line of cosmetics and believed in the death penalty.

"The musical will be sort of like *Tommy*," Stormy continued.

"Titus Bean did the libretto and Willy Roy Rogers scored

it," Hondo said. "It's a country-western outlaw porn with a message."

"I mean, man, there's no euphemisms in this." Stormy licked her lips and quickly indicated the camera and lighting setups. "I've got the finale number. It's what the sixties were all about." She stared, sightless, out toward Ecuador. "My lover lies naked and dead, killed by bigotry and censorship and repression."

I pictured a naked hippie beaten to bloody jelly by William F. Buckley wielding a giant rubber stamp.

"A single spot focuses on me in all my nakedness and I look up in my natural innocence, my body bruised and covered with the drying semen of rapine ejaculations."

"Rapine ejaculations?" I sat up.

Stormy gave me a look of exasperation. "I'm raped by the same motorcycle gang of crazed Vietnam vets that kill my lover." With rapid hand movements she quickly replaced the cameras and lighting, reglazed her eyes and was back in the finale. "I sing this song with the camera coming in close in soft focus until just my face fills the whole screen, then closer, to my lips, and I sing this song of forgiveness called 'What's Forgiving for If It's Not for Giving Head.' " She sat back. "Then I blow them all between verses. It'll be dynamite."

"I see what you mean about no euphemisms," Farah said.

Hondo smiled and winked at me. "I'm trying to package Hopper and Fonda. They're great in motorcycle pictures." Hondo leaned back and looked across the darkening water toward the boat. Flickering torches ringed the dining room and bar. Occasionally someone would take a photograph and the flash would light up the cove.

"Go get us a drink," Hondo directed Stormy.

"Listen," Hondo said, watching Stormy go to the bar, "I don't want you all to get the wrong idea about Stormy and me. It's a professional relationship. She's got talent. I'm doing this as a favor to Ezra. I think a lot of Ezra. It's a principle with me, don't ask me why"—he made an elaborate shrug as if explaining an unwilling theopathy—"but I never fuck my friends' old ladies." He rubbed his chin. "I'll let 'em blow me, though," he added. "You don't have the competition or the emotional involvement."

The sun was gone, leaving the western sky a soft coral. The torchlight from the hotel flickered across the water. The surf against the rock was the only sound. Stormy returned with the drinks. Farah smiled. She put her bare foot in my chair and rubbed the inside of my leg with her toes.

A blue twin-engine Cessna buzzed onto the landing strip in a cloud of dust. Raul was bringing in the last load of Ora Bell's luggage. Red's pickup rattled out of the courtyard and up the hogback.

CHAPTER

THE CIRRUS CLOUDS IN THE EASTERN SKY MADE THE RISING sun look like it was shining down a hall. It was the last day of the Annual Baja Celebrity Fish Tourney. The fishing had been bad all week and everybody was pissed off except Farah and me. We spent the long hot days together. While everyone else competed, we idled away afternoons and nights, tangled in sweat-soaked bed sheets. I felt the stirrings of emotional involvement.

I met Farah for lunch. We ate quietly in the high-ceilinged, whitewashed dining room. The sunlight bounced off the polished tile floor. We had salads and seafoods and wine. Farah signed the bill.

All the men were out fishing and would be gone until nightfall. The cove was empty. Talk about serious competitors—all day at sea, all night awash.

"I like these isolated jet-set hangouts." Farah looked down at the pool. Stormy and the models were in and around the water. The fashion photographer was shooting from the clerestory wall of the Aztec Bar. "The smell of people isn't on everything."

"It won't be isolated here much longer since the government built that tourist highway," I said. "Satellite view of it looks sort of like a catheter draining Southern California."

Farah sighed, "Only a few seasons left for us international sportspersons and this place will be Miami on the Sea of

Cortez. They'll have the Super Bowl here and everything will smell of people."

"I take it that means people stink."

"People stink."

We drank daiquiris and watched the photographer move Stormy around. He seemed to favor poses where she was sucking on something.

As the sun began to sink the celebrity fleet started to drift in and people began clustering around the palapas on the beach. They squinted into the glare, checking for marlin flags. There weren't many.

"You know, in last year's tourney," Farah watched the boats, "Jace slugged a fish for being too small."

"The old killer instinct," I said.

The boats anchored and the Mexican kids were rowing celebrity anglers ashore. The fishermen were all in whiteface, greased with sunscreen. The successful ones stopped at the waterline and had their pictures taken with their catches. None was impressive.

Jace Everett stood smiling for the photographer, holding a small blue marlin. No one would know, watching this tiny grinning man, that he was a fishbeater.

The models and photographer moved to the beach. Stormy Claridge, in a string bikini, stroked Luther Watt's rooster fish while Red, the foreman, showed Nadine how he could blow smoke rings through the hole in his throat. George Billings was flitting at the waterline, helping celebrities with their fish.

"Let's go see Hondo." Farah pointed at the *Gorilla Woman* anchored again in the cove. I followed her. We hailed a kid to row us to the boat. When we got to the *Gorilla Woman* I paid the kid a dollar.

"Jesus, you're killing the exchange rate here." Hondo was looking out the open porthole of his stateroom. "Pipe these fuckers aboard, mate," he yelled to Fernando, his Cuban mate. We climbed aboard and joined Hondo at the fantail table.

Hondo purchased the *Gorilla Woman* with the money from

his first independently produced film—a sci-fi disaster story about a bad batch of birth-controll pills that caused "crazed hormones."

"Fernando! C'mere," Hondo yelled to the Latin man.

Fernando frowned and thumped over to the rail.

"Nobody can swim here." Hondo spoke louder when he spoke to Fernando. I guess to Hondo it meant he was bilingual. Fernando said nothing. It was more like Hondo thought Fernando was deaf instead of Spanish-speaking.

"They cut bait here." Hondo pointed at the water several times, enunciating and forming the words with his lips. "Sharks. There's sharks here." Hondo bared his teeth. Fernando nodded and went below deck.

"Fernando's a good man," Hondo said. "Met him in Bogotá six-seven years ago when we shot that Hell's-Angels-in-the-Angolan-Civil-War picture. I had to figure out a way to keep the whole set from getting busted for cocaine. Jace Everett had some money in the picture and his pilot Raul and Fernando were in Cuba together. Fernando knew somebody in the president's office and gets it fixed for twenty-five thousand dollars. Fernando knows somebody everywhere. There's Cubans all over Latin America. Everybody's somebody's uncle."

"I don't like the way he creeps around and never says anything," Farah said. "Everytime I see him he looks like he's just finished doing something dirty." Farah removed her blouse and was sunbathing. Her nipples were erect. Chill bumps covered the areola. Fernando returned from below deck with two brandy snifters, one filled with high quality Colombian cocaine and the other filled with brown Mexican heroin. The heroin was to smooth out the cocaine.

"This is the real drama," Hondo said as Fernando placed the powder-filled snifters on the table, "the drama of destruction."

I snorted the rails that Hondo offered. They hit differently. The cocaine sliced neatly between the eyes into the front of my brain. The heroin hit like a sawed-off shotgun; brain, spine, balls, stomach, arms, legs, my synapses uncoupled ever so gently. I felt wonderful. The feeling was familiar and terrifying. I made a note to pass any more brown and stay with tequila and cocaine. I smiled at Fernando and leaned back. Anxiety and panic receded.

Everyone and everything was distinctly outlined and in its place. The world was tidy. The red-brown peninsula supported the pristine white hotel to the land's end. The colors of the ocean and sky were brilliant, clear, and vibrant. Up on the hogback near the airstrip stood the village of the Mexican hotel help—shanty houses made of sticks—a village of human thoughts, hopes, and actions. It resembled a brush pile where animals sought shelter.

Water slapped gently against the hull.

Farah had turned on the tape deck and "Motel Time" blared across the water. "Jack Blanchard and Misty Morgan is Hondo's favorite country team." Farah smiled. "Fuck Donny and Marie, and fuck Conway and Loretta. Right, Hondo?"

"Right, babe." Hondo flipped a cigarette butt over the side. I watched the fish nibble on the filter tip and took some time considering the different couplings that Farah had suggested.

"You shouldn't litter, Hondo," Farah said. "Don't you listen to Woodsy Owl?"

"Fuck Woodsy Owl." Hondo banged the table and caused Fernando to spill heroin into his moustache. I refused to consider Woodsy Owl while Fernando brushed the heroin from his moustache onto his tongue.

The boom of a shotgun echoed across the silent cove.

"There they go." Hondo didn't bother to look toward the sound. "The wind's picking up. It'll make it tough shooting." I looked across the choppy blue-white water toward the hotel.

Farah was facing west, trying to catch the last rays of the sun.

"Got the light changing on 'em," Hondo said as a second boom echoed. "Using the air cannon for the first fifty birds and having the second fifty hand-thrown."

Fernando had moved to the bow and was using binoculars, watching a purple-and-white van move slowly through the Mexican village to the airstrip. It was the same van that had been parked by the wreckage of the Jap freighter.

"How much do you think Junior'll win?" I asked.

"Nothin'," Hondo said. "Billy's smarter, a better shot, and he bought off the thrower."

The original bet on the pigeon shoot was the $4,700 that Junior had lost to Billy at gin. Junior was suspicious that Billy had cheated, but he couldn't prove it. George Billings, the astronaut, had watched the card game.

"I played a lot of poker in the Air Force, Mr. Everett," Billings told Junior's father later. "I have seen every kind of cheater there is. This guy just goddamn drew the cards." Astronauts believing they had seen it all was a syndrome that has long been the concern of NASA psychiatrists. Good cheaters, of course, wouldn't be in the Air Force. Billy had cheated all night.

Junior was standing framed in the pointed arch of the hotel terrace, wearing white pants and a matching lightweight safari jacket. Stephano, the hairdresser, stood behind him, smiling. The air cannon, on a rock ledge beneath the hotel, launched the pigeons out toward the ocean. Billy had already shot twice. One pigeon lay in bloody disarray on the rocks while a second circled over the hotel.

"Dumb fucking pigeon." Hondo watched the surviving pigeon head back to its roost in the Mexican village.

It was a half mile from the hotel to the *Gorilla Woman.* The thrower stuffed another pigeon down the barrel of the air cannon. Junior nodded and the thrower pulled the lanyard, launching the feathered cannonball skyward. The frantic pigeon began flapping his wings before the dull thunk of the compressed air charge reached us. The sights and sounds were out of sync. The pigeon went into evasive action, barrel-rolling and making a half turn, getting some distance between him and Junior. Suddenly an invisible hand slapped the bird from the sky. Then the solid boom of a matched Baretta rolled over the *Gorilla Woman.* The bird bounced off a rock into the water. Feathers floated silently in the salt breeze.

"You never hear the one what gets ya." Hondo reached toward the snifter full of brown powder. "The only way to go. Look at the asshole that got away." He gestured angrily in the direction of the village and threw heroin all over the table.

Farah leaned over until her naked nipples raked the tabletop and slowly licked up the brown powder.

Hondo pointed to her smooth brown back. "And you ask, is there a God?"

There was another boom.

By the time Billy missed his fourth straight bird Junior wanted to up his bet.

Billy agreed to the bet reluctantly and asked only the courtesy of not being forced to honor bets in excess of what he had already won. Junior told him piss on that. They tripled the bet. Billy staged it brilliantly, but almost underestimated his opponent.

Junior competed with a rage, but Billy's shooting skill, coupled with the thrower's skill at pulling tail feathers, was too much.

During the shooting Fernando rowed ashore and was up at Jace's plane, talking with Raul and the driver of the purple-and-white van. Red stood off to the side, blowing smoke rings through the opening from his laryngectomy.

By the end of the match, the cliff below the hotel was littered with dead and dying pigeons. The thrower clambered over bloody rocks, wringing pigeons' necks, while Junior paid off Billy. It was a big score for Billy. On the *Gorilla Woman* it had become background noise.

CHAPTER

THE CELEBRITY FISH TOURNEY VICTORY LUAU AND COCKfight was a gala evening complete with fireworks. Farah and Hondo and I sat on the fantail and drank and snorted until Fernando returned to take us ashore. I had had too much tequila and decided to swim.

"Fuck the sharks," I said and thrashed into shore just daring some great white sonofabitch to mess with me.

When Hondo and Farah and Fernando rowed up, I was dripping and leaning against a giant torch talking to Billy Bentson. Billy was looking for side bets on the Celebrity Cockfight. Junior Everett had no idea what sailing on Eagle Mountain Lake with a Fort Worth speedboat cowboy would cost him.

We wove our way through circles of celebrities littered along the beach, all eating at their own whole cooked deer complete with antlers. Famous people dressed in flowered shirts and white double knits squatted in the sand, devouring whole deers with their bare hands. It was pretty weird in the flickering torchlight.

The Everett party only partially encircled their deer, leaving empty spaces near the rear haunches. At least I wouldn't have to look it in the eyes. Ora Bell's hairdresser, Stephano, and Junior were conspicuously absent.

Fernando grabbed up a coconut full of pink something, toasted everyone, and drank it down. Then he leaned over and deftly gouged out the deer's eyeballs and popped them into his mouth. Grabbing another coconut, he walked a few yards into the flickering shadows, lay on his back, and sang into the sky about the cockroach that had no marijuana.

"I gave him the night off," Hondo said. "He had a big day."

"Fine." Jace smiled and winked. "Fine." Jace pointed through the deer's antlers to Luther and Nadine Watt. "Mrs. Watt was just telling us about the book her husband is writing."

"Oh, please call me Nadine, Mr. Everett," Nadine said.

"Call me Jace, Nadine."

They learned each other's first names. Nadine would think that was lucky.

"Well, Luther doesn't actually do the writing. He just talks into a tape recorder. Titus Bean types it out and puts it in order. It's real lucky we can get him," Nadine continued. "He had another book canceled."

I'm glad I live in the kind of universe where I can see other folks benefiting from my entropy.

Billings began discussing his proposed book about the spelunking gap between us and the Russians. "I think I have some relevant things to say."

The fucking spelunking gap.

We sat around and ripped hunks off the deer and stuffed them down our throats and sloshed down pink stuff out of the coconuts on top of the venison. Finally Jace proposed a toast.

"Here's to us winners." He and Luther had won the Annual Baja Celebrity Fish Tourney on their small marlin and rooster fish. The fishing had been lousy. Jace proposed a second toast. "To competition," he said. "It's what built the world. Without it the human race would stagnate."

"Why is it," I asked, "that the rich people discuss competition and the poor people live it?" I was bored by these ersatz athletes.

"Rich people discuss competition because they learned about it getting to be rich people," Jace said. "Stifle competition and you give evolutionary weaknesses unfair advantage. Competition is evolution, it's neither good nor bad, it just is and is necessary. And the first thing to learn about competition is that it's dealer's choice."

I thought Billy Bentson should have said that. Nobody pays attention to their lines. Billy just sat there with his wet little ferret eyes gleaming. Billy never said much unless in the throes of a personality collapse. Then you couldn't shut him up and he'd show you his cheating gadgets and his card tricks. But Billy was a good enough cheater to try and notice when his edges were frayed. Billy paid close attention to that aspect. He was greatly influenced by Jackie Gleason as Minnesota Fats in *The Hustler*. Billy recognized the danger of something being out of place.

"Well, all I know," Farah spoke softly, "is that society is based on cooperation. Competition against one another is a centrifugal force. It's dangerous. It even makes sex competition."

"Honey"—Jace winked at Farah—"love and aggression are the same. You can't have love without competition. It's a social tension that binds us together, and learning to handle that tension is what love is about. Strong relationships are a direct result of strong competition." Jace clenched a fist. "The need to become part of society is the other side of the desire to be an individual, and aggression is how we work out the contradiction. It's a defense of our personal space. Sure sex is competition, it's all competition."

Luther said he thought sex was "just a matter of a guy and a gal gettin' sumthin' straight between them." Then he went "yuk yuk yuk."

I couldn't tell if he was serious. I laughed, but nobody else did.

Hondo and Jace got in a protracted argument over who had found the prettiest pebble on the beach. Finally Farah said that Hondo's rock had the cutest grain while Jace's had the nicest feel. Jace was not satisfied.

"Cutest grain my red ass." He stood and heaved his pebble into the darkness. "Fuck cutest is what I say."

Then Jace took Hondo to see the projections on his Everett Sports Enterprises South American Sports Network. Nadine went off to bed. Stormy went to change. They were planning to shoot fashion stuff around the cockfight.

Junior came and got Farah. They stood just outside the torchlight circle and talked with the redheaded Stephano, Ora Bell's hairdresser. They were arguing in whispers, giving me Buck Binder déjà vu. Farah suddenly threw her drink down the front of Stephano's glove-leather suit.

"Bitch," Stephano snarled and stalked up the beach. The wet leather squeaked with each step. He wove through the partially eaten deer carcasses that littered the sand. I could hear Stephano squeaking long after he was out of sight.

They held the cockfight in the Aztec Bar. George Billings supervised the creation of an arena by circling the cocktail chairs and pouring sawdust on the polished tile floor. It was pretty bizarre—rich people in evening clothes watching Mexican roosters rip each other to bloody shreds. Flashbulbs popped while Stormy and the models struck poses for the fashion phtographer. The celebrities made a great backdrop.

"This is sure something, Mabry." Luther and I sat at a table near the bar and watched the ring of people hooting and yelling at the struggling chickens. "Did you ever think you'd get to a place like this?"

"The question is, will I get out?" I said. "The whole place is meaningless to me. I got no purpose here. I'm like a piece of driftwood. I get picked up, examined, and even stroked, but they'll toss me back to float or sink. It's somebody else's world, somebody else's ocean."

Luther looked at me and frowned. I wasn't a celebrity. It wasn't a good feeling.

When someone is lost in the wilderness, the biggest danger is panic. Searchers often find the bodies of the lost with their clothes ripped off and their flesh in bloody shreds. Terrified of being lost and terrified by disconnection, they panic and run until the underbrush tears them to pieces. I can feel that terror churning in my belly.

"You know," Luther continued, "Nadine's right—we been lucky, and I feel guilty about not wanting to settle down. But you just can't turn yourself off. I been running on adrenaline and nerve too long. I like it. I tried to take some time in the spring and just stay around the house. It was a disaster. I paced around. Bitched at the kid and Nadine."

The crowd around the cockfight began screaming. "Get up, you sumbitch." Junior threw his drink at the rooster he was backing. The rooster had taken one in the throat and wasn't about to get up. The handler picked up the bird and sucked the blood out of its throat and blew air into its lungs, trying to revive it.

Billy Bentson came by and collected one thousand dollars from Junior.

Stormy Claridge, in a hooded blue-and-white striped velour jacket and white cotton pants, walked down the staircase into the Aztec Bar from the dining room. The photographer clicked all the way. Luther watched her closely.

"Would you be happy with all the women you wanted?" He looked at me hard.

"It holds a certain savage appeal to me," I said.

"Me too," Luther said. "I wonder why?"

" 'Cause we're lost in Mexico and afraid to walk out alone."

"I ain't lost and I ain't alone. I got Nadine. How come I want more?" Luther was puzzled. "Nadine says I'm sexist." He chased a shot of tequila with a beer.

"I think you're just horny," I said. "It's the pressure of performing."

Luther watched a woman in a pink cocktail dress at the bar sloshing down a daiquiri. "Did you ever notice," he said, "that all the assholes at the front of the line are just like all the assholes in the back?"

"I guess it doesn't do any good to crowd," I said.

"It's always good to crowd," he said. "You might as well be with the assholes in front as the ones in the back." He kept his eyes on the woman perched on the bas-relief stone barstool of the Aztec god Huitzilopochitl.

Aztec priests once ripped the still-beating hearts from the chests of sacrificial victims to honor and appease this god of sun and war. Now a fat lady from New Orleans in a pink dress squatted on his head and drank a banana daiquiri.

Luther leaned backward and stretched his back, the vertebrae popped loud enough for me to hear. He kept staring out toward the cove. Somewhere on the beach a flashbulb momentarily illuminated the entire cove—the bobbing boats, the granite scarp, the brown rocks. Then it was all swallowed again in black.

"You know, man, this is just like I thought it would be." Luther's eyes gleamed wetly. "All them goddamn years of working stock and borrowing money for entry fees. I imagined it would be like this. It kept me going." The cowboy laughed. "I got it now, Mabry, and I ain't lettin' it go. I'm the champion, the best, and I'm gonna capitalize on it. I'm gonna hold two or three roping and riding schools every year. I'm training more horses to sell. I'm gonna ride it to the end. I worked too hard to get here not to start grabbing with both hands."

He held up his scarred and callused hands. They showed the price he had paid: The knuckles were swollen and the fingers were misshapen; the skin was cracked, scabbed, and dry. Luther slept in Vaseline-soaked gloves to ease the dryness and pain.

"God, the things Nadine had to do. That's a good woman, Mabry. She worked her ass off and never complained. I know she irritates you with that 'We're so lucky' crap, but, man, she worked so hard. I love that woman, Mabry. I need her." Luther had tears in his eyes. His joy was uncontained. He was a success.

Luther looked over at Stormy. He laughed again. "I just can't believe it. It's just like I imagined it from the first. Imagination. That's the key. You have to imagine your life first."

He was right about imagination, but I had never prepared to imagine my life from this point.

Luther watched as Stormy posed against the bar, her hips thrust forward. The fashion photographer shot up from his knees at her feet.

"Listen, buddy," Luther said. "If you need a job, Nadine's daddy, Big Bob, will give you two hundred fifty dollars a month and a damn good house trailer to look after his ranch up on the Blanco River."

I nodded.

Luther stood and stretched and then touched his toes. "Boy, I got myself some bodily cares. I feel like my spirit is shriveling up. I need a hot beef energy injection." He looked at Stormy.

"What about Nadine?" I asked.

"She's already asleep," Luther said. "She needs her sleep more than she needs my pain. A man don't wake up his wife to fuck her."

"Maybe I will," I said. "She's not my wife."

"Sure, go ahead." Luther smiled. "If you want your dick broke off."

He kept his eyes on Stormy, who was bent forward, posing with her finger in her mouth. "That girl likes to perform, she likes the pressure and the pain. She's like us, only younger and tougher. Can't hurt her unless I wear my spurs." He walked over and said something about a filly. The last I saw of them they were walking toward the beach and he was explaining to her what a "heeler" was.

Billy Bentson won $9,500 on the cockfight. He had made a deal with the handlers.

If I ever would have given up my comeback it was that last night in Baja during the fireworks show, when George Billings,

the astronaut, said, "The sky sure makes a nice backdrop."
Something snapped in my head.
"Let's go someplace simpler," I said to Farah.
"For instance?"
"I can get a job looking after a ranch on the Blanco River," I said. "It doesn't pay much."
"Why?" Farah's face was blue from the flash of a giant pinwheel.
" 'Cause I'm tired and I suddenly feel a kinship with fighting cocks, pigeons, and blue marlin. It's not how I expected to end up. In fact, until this instant I never considered ending up at all."
I think she considered it for a moment but it was difficult to read her expression in the bizarre light of the fireworks show. I know I would have gone that night.
"How much does it pay?"
"Two-fifty."
"A week?"
"A month, but we'd get a trailer."
"A trailer? A house trailer?"
I nodded. "Not much security, but some."
A giant red rocket exploded, bathing the cove in a red glare. Everything seemed magnified.
Farah shook her head. "I left El Paso County because I didn't want to end up in a house trailer. I'm not going to start my son out in one. Trey has the right to his family's wealth and power. I'm going to see he gets his share."
"It doesn't seem to be doing his father much good."
"What the hell would you know about it?" Farah flared. "Listen, please just stick with me on this. It's gonna be a good deal."
"I've heard that before."
"I've already spoken to Jace," she said. "He wants you to come to work for him in Dallas. WBAR needs a midnight-to-six-A.M. disc jockey. They'll try and take advantage of your name—you may be a celebrity yet."

I accepted with the confidence of a man who thinks that listening to radio qualifies one as a radio expert. I imagined I would be a great celebrity. Imagination. Discipline. Confidence.

That night I couldn't sleep. Thoughts of my future with Farah kept colliding with the sight of me thrashing in the cove, almost fatally out of my element. It was more deathbent than I've ever been.

JAWS CHOMP JENKINS COMEBACK; FANS MOURN

I can't believe I did it. I'm terrified of being eaten alive.

"FUCK THE SHARKS" JENKINS' LAST WORDS

The moon put a phosphorescent shimmer on the cove. I thought about Farah and wondered if my being dependable would really be enough. I doubted it and I doubted that I could be dependable. I wanted power too. Football had made me feel powerful. I missed it sorely. I didn't really want to live in a house trailer on the Blanco River. I thought about Luther off with Stormy. Nadine would be alone in her room. Getting the women, that's the real competition. My cock began to stiffen.

I was thinking about jacking off when Farah burst into my room.

"I told Junior about us . . . the way I want it." She flicked on the light. "Oh, Christ."

I stared at her, my cock in my hand.

"Well . . . ah . . ." she stammered, ". . . ah . . . he's run off on the motorcycles with Stephano. . . . Ah, I think he's out of the closet." She closed the door and flicked off the light. "Here, let me do that."

She knelt across the bed and began stroking me gently, then she leaned forward and began sucking. She stopped. Her hair fell across her face as she turned her head to look up. Her lower lip was wet.

"I'm only doing this because you look so pathetic." She smiled and brushed her hair back and began sucking again.

Mr. Pathetic gets a blow job, I wanted to say, but I didn't. I was afraid she would stop. I think that's what she means about sex being competitive. I just watched her head bob and felt the warmth of her mouth. Her lips had some genuine heft to them. It wasn't all lip gloss. Jesus, what a treat.

As I came, filling her mouth, I imagined the satellite view of me on the very tip of the Baja Peninsula with this beautiful woman kneeling between my legs, sucking noisily. Very phallic. Very sexual. Very gratifying. I exploded into her mouth and felt like things were getting better. I felt powerful.

On the other hand, it could just be an ego thing.

PART THREE

FUTILE ATTEMPTS

He may be dead but he's still mean
I wrapped him in the white and green . . .

CHAPTER 1

I PLAYED WILLY ROY ROGERS' GRAMMY-WINNING "I BURIED My Dog in My High-School Sweater" as the last cut on my midnight-to-six-A.M. shift on WBAR, the Dallas Country Place. I closed out the show with a moment of meditation sponsored by the Transmission Clinic and segued into the news.

The news was sponsored by Standard Oil and Johnny Cash was fronting for them. It was like Woody Guthrie doing spots for Peabody Coal.

As I unplugged my earphones, Nit and Nat, the morning drive-time team, bustled into the studio. They had the air from six to ten and the ratings to hold it. Their numbers were a little soft from six to seven, when they needed an hour to draw back all the listeners I drove off from midnight to six.

Nit and Nat erected their sound-effects gear, getting screwed down for four hours of prime-time radio. Their eyes had a wild cast. Panic at six A.M. They did a tight show with no dead air, using cartridge-tape rooster crows and a cowbell a lot: "Clang clang clang, cockadoodledoo" and into the country hymn of the hour. They strained to be country and made a lot of jokes about Levi's, boots, and cow shit.

I pushed my earphones into my mailbox and turned to leave the studio.

"George Billings is in the program director's office—he wants to see you."

“Thanks, Nit,” I mumbled. My mind crackled and my ears rang.

“Nat.”

“What?” I turned back.

“I’m Nat. Jesus, Mabry you been here three months and you still can’t tell us apart.”

“Sorry, Nat.” I apologized and stumbled out of the studio past the newscaster, who was quoting John Connally as wishing that more Americans were as decent as the Shah of Iran.

“It’s six A.M. and the world’s still spinning. This is Big Red with the news.” Big Red put that little Paul Harvey squeal into “news.”

I don’t know why I couldn’t keep Nit and Nat straight. Nit is in his mid-forties and bald, while Nat is a full-headed blond about twenty-six. But on the radio they sounded exactly alike, and I seldom saw them except at six every weekday morning—and at the small-time celebrity events where a local merchant rents “the whole WBAR Gang” to showcase his products. At these events ex-astronaut George Billings, Everett Enterprises Celebrity Coordinator, required us to dress up in cowboy costumes complete with cap guns. He wanted an authentic-looking “WBAR Gang.” Billings called himself coach and gave pep talks about the necessity of celebrity events as public relations for the station.

“I love the challenge,” he would say. But he never dressed up in cowboy drag and ran around in public like some escapee from day camp. Beware of a goddamn eager astronaut.

Last month during State Fair General Motors hired us to dress up and run around in a posse at the Automobile Building “arresting” people to come look at the new Buicks and Cadillacs.

Ford had the Punt, Pass, and Kick tie-in with Ezra Lyttle and Sonny Jeeter while Stormy Claridge and a magician worked the Chrysler exhibit.

General Motors had “The WBAR Gang.” Nit and Nat promoted it all week in between the Honda giveaways. We spent the week hijacking people at gunpoint to come look at the GM cars. Everybody was always over at the Chrysler exhibit watching the magician saw Stormy in half.

A cowboy from Fort Worth punched out Big Red to escape a WBAR Gang Celebrity Customer Roundup.

"You ain't taking me in," he yelled and just knocked the shit out of the tiny newscaster. Big Red is only about five foot two. He has a big voice. It's the nature of radio.

I walked down the hall as Big Red finished the news with a report that the city of Houston is sinking.

George Billings was sitting at the program director's desk. He had the current Arbitron ratings in front of him. As celebrity coordinator, Billings was troubleshooter for WBAR and Jace Everett. It was a perfect job for a retired colonel.

"Your numbers stink," he said.

I wasn't surprised. Last month my show didn't even register on the ratings charts. I knew it was only a matter of time.

While all America hungered for the chance to be a good audience, I couldn't strike a responsive chord. I felt it was unfair that they didn't give me any money or Hondas or trips to Six Flags to give away. I hated the job. The manic, insane, babbling nights were taking their toll, turning my nervous system inside out. I began hearing the phrase "the long slide down." It just sort of repeated itself again and again in my head, my right cerebral hemisphere trying to make something clear to the left, wearing out my corpus callosum. I was suffering a peculiar sensory deprivation. I was talking and no one was listening, not even me. . . .

"The long slide down" . . . I would wake up with it ringing in my ears.

"Did you have Smoking Jim Stewart on your show last night?" Billings turned another page.

"Yeah, we talked philosophy to those waiting for the effects of their drug overdoses." Smoking Jim had stopped by at three A.M., drunk and depressed about his injury grievance. The club had claimed he was a junkie.

"I thought so." Billings sighed. "That guy from the ACLU called me at home last night and said you two were saying "nigger" again on the public airwaves. We would rather you interviewed active players. People aren't interested in has-beens. Stewart's over the hill."

"Sorry, George, but active players are tough to get at three A.M."

"I don't care, man," Billings said. "Mr. Everett said to put you on, we put you on. Call your old teammates and interview them over the phone. They'll still take your calls, won't they? We gotta keep trying to get these numbers up." He turned another page. "We gotta saturate the market. Since we own your name now, we gotta make it worth something."

Before WBAR would spend money on advertising I had to sign over exclusive rights to my name to Jace Everett. In three months it hadn't done them much good. Not that Jace didn't try. He put my face on billboards, ran radio and TV promos. *Mabry in the Morning*, the show was called. There wasn't a place in Dallas a person could escape some media reminder of me. It seemed the perfect revenge. Except nobody listened to the show.

"You're going on Celebrity Assignment to the Midland/ Odessa Battle of the Celebrity Sexes Golf Tournament today," Billings announced. "See if you can't win the sonofabitch. I don't know how good I'll be. I got a groin pull playing tennis." He rubbed his groin enthusiastically while describing the specific steps and stroke that overtaxed his crotch muscles.

"You know"—Billings quit rubbing his groin and sat back —"I was a pretty goddamn good second seed when they cut me off the New Trier tennis team. They said I was just too short." The astronaut leaned back into the seat and stared vacantly out of the window. "I guess it all worked out for the best. I wouldn't have DeeDee or anything, probably."

I watched him stare out the window for a while.

"Well." Billings snapped out of his daze. "They gonna beat

the Redskins?" Dallas and Washington were fighting over a play-off spot.

"Sure," I said. "If the secondary holds up. They're not sharp . . . smart, you know what I mean?" I never mentioned my underlying premise that something had gone out of professional football the day Mabry Jenkins announced he was retiring to look after his business interests. "I always watch the game from a defensive secondary viewpoint," I added. I didn't watch much. Playing was all I knew. I didn't, know about watching. I didn't tell Billings that. He firmly believed you could understand things in the abstract. Who knows? Maybe you can.

"They've only been scored on three times through the air," Billings argued. "How can you blame anything on the secondary?"

"It's not the scoring," I said. "It's the field position. That's where NFL games are won." I acted like it was a verity. He didn't know. "The secondary gives up too much to the pass between the twenties." I pressed my case. "It forces the linebackers to play deep and the linemen to constantly rush."

"What about the linemen?" Billings was puzzled. "Titus Bean says LD Groover is having a miserable year and the defensive line is the trouble."

"That's how little Titus knows." I laughed to show my confidence with the subject matter. "LD has to play pass so much that they're trapping and influence blocking the shit out of him. It's the secondary, I'm telling you."

"Well, you can see where it might look biased." Billings softened. "You being who you are and all. And nobody else even mentioning the secondary. Some writers are saying this is the best secondary Dallas has ever had."

"What do they know? They're watchers. I know what goes on out there. I'm a player."

"No, you're not." Billings shook his head. "You're just like everybody else, a watcher who thinks he's a player." He waved me out of his office and went back to studying the Arbitron.

Down the hall, Nat ducked out of the studio and into the bathroom. It was one sure way I could tell Nit from Nat. Nat threw up every morning at showtime. Panic at six A.M.

It was cold when I left the station. The sun wouldn't be up for a while. The Dallas morning traffic was thin and I crossed the street in the middle of the block to Pinky's All-Nite Eats. I stepped into the sour-smelling white porcelain glare and shivered as I sat down at the counter.

"Possum on yer grave," Irene, the waitress, said. She stood behind the counter, a big woman in a dirty white apron. Her bright red lips and black eyebrows were painted on a white powder face. Her hair was dyed black.

"Just cold," I said and shuddered again.

"A fella ain't a man 'til he learns to shudder," Irene said. "My granpappy told me that. He learned to shudder in Detroit." She turned back to the grill.

"I never learned to shudder," I said. "I think I'm a natural."

"You want coffee?" She poured it without waiting for a reply and plopped a piece of pecan pie in front of me.

"The pie's on me," she said. "It's gettin' old."

Irene switched on the radio behind the grill. Nit and Nat bubbled out. They were straining to hit stride. Nat was still clearing breakfast from his sinus cavities.

Irene worked from midnight to noon and never listened to my show. "I dunno, Mabry, it's yer voice, I think, it depresses me."

It had depressed Billings too, but Jace Everett told him to keep me on.

"Bad news . . . bad news . . . we could have a thunder thingy or two this afternoon." Nit/Nat was giving the weather report. We were in the middle of a two-year drought and the disc jockeys still thought rain was bad news.

The door creaked behind me and a small man with a five-day beard staggered into the diner. He winced at the brightness, then swayed to a stool at the end of the counter. The traffic outside was picking up and the flashing red and green lights seemed less purposeless as they arranged the small streams of headlights into downtown.

"Jes' coffee." The man looked up from beneath the bill of his black-and-white checked wool hat. His face was weather-reddened and the skin was tight against his eye sockets and eyeballs. He looked slightly reptilian.

"Any bars open around here?" He sipped his coffee and watched me from the corners of his eyes. Irene wandered off to scrape the grill.

"Not yet," I answered without really knowing.

"Goddamn. I jest got in from Florida," the grubby man said. "I got this friend down there I can work for anytime. Instead I get six goddamn months in the hospital." There was a pause. He expected a response.

I was silent.

He began again.

"Mugged." He whipped off his hat and bent forward to reveal a half-shaved head and a jagged scar that ran from just above his right eyebrow over the top of his head to disappear into the turned-up collar of his dirty gray cardigan sweater.

"Jesus." My stomach turned over.

"Lead pipe." He replaced his hat. "The bastards threw me off the pier. Lucky for me the tide was out. Broke my arm, though." He fumbled with his shirt-cuff buttons, getting tangled in the frayed sweater sleeve. "Aw, fuck it." He gave up.

Irene glanced over her shoulder, continuing to push dirty grease into the trough at the back of the grill.

"I coulda still worked for this guy, but I come back here to straighten some things out. My wife and kids are around here somewhere." The man was talking into his coffee cup. "I'm a good worker."

I nodded.

"What time *do* the bars open around here?" He acted like I closed them. I shrugged and got to my feet. I was anxious to be back outside.

"Well, good luck." I attempted the same casualness I postured at the State Fair Side Shows.

"Yeh, sure." The man eyed me like a hermaphrodite. "You don't look like no stockbroker yourself, Mac." He pulled my pie over in front of him.

"What do I owe you, Irene?" I took a piece of bubble gum from the box by the cash register. Irene just waved me off and never looked around. I left a quarter next to my coffee cup. I read the gum wrapper comic and fortune. I had been taking the advice lately. The fortune read "dedication will pay off in dividends." The cartoon was in Spanish.

I stood on the sidewalk watching the traffic. The morning was overcast and smelled bad. WBAR flashed in blue neon across the street. A metro bus rumbled past. MABRY IN THE MORNING WEEKDAYS MIDNIGHT TO 6 A.M. WBAR was printed in twelve-inch red silk screen letters on the side card. My face grinned in Day-Glo from the side of the bus.

"Hi, Mabry. Cold sonofabitch, ain't it?" The disembodied voice came from the darkness of the storefront doorway of Men, Inc., a day-labor contractor. A small cluster of men huddled out of the wind waiting for Men, Inc. to open. A barrel-chested man with one leg hobbled forward on crutches.

"Oh, hey, Legs." I turned and shoved my hands into my hip pockets. Legs hobbled up, turned sideways to me, and leaned on his crutches. We didn't look at each other.

I had gotten to know Legs because of the proximity of the WBAR parking lot to Men, Inc. The nickname was Legs' idea to get hired more. I thought being one-legged was a sufficient attention-getter.

"No, man," Legs had offered. "It works, believe me. I'm a celebrity here."

I believed him. Legs *was* the only name I knew out of many familiar faces.

"What's goin' down, man?" Legs always talked like he was on *Police Story*.

"I got bad numbers."

"Bad numbers? That's okay, man, you're still the tops of the pops, the tops of the pops." Legs didn't know what "bad numbers" were. He didn't even own a radio.

"Not anymore."

"Well, shiit." Legs shook his head and scratched his stump.

"Yeh. My audience turned on me."

We exchanged tentative glances.

"Well, good luck." Legs smiled slightly and dropped his gaze. Downtown Dallas before daylight was a brutal place. Today I *felt* like a hermaphrodite. I walked on to my 1961 white-on-pink Cadillac convertible. The bank came and got my new Lincoln.

I ran a hand down the Cadillac's sharp tail fin, jerked open the door, and slid onto the cold white leather. It took a couple of turns before the engine caught. I pulled onto the street behind another metro bus. The bus's rear placard had a full shot of me in game uniform holding a microphone: INSIDE FOOTBALL WITH MABRY IN THE MORNING. LISTEN WEEKDAYS MIDNITE TO 6 WBAR YOUR FRIEND IN THE COUNTRY.

I turned on the radio and punched up WBAR. A rooster was crowing and a cowbell was clanging.

"C'mon, Ernie." They called their cartridge-tape rooster Ernie. "It's time for the country hymn of the hour, sponsored by Herbert Funeral Parlor."

Up came the strains of "Drop Kick Me Jesus Through the Goal Posts of Life." The show was tight. Not one empty sine wave escaped the transmitter. Silence was an unpardonable sin at WBAR.

In the next hour they would start giving away the motorcycles, tape decks, cold cash, and Panther Hall tickets to anyone who would call the station and say they loved WBAR more than Momma.

The traffic was getting heavy as I headed out Cedar Springs Avenue. A lighted billboard of my face dominated the Pearl Street intersection. "The Gridiron Goofball Midnight to

6 A.M. WBAR." Across the intersection a Dallas scion headed into the business district in a Cardin suit and a 450 SL. He leaned across his steering wheel and snorted up two spoons of cocaine. He winked at me as we passed. It was seven A.M. when I pulled into the Lucky Duck Apartments underground garage. I parked in the space where a man had raped a Braniff stewardess. It was the third episode in as many weeks. The papers called him "The Grateful Rapist" because he always said thanks.

LD had left a note on our apartment door: "Am working on tome—would appreciate any cooperation." Since LD is six foot seven and weighs 270 pounds, I crossed the hall to Farah Everett's apartment.

Farah left Junior after he ran off on the motorcycles with Stephano at the Baja Celebrity Fish Tourney. He had finally publicly embarrassed her. Farah and Jason Everett III (Trey) moved into the Lucky Duck Apartments, across the hall from LD and me. Junior and Stephano Valentine had moved into a house near Oaklawn. Stephano did the decorating. Farah called it "Early Fellatio." Farah and I went there to a dinner party one night. They had a black fag butler and all three of them got in a screaming fight over the placement of the fish knives. I knocked on Farah's door. She answered in a floor-length terry-cloth robe. Her pretty face was still wrinkled from sleep. She leaned against the jamb and yawned. "Is LD working?"

I followed her inside. The robe was tailored and clung nicely to her backside. Jason III was on the floor in front of a big Zenith floor model, watching the farm report.

"Hey, Trey." I waved at the boy.

"Hey, Mabry," the boy answered. "Look at this fool."

I wandered over toward the television. Farah disappeared down the hall toward the bathroom.

"This guy is talking to a pig."

The gray-haired local farm reporter was carrying on a conversation about "high octane hog chow" with a Hampshire hog.

"Can you believe this?" The ten-year-old shook his head in disgust. "Christ, morning television is getting as bad as prime time."

"Who's on *Dallas* A.M.?" I asked.

"Stormy Claridge. She's guest hostess. They call her a sports analyst." Trey shook his head in disgust. "She doesn't know doodley squat. She just asked Bobbyday Burke what sign he was." Trey was also a sports expert. His grandfather loved him. He was a good boy.

"I heard your show this morning." Trey was flicking the channel tuner around its circuit. "Not bad." He stopped at a commercial that featured Sonny Jeeter endorsing "Old Tyme lemon flavored drink, just like old-fashioned lemonade that my momma used to make." Except that it wasn't lemonade. Sonny's face looked almost featureless. Makeup had obliterated the lines around his eyes and mouth.

"Was that Smoking Jim on with you?" Trey asked. "I thought you guys said 'nigger' an awful lot last night."

"It's tough to think of things to say at three A.M."

Trey tuned to *Dallas* A.M. Stormy Claridge's face filled the screen. Ezra had gotten her the job. Trey turned the sound up. Stormy was wrapping up a discussion of her upcoming Hondo Higgins film.

"There's nothing euphemistic about this," she said. "It's raw art." She couldn't have put it better.

Trey and I watched the show while Stormy discussed her adventure covering the rodeo circuit. The camera focused on the photos she had taken. A large number of them were of Luther Watt. On Friday she would have Billy Bentson on to help her handicap Saturday's and Sunday's games. She called him "Billy the Geek."

Stormy went off the screen and a denture-cleanser commercial flashed up. Trey turned down the sound.

"Coffee, Mabry?" Farah was back from the bathroom, fully dressed. She was standing by the yellow formica drainboard in the tiny kitchen. Trey looked at his mother.

"Foxy," he said and turned the volume back up on the television.

I slouched in one of the yellow dinette chairs. "Yeah, I'd like some coffee, thanks." I exhaled loudly. I was tired and tense. "It's been an early day."

"How was the show?" Farah poured the steaming coffee from an electric percolator, then joined me at the dinette table.

"My numbers are bad," I said. "It's getting me down."

"Don't worry about it," she said. "They're just numbers."

"That's easy for you to say, planning your comeback against Junior's finances." I sipped my coffee. "You got good numbers, I got bad numbers."

"Well, you're not very good," Farah said. "You talk too slow."

"It takes time to think of things to say," I said. "I don't want to sound stupid."

"That's a good one." She giggled.

"I sound stupid, don't I?" I knew I sounded stupid. I *was* stupid.

"You talk too slow. Nothing sounds more stupid then empty air."

"Goddamn, I took this job because you wanted me to. I'm making a complete asshole out of myself six hours a day, five days a week."

"Don't worry." She grinned. "Nobody listens. Anyway, it's good experience and better than wasting your time at the spa working on your mythical comeback."

"It's not any more mythical than the power you think you're going to get for that boy."

"You don't know what you're talking about." Farah spoke softly. She glanced at Trey, who was engrossed in the television. "A man can't be allowed to disown his responsibilities no matter how rich he is."

Maybe that's what stood between Farah and me—our concept of responsibilities. That and being an electronic idiot from twelve to six every morning. Whatever it was, our relationship was faltering and we seldom fucked anymore. When I wanted to she didn't and if she wanted to I was at the radio station.

"Your problem," Farah continued, "is your manhood is all wrapped up in work. Don't worry about success—just be dependable. I need someone I can depend on."

"Big talk from somebody whose only job was selling gorny dogs and Mistah Peppahs. You're so cool, collecting separate maintenance and telling me to be dependable. Working ain't that easy. It wears a man down."

"You don't have a child to worry about."

"I worry about him. I see what's in store for him," I said. "Shit, I can't imagine succeeding at anything anymore."

"You could if you were more like Jace."

"Jace ain't got anything on me but technique. It's just learning. If I survive I'll learn."

"Don't be so dramatic," Farah said. "I hate dramatic disc jockeys."

"I just got them ol' post-industrial blues, facing another drop in my career trajectory."

Trey flicked the channel tuner. He stopped at a commercial about a man who died without life insurance and left a young boy facing the long slide down.

"Dad just didn't figure on dyin' . . ."

The asshole.

"Hello, reality fans." LD Groover, weary from the typewriter, stood gigantic, red-eyed, and smiling in Farah's doorway. Waylon Jennings blared "Ain't No God in Mexico" out the open door of our apartment.

LD had been working on his book, entitled *The God Squad*, by LD Groover with Titus Bean. Who else? They sold the book as a "Vietnam veteran and professional football player's spiritual revelations" in which LD describes visions and messages from God during particularly strenuous moments in his life. The first chapter is entitled "A Funny Thing Happened on the Way to Khe Sanh." It could mean big money and a chance at television.

"I could be the next Alex Karras," LD explained. "I'm a natural. I'm a better player and I understand the game." LD had been trying for years to scheme his way into a rich retirement. He yearly announced his retirement and then renegotiated his contract with an angry but frightened general manager. LD was the right side of the defensive line. This year LD was more intense about lining up an outside job. "It can't last forever," he said.

The book seemed like LD's best chance, since he had mortgaged his ass on the Celebrity Bar & Grill.

Titus had given LD the idea of a book and even put him in touch with an agent. From there a ten-page outline of "an international working-class hired killer's" memoirs sold in the low double figures with more on delivery of manuscript. LD couldn't stand to talk into a tape recorder and was glad he had taken typing in high school. LD knew how to take criticism, which gave him a big jump on sensitive artists. Besides, he expected to terrify many would-be critics.

"Mabry, you got any speed?" LD closed the door and joined Farah and me at the table. "We're practicing at ten this morning."

I dug into my jacket pocket and handed LD the small pill vial. The big tackle shook six pills into his hand. LD took amphetamines all season long. I never took speed until I got my job as a disc jockey. An NFL defensive tackle and a disc jockey have things in common.

"This all ya got?" He was disappointed.

"I can get some more. Just leave me two." I motioned for him to return the bottle.

"But that'll only leave me four." He was whining.

"That's mathematics." I reached over and took two pills while LD stared sadly into his palm.

"Coffee, LD?" Farah made to rise.

"No thanks. Makes me sick." LD grimaced. Farah settled back and glanced at the kitchen clock. "Hey, I listened to you all this morning." LD shook his block of a head. The curly hair sprang in all directions. "You guys sure said 'nigger' a lot."

"You weren't the Lone Ranger."

"You had listeners?" LD was surprised.

"Two that I know of." I pointed over to Trey, who was listening to our conversation and watching the soundless television. "And the guy from the ACLU again."

"You mean you can't say nigger *even when you got one with ya*?" LD was outraged.

"I guess he wants to pick the niggers himself." I sipped at my coffee. "Either way, my future looks bleak."

"For saying nigger?" LD had moved to abject despair over the state of the broadcasting industry.

"No." I shook my head. "Christ, last night had to be the most listeners ever and we still had more people *at* the station." I shook my head in embarrassment. "That lawyer must be one desperate man to listen to my show."

"The desperate are up late every night." LD observed. "That's why I'll be the next Johnny Carson and you can by God bet that I'll say nigger when I please." LD walked to the sink and turned on the faucet. He popped an orange heart into his mouth and washed it down directly from the spigot. He wiped his mouth. "Last night I wrote about the perversion of winning and losing and the security of being a has-been."

"I don't see a lot of security in it," I argued.

"You can't fuck up something in the past," LD pointed out. "I have to run." He eased to the door favoring his arthritic knees. "I see my hypnotist before practice."

I followed LD to the door.

"He gave me a new mantra," LD said, grinning. He began to drone. "Don't fuck up . . . Don't fuck up . . . Don't fuck up."

Farah shook her head and laughed.

Trey waved but kept his eyes glued to a commercial about elves making cookies in a hollow tree.

LD left for the practice field. I watched him limp through the courtyard and into the underground parking lot. A McDonald's drink container floated in the swimming pool.

LD had been a staunch and loyal friend. I wondered if our friendship would inevitably wither without the glue of mutual struggle in professional football. I hoped not. I seldom saw any of my old teammates. They were too busy, all still on the edge, clawing and biting and high. No matter what I had been, now I was just a spectator and it was not the same.

Alex Hart came by drunk once to complain when Buck started Sonny Jeeter the third regular-season game. Jeeter's recovery had been phenomenal. They had to tape his leg from hip to ankle just for workouts but he kept the team neck-and-neck with Washington. The game in D.C. at RFK would tell who went to the play-offs. Dallas and Washington always had great rivalries. I used to be a part of them. I miss being disliked by Roy Jefferson and Charlie Taylor.

Ezra Lyttle was a pleasant exception. He came by frequently. He and Stormy still hadn't gotten married. She didn't have her own line of cosmetics, but was doing sports bits from Dallas for ABC. Ezra knows Roone Arledge. Her career was moving. Her ratings were certainly better than mine.

"Stormy's so good to me, man," Ezra said to me the night he came over to help LD choose drapes for the Celebrity Bar & Grill. Junior's friend who designed the Disneyland ride through the human endocrine system had taken a $5,000 consultant's fee and promptly disappeared, so Ezra and LD were doing the decorating.

"If Stormy wasn't so busy, we'd get married right away," Ezra said, "but I can understand it, man. She wants a chance to express herself. It'll strengthen our relationship, man. It'll turn out for the best, you'll see. She just wants a career."

He acted like I was arguing with him. I smiled and nodded. Hell, *I* wanted a career.

I like Ezra. I can't help it. He cares about me.

"I hear you're trying to catch on with the Giants," Ezra said. "They could sure use you and, man, will you like New York." Ezra spent three weeks in Manhattan, going to stockbroker's school. "It's a terrific place. You can stay up all night," Ezra enthused. "Have you ever had shoestring spaghetti?" He wrote down the address of Mamma Leone's—"the best shoestring spaghetti in New York."

"Yeh, that's nice," I said distantly. I was trying not to talk too much about my comeback attempts anymore. I worked out in an old men's spa over on Turtle Creek. Old men understand the need to believe in coming back. Besides, the Giants weren't the least bit interested in me. The fucking Giants.

"Man, the guy who thought up that New York subway system was a genius," Ezra said. "I mean, the subway that goes to Brooklyn, how did they know that all those people were gonna live in Brooklyn? If I could get a guy like that on our board of directors . . ."

"Ezra, I don't think the subway came first," I said.

"It had to," Ezra said. "They couldn't have put them in after all the buildings were on top."

"I think so."

"Oh, yeh?" Ezra was crestfallen.

We were silent while LD chose between a drape that would make the Celebrity Bar & Grill look like a Russian whorehouse and a drape that would make it look like a Chinese whorehouse.

"Well," Ezra said, finally brightening again. "You'll like New York, anyway."

That's what I mean about Ezra. You can't help liking him. He's such an optimist.

CHAPTER

It was ten A.M. when I was awakened by pounding on the apartment door. It was Junior Everett and Stephano Valentine. Junior was carrying a briefcase. The spider monkey Stephano gave Junior as a housewarming gift was riding on his shoulder. They made a great threesome.

"Where's Farah?" Junior asked.

The monkey chattered and ate part of a Three Musketeers bar.

"I don't know," I said sleepily. "Come on in. I have to sit down." I plopped onto the couch, closed my eyes, and fell over on my side.

"What about the kid?" Junior paced nervously up to the couch.

Stephano slunk to the window and kept watch.

"Doesn't he go to school?" I kept my eyes closed. My throat was raw. The room filled with the smell of Tea Rose perfume.

"Oh, yeh."

Trey attended the same North Dallas private school as his father and grandfather before him. Trey hated the school. The teachers were all afraid of the students. Tuition had skyrocketed since busing.

"Shit." Junior paced nervously into the kitchen and stood looking around. He eyed my two-by-four-foot blow-up of George Jones at Panther Hall. It was a gift from Titus Bean, who was a charter member of the Fort Worth George Jones

Fan Club. That was pre-Tammy George—he still had a flat top.

"I wanted the kid to check this stuff with his chemistry set," Junior said.

"What stuff?" My eyes were still closed. The lids were gritty.

"This." Junior returned to the couch and dumped five baggies of white powder out of the briefcase and onto me. "The God of the Peruvian Indians." He paced to the window and looked out. He and Stephano exchanged glances. The monkey chattered. "I want the kid to check its purity. He knows all the tests."

"You don't?"

"No. Well sort of." Junior refilled the alligator case and headed toward the kitchen. "You have any Clorox?"

I shook my head and swung my legs wearily off the couch. Tiny spots of light flashed in my brain and creatures swam across my eyeballs. "Let's snort some," I suggested. "That's always a good test."

"Just a minute. Just a minute." Junior filled a glass from the kitchen faucet, set it on the drainboard and opened one of the bags. His 22-carat neck chain was fastened to a gold coke spoon shaped like a miniature cock and balls. He dipped some powder and dropped it into the water glass. The whole wad fell to the bottom like lead shot.

"What does that mean?" I asked.

"I'm not sure. It either means it's almost pure cocaine or almost no cocaine."

"I think it means almost no cocaine."

"Me too. Shit!" Junior slammed his hand on the counter. "I knew ten thousand was too cheap. Fucking Cuban ripoff artists. I'll show their ass." He looked at Stephano. "We've still got that diary." Stephano nodded. Junior scratched his head, digging through a full-blown black six-inch natural hairstyle. Pancake makeup was caked on his upper lip. He chewed nervously on his thumbnail.

"Let's try the burn test." Junior was rummaging in a drawer for aluminum foil. He tore a silver wedge from the Reynolds Wrap, dropped some powder on it, and held his flaming gold Dunhill underneath. The powder boiled and grew into an amorphous black lump.

The monkey squealed and chattered.

"Shut up, goddamn you." Junior took a swipe at the monkey.

"It looks like one of those things you burn to make worms," I observed as the mass blackened, twisted, and turned above the flame.

"Here, let's sniff some and see what happens." Junior held out a full spoon of white powder.

I snorted quickly with my left nostril and felt it hit up next to my eye. My sinus burned with a familiar alcohol medicinal taste. Junior filled my other nostril and then took two spoons himself. We stood around trying to decide what, if anything, was having which kind of effect on either of us.

"How do you feel?" Junior asked.

"Not bad." I nodded my head. My eyes watered.

"Well, did you feel bad before the hits?"

"I think so. I don't remember."

"You don't remember. That's good enough for me. It's coke." He closed the bag and licked the tip of the coke-spoon penis. "You want to buy some?"

"My teeth aren't numb."

"Good coke doesn't always numb your teeth." Junior was a great salesman. "Some of the best is really smooth. You hardly notice it."

In Baja I had seen Junior snort crushed up No-Doz tablets.

"How much?"

"Fifty dollars a gram."

"Let me think about it." I sniffed. My nose began to run.

"I don't have a layaway plan." He replaced the bag of powder in his briefcase. "Say, I heard your numbers were bad again this month."

The monkey picked through Junior's curls, first inspecting, then eating his finds.

"Yeh, Billings showed me this morning."

"Well, you're not very good." Junior's voice was tentative.

"Goddamn," I said. "Suddenly everybody's a critic. I didn't know you listened, Junior." I stalked into the living room. "I figured you didn't have time what with your hairstyling, gambling, oil and dope deals, and raising Astrakhans."

"Afghans."

"What?"

"Afghans." His tone was firm. "We raise Afghans. It's quite profitable. Stephano knows all about it. You don't have to get ugly. I was only trying to help." Junior Everett gathered up his alligator briefcase and bags of powder and was out the door, the monkey clinging tightly to his cloud of curls. Stephano brought up the rear and smiled at me as he pulled the door shut.

The phone rang. It was Mr. Green from American Express.

"Hello, deadbeat."

I hung up.

I packed a bag with my golf clothes and WBAR Gang costume and drove out to the airport to catch my flight to the Midland/Odessa Battle of the Celebrity Sexes Golf Tourney and Charity Telethon.

I picked up a newspaper at the airport. Titus Bean had a copyrighted story on the front page. A group of Everett Chemco employees from their Midland plant were suing the company over being turned into "alleged zombies" through contact with PRP, a base chemical in both Chemco artificial stadium grass and "agent blue," a herbicide manufactured for the Defense Department and currently being sprayed on the Mexican marijuana crop by the DEA. Everett Chemco denied everything and referred to the employees as "perpetual malcontents." There were no pictures of dead babies.

The flight was a Continental jet to L.A. with stops in Midland/Odessa and Albuquerque. I knew the stewardess and she brought me a magnum of champagne and wished me luck in the next game. It's funny how people don't compute.

I drank the full magnum of champagne and arrived in the Permian Basin an alleged zombie. I had only tried for perpetual malcontent.

George Billings had arrived earlier; he met me at the airport. Everett Sports Enterprises and Everett Chemco were the sponsors of the Midland/Odessa Battle of the Celebrity Sexes Golf Tourney and Charity Telethon. George was Official Host and Celebrity Coordinator.

"You're drunk," Billings accused. He handed me an outsized red badge with my name hand-printed in blue Pentel above the typed words "Radio Star." Penciled in below were the words "Ex-Pro Footballer."

"I heard everybody out here was an alleged zombie. I didn't want to feel out of place."

"Hey, Jesus." He shushed me and looked around. "Don't be joking about that. We have radio and television people coming."

"I'm radio people, George."

Billings frowned at me. He was learning to accept my assault on his sensibilities as his job. He would rock back on his heels like somebody taking a punch. Then he would shake it off.

Shake it off. Run it out.

I stopped at a newsstand and bought a pair of chrome-rimmed wraparound sunglasses. West Texas is much closer to the sun than Dallas. The reflector lenses made me look like Plastic Man with a broken nose.

"My whole life is being taken up with egos," Billings said. "Can you even play golf?"

"I'll be okay."

"You were never okay," Billings said matter-of-factly. "You wouldn't be here if you were okay."

He had me there. Shake it off. Run in out.

"I wish my groin was better," Billings said. "Mr. Jace would like somebody from his organization in the winner's circle."

My tee-off time was at two. I checked into the Airport Motel, showered, and changed into my Johnny Miller shirt with matching red slacks and shoes with tassels. I topped it all off with my red Super Bowl X baseball hat. I was feeling better.

My partner in the Battle of the Celebrity Sexes Golf Tourney was Stormy Claridge. It wasn't a battle of the sexes at all, but a tournament of mixed teams. Billings explained that Battle of the Celebrity Sexes tested better in market surveys and was more alliterative.

Stormy was waiting for me on the first tee, wearing a white skirt, a matching short-sleeved pullover, and a white visored hat. Her legs were a little thick at the ankles, but she had a nicely developed upper torso and knocked the shit out of a golf ball. She wore a red silk-screened badge with her name and "Miss Massey Ferguson" in blue Pentel. Typed across the bottom was "Talent Winner, Miss Texas Pageant." She looked great.

George Billings and his wife DeeDee rounded out our foursome. DeeDee was stubby, with short dark hair and played intently in blue Bermudas, varicose veins, and a blue visored hat. She had been CINCPAC Woman's Golf Champion and in college was the Air Force ROTC Sweetheart. By the fifth hole she and Stormy were locked in deadly combat. There is a basic animosity between beauty queens.

Several times during the first nine holes, a security guard would zoom up in a golf cart and confer in low tones with George Billings.

"Trouble?" I asked Billings as he mopped his brow. The guard had just driven away. We were making our tee shots on nine.

"Demonstrators up by the clubhouse." Billings scanned the fairway. Down by the ninth green a gallery of several hundred West Texans baked in the sun. The red flag waved in the hot wind. "They want to turn this PRP contamination thing into a media event. Make it seem like a big deal. But we're ready. I invited a couple of Texas Rangers to play in the tourney. They're over on four. You know that little par three over the water?

"I figure," Billings continued, "a couple of celebrity Texas Rangers with nine irons should handle any troublemakers. Your buddy Titus has caused all this trouble. We'll get his ass, too."

I topped my tee shot with the heel of my driver. The ball bounced off my leg and rolled off into the rough. I hopped around on one foot, rubbing a knot the ball made on my shin. Stormy stared dully at me. Her disappointment in my golf game was obvious. I limped into the rough and found my ball under a jack pine. I slashed the goddamn little thing about twenty yards out onto the fairway. I was still away.

Stormy snorted and shook her head.

I pulled out a three wood and with a discipline and concentration spawned of deep humiliation, hit a low screamer that sliced over the practice green, caromed off the clubhouse ball washer, hit a wheelchair in the gallery, and rolled about five feet shy of the cup.

"Damn," I said, slamming the club back into my bag. "Short."

Billings holed out on nine and quickly left for the clubhouse, carrying his nine iron and a can of mace. DeeDee followed with a putter and a tear-gas pen. She did the light work.

Stormy was lining up her putt.

"Look at the tits on her." Several tool pushers in red and yellow hard hats were watching Stormy line up her putt. "Bend over, honey, I'll show you a real long drive." A tall man in a red Exxon hard hat yelled. Several people laughed. "Come on, lemme check yer lay. Hah hah hah." The bright red and yellow hard hats speckled the crowd. There were an alarming number of them.

"Aren't you going to do something?" Stormy looked at me.

"You want me to putt first?"

"Hey, baby, if you play with me," Exxon yelled, "I'll give you twelve *extry* strokes." The red and yellow pods bobbled atop the crowd as the roughnecks yukked it up.

"Okay, fellas, let's give it a rest."

"Fuck off, dickhead," Exxon snarled.

I turned to Stormy and shrugged.

"Some teammate," Stormy sneered. "No wonder you're washed up." She bent down and missed a five-foot putt. "Goddamn fuck." She glared at me. "You chickenshit."

I quickly replaced my ball and hurried to putt and get out. Stormy disappeared into the crowd with her putter. I was on my backswing when I heard a sound similar to beating a rowboat bottom with a cane pole—sort of a whooosh-boing. The red Exxon hardhat came sailing through the air and landed about twelve feet from the pin. Not a bad shot.

I putted out.

Walking to the tenth tee, Stormy and I crossed the parking lot, site of the confrontation between the demonstrators and the celebrity Texas Rangers. All that was left was a crudely painted sign reading "Everett Chemco Poisons Americans" with a rough drawing of what looked like a flipper-headed baby. Midland-Odessa activists aren't very artsy-craftsy.

Billings was talking to two burly men wearing red celebrity badges with their names in blue Pentel and "Texas Ranger" typed below. The taller of the two Rangers had "hippie-eater" penciled on the bottom of his celebrity badge. They stood by the cart rental. Billings was wiping off the head of his club.

On the second nine DeeDee Billings was no match for Stormy, who was recharged by her chip shot off the redneck's head. During the confrontation in the parking lot DeeDee had misjudged the wind and tear-gassed herself. Her eyes watered throughout the back nine.

"If those goddamn environmentalists had their way," Billings said to me on the fourteenth tee, "there wouldn't be any goddamn progress."

DeeDee was over at the ball washer, wiping her eyes, and

Stormy was addressing the ball. "*Think* it causes cancer. *Think* it causes birth defects," Billings continued. "Goddamn, everybody's got a natural level of PRP. A little poison never hurt anybody."

Stormy hit a tremendous shot. The white speck soared through the brown-blue West Texas sky. It was a hot day.

Stormy and I finished second, behind a celebrity orthopedic surgeon from Houston and a Dallas Cowboy cheerleader. The cheerleader did all eighteen holes in her game uniform. Stormy made it clear who she thought cost us first place.

That night at the banquet prior to the Charity Telethon George Billings gave his talk. He got everyone's attention by clinking his water glass with his fork.

I was dressed in my WBAR Gang cowboy drag with two cap guns and fake turquoise-studded belt and holsters that matched my gauntlets.

"Attention . . . attention," Billings started off. He sounded a little belligerent. "Right here on TV tonight we're going to show all of West Texas and eastern New Mexico the technique of raising money for charity."

Billings waved his arms and the curtain on the stage behind him parted, revealing a scale model refinery flanked by a miniature oil derrick and a railroad siding complete with tank cars. The cracking plant was designed to hold the banks of telephones where volunteers would accept pledges from telethon viewers. The pledges were written on slips of paper and deposited in the tank cars while the total dollar values pledged were marked out up the height of the derrick from $0 and "Duster" all the way to "Gusher" and the one-million-dollar goal. When the curtain parted to reveal the designer-built set the crowd went "aah."

I went "aah" too. It caught me by surprise.

"And let me start the drive off." Billings held up a check. "First, a little gift from the free enterprise system and Everett Chemco, the profits from the Annual Midland/Odessa Battle of the Celebrity Sexes Golf Tourney." He waved the check around. "Five hundred and eighty-nine dollars." He handed the check to Stormy. "And I'll ask our special guest, Miss Massey Ferguson, Stormy Claridge, to deposit this money in the specially designed tank-car pledge banks." The assembled celebrities and members of the Permian Basin Community Chest applauded wildly. Everybody got off on charity.

Stormy dutifully climbed the steps and deposited the $589 check to the accompaniment of some heavy breathing and a lot of coughing and chair scraping.

It cost Everett Chemco $11,000 just to promote the Golf Tourney. And that didn't count the celebrities' fees and expenses. Outgo always stayed close to income. Charity got the difference—$589. It was the old trickle-down effect.

"Let me get serious for a minute." Billings pursed his lips. Everyone quieted and leaned forward. "As Official Host I can tell you how honored we at Everett Chemco are to help out every year with the charity campaign. We think we've got a pretty good team out at Chemco, and with the help of you volunteers and all these wonderful celebrities . . ." The audience applauded "celebrities." There were a few whistles. Stormy blushed. I blushed. ". . . we can put together a victory tonight." He looked at his watch and held up his hand. "It's a twenty-minute countdown and we're on the air. So"—he pointed to the top of the derrick—"let's *go* for that goal." He pointed to the volunteers ready to answer the phones in the miniature cracking plant. "And *fight* for those pledges." He held both hands over his head, signaling a touchdown. "And let's *win* this charity drive. Go Fight Win Go Fight Win." Billings was screaming and turning red in the face. The crowd was yelling along with him. Stormy was up hollering and waving her arms.

It was all pretty exciting—the crazed mob ambience.

"That was fun." Stormy collapsed onto our table, her breasts crushed against the red-and-white checked cloth.

Billings made his way through the applauding and cheering people. He handed me a small white envelope.

"We'll be on the air until eight tomorrow morning," Billings said. "The doctor says not to drink too much when you take these." He handed another envelope to Stormy. Inside each envelope were ten orange Dexadrine hearts, enough to keep the cast of the Gong Show up until next week. Billings searched out the other celebrities.

"Might as well." Stormy washed one down with her wine. "It's for charity."

Nobody knows what went wrong. Despite a videotaped plea from Hondo Higgins on horseback and Stormy dancing twice to "Ragtime Cowboy Joe," we didn't raise much money. The phones in the designer-built cracking plant seldom rang and the derrick's oil spout hovered just above "Duster." First Billings blamed it on not being able to get a real football player. "You can't have a telethon without a real football player," Billings cried. "We're just a bunch of losers." Then Billings decided that it was "because of all those lies Titus Bean wrote about PRP." So, between four and five A.M., retired astronaut and Air Force colonel George Billings "put those false stories to rest forever" by eating a handful of PRP on camera.

It didn't help the charity drive and made the tiny astronaut violently ill. He was outside throwing up when the television station manager came around demanding up-front cash for any more air time.

"What about the crippled children?" Stormy followed the station manager into the control booth.

"Fuck the crippled children," he said. "I've got a business to run."

At five thirty A.M. Stormy began an emotional appeal for donations. She was on the bottom side of four Dexadrine and too much wine.

"Why haven't you people responded?" Stormy pleaded into the camera. Her smile dissolved into a twitch that pulled at the right side of her full mouth. "Is it something we've said? Or done? How have we offended you?" She began to sob. "How can you not help little children? You *must* send your pledges. How can you reject us like this?" Stormy choked back tears and tried to collect herself.

Billings came back into the studio, wiping his mouth. He was ashen.

Stormy continued talking into the camera. ". . . I . . . I was a defective child myself . . . I . . . I had a club foot." Her shoulders shook and her eyes rimmed with dissolving mascara. "I know the heartbreak," she sobbed, "the struggle. But what do you care about heartbreak, or sadness, or struggle?" Her lower lip quivered and her chin cauliflowered. She turned angry. "*You* don't worry about others and their pains. Sitting there drinking beer." She was yelling at the camera. "*You* don't care."

"You better cut her off," Billings said, his gray face covered with sweat.

"You lousy no-good cheap chiseling . . ." Stormy's eyes blazed.

"Cut her off."

". . . redneck . . . MOTHERFUCKERS!" Stormy shot the camera the finger.

"*Cut her off!*"

They cut her off.

The phones began ringing for the first time all night.

Billings dropped Stormy and me off at the Airport Motel. The sun was coming up. It doesn't take long for the sun to get up in West Texas. Stormy and I retreated to her room and ended up in bed. She had calmed some.

"I love that." Stormy had insisted on the superior position and was straddling me with her head on my chest. The mass of her breasts was a comforting weight.

"Do you and Farah do this?" Stormy licked and whispered into my ear.

"We've never even been to Midland."

She wiggled her buttocks to seat herself better. "Sometime let's do this with Farah." She was gripping me with muscles I didn't know people had. "I want to watch you suck each other."

"Sure . . . sure . . ."

Then she started to convulse, her eyes half lidded. "Oh, my God . . . my God . . . I'm coming . . . I'm coming . . . talk dirty to me . . . talk dirty . . ."

"You no-good dirty sonofabitch." It was all I could think to say. It took something out of it for her.

"I never said I was Warren Beatty." I lay back.

"You ain't even Roone Arledge."

After a few moments, Stormy began to fellate me.

"You didn't come," she said. She was right. Her lips went to work and I was soon erect. She straddled me again and fucked me for ten minutes straight. Nothing. She sucked again. "Okay, baby," she coaxed. "Give . . . come on . . . give . . ." Nothing. "Come on now, don't hold back . . ." She was stroking me with her hand. "C'mon . . ." She began flogging me.

"Hey . . . hey . . ." I winced. "Easy . . . easy . . . take a rest . . . I don't mind."

"No, damnit, this sonofabitch . . ." She started sucking again and the erection returned. She positioned me on top. I got tired. I wanted to quit.

"Quit?!" She was shocked. "What kinda loser are you? Okay, okay, I'm sorry about the Roone Arledge remark."

"I don't think it matters." It didn't.

I left a half hour later.

"Mabry," Stormy said as I opened the door. It was bright and hot outside. "It could be 'cause your numbers were bad."

I nodded and stepped into the West Texas heat. I was still dressed in WBAR Gang cowboy drag. I had lost a capgun and both of my fake turquoise gauntlets.

The long slide down.

CHAPTER

WHEN I RETURNED TO DALLAS LD'S NEW MERCEDES DIESEL was in the Lucky Duck Apartments garage. He was on the phone in the apartment.

"Tell them I want cash up front. I don't want any points. I'm not betting on a bag of queers and Jews getting any movie made." LD was talking to his Los Angeles agent. He lay on the couch, an ice bag on his knee. "I have a goddamn football contract to negotiate this May." LD drank from a sweating can of Pearl beer. A Number Two washtub full of ice and beer cans was sitting atop LD's fur-lined Coldspot. The floor was littered with empties. "I want my tax situation straight. I am not getting myself fucked by those goddamn cross-collateralizing sons of bitches. I want it all paid by next year. My goddamn deferred starts in two years." LD took the phone from his ear and cupped his hand on the mouthpiece. "I can't believe I'm hearing this shit." He looked at me in amazement. "I'm telling this guy his job."

"What's a cross-collateralizing sonofabitch?" I asked, collapsing in a chair across the room.

"Hey," LD resumed his phone conversation, "let's pull the book off the movie market and if we win the Super Bowl we'll auction it. How's that sound? Great. Ciao." LD hung up immediately.

"Ciao?" I had never heard LD speak Italian before.

"They say it all the time out there." He waved toward Fort

Worth and the West Coast beyond. "It means 'adios, motherfucker.' " LD sat up and searched the sweating washtub for the few survivors of a full case of Pearl. He found one and popped it open and offered it to me. I shook my head.

"You coming to the grand opening of the Bar & Grill?" LD poured the gold beer directly down his throat. "It's tonight."

I rubbed my eyes. "I've got to work out first. I feel bad."

"You'll feel better if you jack off more," LD offered, moving the ice bag on his knee. "Jacking off is the only answer. I think *I'll* jack off." He unzipped the fly of his plaid Bermuda shorts, then jerked open the door to the converted Coldspot. The light came on inside. The rabbit fur looked moth-eaten.

"Gotta break down that body armor," he said as he sat in the refrigerator and began getting his stroke rhythm. "Charge up the old system. Big game this weekend."

"Lost in the orgone again," I said, walking to my room.

It all seemed like a dream. I wasn't sure I hadn't dreamed everything. Physical pain on Monday mornings reassured me something very real had happened on Sunday—I had the bruises to prove it. Not anymore. It left me without moorings.

The doorbell rang. LD was finished. He wiped his hand on his Texas Tri Delt T-shirt as he answered the ring. It was a strangely erotic gesture. Smoking Jim Stewart stood in the hall. He looked terrible. His face was lined, his eyes pained.

"I have to get my back fixed. I can't stand this." Smoking Jim sat down and leaned forward, resting his elbows on his thighs and supporting his weight. "This grievance procedure is taking forever. I'm dying." He had tears in his eyes. "I can't sleep. I can't do anything." He sounded desperate. "I lost the Wig Rental. I can't take care of business. Shit, I can't stand or sit for more than a minute. I'm out of money." He took a yellow pill and washed it down with a beer.

"Well, get your back fixed," LD said. "Isn't there something that can be done?"

"My doctor says for five thousand dollars and five months rehabilitation I'll be fine"—Stewart shook his head—"but he's in the back fusion business. Besides, I don't have the money or the insurance for any of it and if I get it fixed then I'll never collect from the club." He grimaced with pain and then swilled his beer. "They owe me, man, they owe me." It was unnerving to see a man of Stewart's size reduced so completely. "Christ, my wife thinks I'm crazy and Dr. Badd says there isn't anything wrong and if there is something wrong I could have done it stepping off a curb after I was cut. Friedman says I'm addicted to pain pills. Jesus." Tears filled his eyes. He was in great pain physically and spiritually. He wiped his eyes and groped for words to explain his agony. "God, I feel so . . . spineless." He banged the arm of the chair with a clenched fist. The jolt shook the tears loose and they ran down his cheeks and disappeared into his three-day beard. He looked desperate. I wished he wouldn't cry in front of me—I wasn't the player rep. "If I could get my hands on Buck, I'd . . ." He made a throttling motion with his hands. "I lay there all night in the dark thinking about all the shit I'd do to that motherfucker."

Smoking Jim let his hands fall into his lap and he rocked forward in pain. "My back is killing me, man. I'm telling you it's killing me." He glared at LD. "You don't think I'm lying, do you?"

"Hell, no, man." LD was uncomfortable in the presence of this pain.

"I have to get hold of myself. I don't know, maybe I'm not hurt." He began to argue with himself. He stopped and stared at the floor. "I have to call my lawyer. Can I use your phone? This guy's a buddy of mine. He isn't charging me anything." Stewart struggled painfully to his feet. "He thinks I have a real good workman's compensation case." Stewart was happier talking about his lawyer. "They gave that pitcher from Detroit lifetime disability."

"I don't know, man," LD said. "I don't think it's the same."

"What the fuck do you know about it?" Smoking Jim said. "You guys are all against me."

"I'm sorry, man. I don't know shit."

"Don't you see?" Smoking Jim pleaded. "They know I'm hurt. They can wait until I go under." He stepped closer to LD. "Look at this face. Look at these creases and lines. It isn't even my face. I have to keep them away from me." Stewart hobbled toward LD's bedroom and the phone. "Garvey handles the actual grievance procedure anyway. This guy is just sort of my advisor and he's a friend. And God knows I need a friend." He disappeared into the bedroom.

A few minutes later Stewart came out. Between the lawyer and the yellow pill his mood was improved. "He says everything's going to be fat. The arbitrator is an old buddy of his and he's putting pressure on the league office right now to settle. A man needs a lawyer nowadays, I guess." Stewart continued on to the outside door. "LD, I'll call you later." He closed the door behind him. I could hear him shuffle across the landing and down the steps.

"That lawyer friend," LD said to me, "will defend him to his last dollar."

"I wonder if he's tried not minding that it hurts."

Titus Bean stopped by to watch the evening news. Titus really knew how to talk back to the television. He loved the news and would scream and yell at various anchormen and correspondents. It was a great show.

During the news story about the House Committee on Assassinations, Titus was on the floor yelling at Walter Cronkite.

"You old fool," he screamed. "Can't you see it . . . it's the goddamn Korean CIA and the bribes. The CIA is pressuring Congress to call off the assassination inquiry. They caught all them Congressmen with their hands in the gook's pocket."

The newscast also mentioned the herbicide PRP and Everett Chemco employees who were bringing suit. A spokesman for the FDA said there was no danger. They interviewed George Billings.

George had gained instant notoriety for eating PRP during

the Midland/Odessa Charity Telethon. He said he felt great. George said there was no danger. His skin looked gray.

"No danger? No fucking danger?" Titus was right against the screen, screaming, "Tell that to all the dead babies, you asshole. It's a goddamn cover-up. They send old George Billings into the breach. Who's gonna argue with an astronaut?" Titus had a good point. Who *was* going to argue with an astronaut?

When the news ended, Titus stood up. "I gotta meet Willy Roy Rogers. We're working the noodles out of Stormy's big finale for Hondo Higgins' porno musical."

I walked Titus to his car. Junior Everett and Stephano Valentine pulled up in his Ferrari roadster. He had a two-pound brass ship's cannon strapped to the boot.

"I just bought it." Junior rubbed the barrel of the small brass cannon. "I'm going to load it with roofing nails, sit her at the head of my stairs, and when they get halfway up I'll give them the whole load." Junior had paranoid fits.

"Who are 'they'?" I asked.

"The same people who drowned Momma. Who did you think?"

Junior took Trey with him out to the Dallas Gun Club. He was anxious to try out the cannon. They sure looked strange driving off in that one-cannon Ferrari—Junior at the wheel, Trey in the middle, and Stephano on the outside. The spider monkey clung to Junior's curly black locks and hunched the nape of his neck.

Ezra and LD's Celebrity Bar & Grill was in Jace Everett's Flags of All Nations Shopping Center. Everett Sports Enterprises handled the promotion of the grand opening. George Billings came up with the idea of the First Annual Texas Celebrity Turkey Trot. He was getting the hang of the celebrity business.

Each celebrity in the Turkey Trot was teamed with a large tom turkey in a race through the mall. It was a great starting grid, with LD on the pole, Ezra in second position, and Willy Roy Rogers on the outside. I was in the second line with the whole WBAR Gang; we were all in cowboy drag. I was still missing my gauntlets and one capgun. LD and Ezra wore their game uniforms, while Willie Roy Rogers was in his new outlaw black. The turkeys seemed nervous.

The winner would get fifty dollars donated to his favorite charity. The start and finish line was Ezra and LD's Celebrity Bar & Grill. WBAR had promoted the event all week and a big crowd lined the circuit.

Stormy Claridge was interviewing celebrities for *Dallas* A.M. George Billings was the official starter.

At the gun, LD tucked his turkey under his arm and took off at a dead run. The crowd went wild. Ezra was a close second, but made the tactical error of holding his turkey by the neck and was slowed by the bird's frantically flapping wings. I stepped in some turkey shit and went down in a heap, ruining a brand-new bandanna-print shirt with peak yokes front and back. It was part of the coordinated WBAR look. The rest of the WBAR Gang hauled ass after LD and Ezra. Willy Roy Rogers pulled a knife and tried to threaten his turkey into running.

LD had a substantial lead at the Baskin-Robbins halfway mark when his turkey shit down the front of his jersey. In a rage, and urged on by a blood crowd, LD Groover stomped his turkey into giblet gravy all over the imported Mexican tiles in front of El Chico.

Nit and Nat won as a team. In the heat of the race they had broken their turkey's wings. They were vicious little competitors. The two disc jockeys took a winner's lap, holding the turkey overhead and chanting, "Number one . . . Number one . . . Number one."

After the Texas Celebrity Turkey Trot I changed clothes, cleaned off the turkey shit and met Farah inside LD and Ezra's Celebrity Bar & Grill. It was packed with frantic Dallas first-nighters.

LD and Ezra both had changed to top hats and tails. They

were circulating through the crowd. LD looked like a full-dress Gulliver among the Lilliputians. Ezra was wearing his handmade ostrich boots. The boots were a "play of the week" award from the local Sportsmanship Club for running into the short end-zone wall at Wrigley Field and not bleeding.

Stephano and Junior arrived. Both men were wearing patent leather Mary Jane pumps and billowy silks. Stephano was wearing a gold ring sculpture of a man performing autofellatio.

Farah watched Junior standing next to the entrance drapes. LD and Ezra had chosen the Russian whorehouse style. Farah frowned as Junior worked the crowd. "Jesus, will you look at him," she said. "He's sure not like his daddy."

Coach Buck Binder walked by our table.

"Hey, Bucko." I grabbed his arm. "Lose my phone number?"

"Well, Mabry, how you doing?" Buck was drunk.

"Fine, Buck. Fine. Never better." I slapped my knee. "Join us?"

He sat down.

"Gonna beat Washington?"

Buck nodded. "Well, Mabry, how you doing?" Buck smiled.

"Fine, Buck. Fine. Never better." I drank. Buck drank.

"New Orleans sure hit that back a lot on the short square out last week," I said.

Buck nodded and rattled his ice. I rattled my ice.

"I don't know, Buck. I don't think Bobbyday Burke works well at my old corner."

Buck looked at me and rattled his ice.

"You're probably right," Buck said, his eyes bleary and half lidded. "We need more old guys, more experience. That's what's wrong with us this year. We could sure use more old guys like you, guys that don't care about little aches and pains." Buck was an old guy.

"Well, Buck, I'm ready to go. I've been working out every day." I held up my glass. "I'm only drinking tonight because of the opening. Besides, I'm not that old."

"Yeh, that would sure be nice." Buck looked quickly to

his glass. "Well, we'll see what we can do. You know how it is." He shrugged and looked for a waiter.

I didn't know how it was.

"Well, Mabry," Buck said after a long silence, "How you doing?"

The debut of the Willy Roy Rogers Outlaw Show was the highlight of the evening. Willy was resplendent in skintight black leather with turquoise accessories. An Austin leather-crafter had made Willy Roy a hand-tooled belt with an attached mother-of-pearl pistol grip that made it look like Willy was packing. It was very clever. Willy Roy had replaced the Blackland Farmers with a new backup band called the North Texas Thugs. Willy Roy's first three songs were about various types of gunplay and love. He did them medley style.

Willy Roy's act sure had changed. Instead of the smiling, sleepy-eyed, melancholy drunk he was a strutting, threatening bad guy. He snarled, cussed, and spat at the audience. He no longer despaired, he seethed. He finished the set with an original composition about a guy who kills his homosexual cellmate with a mop wringer while doing six months on a bum armed robbery rap. The audience screamed for encore but Willy Roy gave them the finger and disappeared backstage.

The crowd loved it.

Willy Roy joined Farah and me at our booth. A plump woman asked for his autograph.

"Buzz off, fatso, I don't do autographs."

The woman scurried away.

"God, I love being an outlaw." Willy Roy grinned. "These people need me to do their feeling. They love outlaws. I don't put up with any shit. I do and say what I want. I tell it like it is. I don't have to drink or get loaded near as much. I'm just mean and I feel wonderful." Willy beamed. "Wait until you hear my new rodeo song, 'Redneck Fuckers.' We're going to record it live at the National Finals Rodeo. Hell, I'll show those cowboys how to *really* be mean in public." Willy Roy's eyes sparkled.

The kitchen construction wasn't finished, so the food was catered, buffet style. Stormy Claridge left her camera crew and filled a plate with food. She sat with Farah, Willy Roy, and me.

"Boy oh boy." Stormy bent to her food. "We're gonna franchise this." Ezra had cut Stormy in on the Celebrity Bar & Grill.

"I think Swanson's already has the market." I chewed on the stringy steak and soggy French fries.

"Franchisin'," Stormy said. "That's how to make the money today. A small business can't make it anymore. You have to be a big corporation with federal government tax loopholes and lobbyists like Colonel Sanders and Ronald McDonald." Stormy talked excitedly while she ate. Food fell from her mouth to her plate, quickly making the return trip on her fork. She ate with the same steady rhythm with which LD Groover jacked off.

"The Colonel shore has himself one sweet deal." Stormy acted like she knew the colonel. "Take it from the Colonel," she sang out, spitting food particles onto the tablecloth. "Franchising is a good tax shelter," Stormy said. "I spent yesterday with my accountant. It took us all day to hide assets."

"I know what you mean, man," Willy Roy said. "You oughta not pay taxes. Some great outlaws were tax resisters."

Before Willy Roy went back to do the second show he handed me a brown paper bag. Inside was a 45 rpm record.

"If you could get Nit or Nat to give a listen they might add it to the play list. Ciao." Willy Roy headed backstage.

"It's eleven thirty," I said to Farah. "I've got to get over to the station."

"Don't worry about it." George Billings sat down at our table. "Stormy'll be taking over your show. You're going on celebrity special assignment to the National Finals up in Oklahoma City. You'll do *Redneck Rodeo Reports.* Try and get your picture in the papers with your buddy Luther Watt. I got you some new gauntlets and guns for your gang outfit. I deducted them from your check.

"*Stormy in the Morning.*" Billings accented each word. "Sounds great, doesn't it."

Stormy smiled.

The long slide down.

CHAPTER 4

IT WAS A BRIGHT SUNNY DECEMBER AFTERNOON AS I CROSSED the Canadian River and closed in on Oklahoma City. I checked into the Hilton Inn and then headed over to the State Fair Arena for the evening performance of the National Finals Rodeo.

The National Finals Rodeo is ten go-rounds between the fifteen top cowboy money winners in each of the five standard rodeo events: calf roping, team roping, bulldogging, saddle and bareback bronc riding, and bull riding. There is also women's barrel racing. Every contestant competes in each performance for the day money and a chance at the average for all ten go-rounds. After the final performance the world champions in each event will receive their buckles. Luther Watt is leading in the calf roping and bull riding and looks like he will take his second All-Around Cowboy title. He has won over sixty thousand dollars so far this year.

It is a grueling eight days, the top cowboys going up against the best stock. It is the finest and most exhausting rodeo in the world. It is only for champions. The pace would kill a lesser man. The thunder of horses' hooves and the yips and howls of exuberant cowboys started my adrenaline pumping as I walked up the dark tunnel toward the contestants' entrance, through swirling storms of light and dust. A gray mottled Appaloosa cantered by carrying a statuesque woman in pink sequined Western suit and jet black hair. A flagstaff was stuck in her stirrup and she gripped it tightly. The stars and stripes rippled and rattled over her pink cowboy hat and perfectly manicured face. Sparkling and mysterious in the dust-filled backlight of the tunnel, Miss Rodeo America was leading the grand entry. She disappeared down the tunnel toward the white glare of the arena.

I walked up to the contestants' entrance.

"You don't look like no contestant to *me*." The official spat a brown stream dangerously close to my blue Adidas.

"I'm supposed to meet Luther Watt." I choked in the dust the horses were stirring.

The official started at Luther's name. He folded his arms and looked me over carefully. "He said you might be a little strange looking. But my God, how's a man s'pose to know anymore?" He shook his head and waved me through.

I pushed past the guard and walked slowly through the crush of people in the contestants' area. I had trouble locating Luther: Brims were bigger this year and hid faces. I stepped over canvas bags, saddles, chaps, bareback gear and bull ropes. I threaded my way past cowboys rocking on the floor astride horseless saddles. The smell of horses, men, leather, analgesic, and stale beer hung in the hallway like a Corpus fog, I spotted Luther talking to the occupants of a sponsor's box. I caught his eye and then stepped back out into the concession area. It was a sea of cowboy hats and quilted coats.

I stepped to the drink stand and ordered two beers. The fans and contestants mingled in the concession area. The National Finals Rodeo was a personal spectacle.

Two bullfighters talked to a heavyset California cattleman, his wife, and their two kids. The bullfighters, purposely ridiculous in grease paint expressions, would soon be dodging and distracting raging Brahmas to give the riders room to escape the horns and hooves. Both men wore tattered clown's clothing and hats, and forty-dollar Adidas soccer shoes. The California family, all in Diamond-style American hats, looked like a matching set of condiment canisters.

"I suppose this is a fucking Falstaff." Luther Watt walked up, picked up his beer and took a long drink.

"Who were you talking to in the sponsor boxes?" I asked.

"They're interested in rodeo teams. You know, signing cowboys to contracts. They say it converts to television better that way." Luther took another long drink. "Say, you seen my ad in the program?" He looked around, finally borrowing a rodeo program from a woman in a towering platinum beehive and a rough-out leather Western-cut suit with three-inch fringe. He turned the pages to a four-color full-page insert featuring Luther seated in a ten-thousand-dollar Ryon's saddle astride his roping horse. Stormy Claridge stood next to the horse, stroking and kissing Luther's lizard boot. "In the saddle or just walking around, Top Hand Boots for the complete cowboy." Top Hand Boots is a wholly owned subsidiary of Everett Chemco.

Stormy looked like she was enjoying herself.

"It looks to me like Stormy's got herself a fetish," I said.

"In the saddle . . . weeoo." Luther shook his head and gulped his beer. "It took two days to shoot that shit in Dallas. George Billings was in charge. Jesus, what a time."

I thumbed through the program. Jace Everett's companies had taken several ads. Opposite one ad was an open letter from Mr. Jace saying that sports and competition make a stronger America. Jace used the words stronger and powerful several times. He mentioned the East Germans twice and warned about reliance on "undependable Arabs" for our energy and explained that through the use of fertilizer and pesticides nature is being taught to be more compassionate.

Jace also had a full-page ad announcing a Santa Gertrudis sale at the Adobe Ranch next week.

"Jace is really going to get big into sports," Luther said. "He wants to get the East Germans."

“He can have ’em. Maybe he can afford to keep them in hormone pills.”

I signaled the counterman for two more beers. “How you doin’ otherwise?”

“I feel so bad I have to lean against a gate pole to cuss.” Luther gulped down the last of his beer, slamming the paper cup to the counter. It made a tiny pop.

Luther’s high, angular cheekbones stretched his brown skin tight and accented the crow’s-feet that were slowly etching out from his eyes. The facial scars seemed by design rather than a random hoof, horn, or fist. The long white slash through his right eyebrow happened at Calgary. It took five Mounties to take him in that time.

Luther bowed his back and stretched his arms over his head to ease the tension. He shuddered and then shook his shoulders.

“Goddamn, I’m sore and I got a calf to rope.”

Luther Watt’s calf came out wild and cut back in front of his horse. Horse and rider went head over heels. It was the same way Leon Hasley and his horse were both killed.

Luther hurt his wrist but still rode in the bull riding. He went last because the doctor had to tape the left hand.

The crowd roared as his white-wrapped arm waved wildly in the dusty arena light. Then he missed his dismount and fell under the Brahma, getting his right foot stomped before the clowns got the bull off him. He only scored a 67 and finished out of the money.

“That was a lucky break out there.” I approached Luther back of the chutes as he was packing his rigging.

“Yeah.” Luther nodded, his lower lip pushed out and his teeth brown with snuff droolings. “I coulda got hit by a streetcar.” His breath was coming in short gasps.

Luther leaned against the concrete-block wall, pulled his Levi’s to his ankles, unwrapped his Ace bandages, and removed the paddings from his knees. Luther had early developed the theory that the best treatment for injuries was not to have them. He was constantly experimenting with special exercises, braces, and pads. It seemed sensible enough to me, but I wouldn't get on the back of a Brahma bull if you wrapped me in inner tubes. Other cowboys stood and sat around, packing up. The concrete floor was cold and damp. The cowboys were lighting up cigarettes and pinching snuff.

I squatted and helped Luther roll his elastic bandages and pack them away in a blue canvas bag. I am expert at rolling Ace bandages. Luther packed away his last gadget and helped me to my feet. My knees crackled and ground. Luther picked up his bag and walked stiffly to the exit.

Luther Watt hurled himself around the continental arena, flying and driving to as many rodeos as superhuman endurance, high-octane fuel, and long-distance telephone calls make possible. Last month Nadine had made him sell the Cessna after he took the top off a tree in East Texas. It hadn't slowed him down. Getting on as much stock as possible while desperately trying to maintain his bodily machine, Luther had gone to the limits. In the last three months Luther had made lots of money in his mad chase after the All-Around Cowboy buckle, but he had pushed too hard. It showed in his cautious, painful step. He had aged considerably since Baja. The last dash for the buckle had really taken it out of him. He never completely recovered.

We were halfway back to the hotel before Luther's breathing returned to normal. We went up to bulldogger Anson Cross's room for a drink and to watch the videotapes. Luther and Anson taped each other's performance, then reviewed the tapes after each go-round.

We watched Luther's accident, his bull ride, and Anson Cross's bulldogging, a 7.1 that took second money. Then we went downstairs to the Gusher Club.

The room was full of cowboys and their groupies—everything from parents to part-time sweethearts. Large quantities of shellacked hair. The crashing of the North Texas Thugs and the rattling of glasses punctuated the drone of conversation. Willy Roy Rogers wasn't on stage yet. The transparent dance floor was lighted, multicolored, from underneath. Men and women in quilted vests, flashy leathers, and Western suits drank, danced, discussed the progress of the Finals, or just hoorahed each other across the room. The equipment and technicians were all in place to record Willy Roy's first outlaw album, *Live at the NFR.* I couldn't wait to hear "Redneck Fuckers."

Nadine Watt appeared in the backlighted doorway. Her pretty face was drawn. She was wearing boot-cut pants, brown rough-outs, and a gray crew-neck sweater. Her dark hair was pulled back and tied with a brown ribbon between her shoulder blades. It was longer than I remembered. She scanned the room, finally sighting us in the dim light. She shoved her hands in her back pockets. A frown lined the corners of her mouth and her brown eyes looked tired. She walked slowly to the booth, her flared pants legs slapping against each other.

When she got to the table I started to rise. She motioned for me to sit and turned to Luther, who was looking in his lap.

"Luther, these guys are gonna have to jerk themselves off without you. I wanna talk to you now." Her voice was firm, monotonous and loud enough to hear over the band. She turned on her heel and walked out.

Luther betrayed no emotion as he watched her out to the elevators. He remained silent, sipping his drink, until the elevator gathered her up. Then he turned back.

His lips were a thin line. "Boys," he said, "that's the difference between a request and a command." He got up and strolled out, stopping only long enough to look at something he'd probed out of his teeth with a toothpick.

Willy Roy came strutting on stage with the same macho stride he had opened the show with at Ezra and LD's Celebrity Bar & Grill. When Willy Roy finished his opening gun/

love medley the crowd, already unruly, was beginning to get hostile. An Oklahoma City postperformance National Finals Rodeo crowd is different from your North Dallas opening night bunch. When Willy Roy snarled, they snarled back. Sometimes the audience would drown Willy Roy out. That drove the record-company people nuts. By the middle of the act, when Willy did "Redneck Fuckers," a musical insult to rodeo cowboys and their mothers, the place went up for grabs.

Five cowboys started for the stage, snapping open their Buck knives like castanets. They chased Willy Roy and the North Texas Thugs to their bus.

We went to Anson's room. Luther joined us. The scene was wild. Word of the party in Anson Cross's room had spread through the grapevine, and people filled the little eleventh-floor room when the Gusher Club closed and the fainthearted called it a night.

When Luther bloodied Roy Duncan's face it seemed to just give the party added impetus.

"Luther," Duncan had begun his complaint, "your goddamn wife cussin' you out this morning drove my whole family out of the coffee shop for the second time."

Luther stood a couple of inches taller than the stockier Duncan and got his shoulder behind the downward blow. The added weight of the Buck knife Luther had clenched in his fist split the bulldogger's cheek like a ripe plum. Duncan went down in a heap.

Duncan's two friends, another bulldogger and a stock contractor from Fort Worth, both started toward Luther. The click of Luther's knife blade locking open stopped them. They scooped up Duncan and left, vowing revenge.

Anson Cross held open the door and bowed, waving the men through with an empty Wild Turkey bottle. I stood behind Luther, my mouth hanging open. The other people were mumbling among themselves. A new momentum was added. Everyone seemed excited and the party surged on.

"Shit, that ain't nothin'," Anson laughed, looking at the reenergized crowd of cowboys and groupies. "Last year in Fort Worth Luther hit an old boy in the back of the head with a two by four and popped out his eyes. Jest like they was on stems." He put an index finger beneath each of his eyes and waggled them. Luther ignored the praise and jammed the knife into his Levi's pocket.

He pushed into the bathroom to get a beer from the two cases iced down in the bathtub.

Miss Rodeo America, in her black pigtails and pink sequins, was squatting on the commode, her mouth opened in shock.

"If you scream," Luther said quietly while digging for a beer, "I'll piss in your lap."

She remained soundless, her mouth open.

"You better not be shittin' in there," Anson yelled from the bed, where he was throwing his rope around last year's Miss Rodeo Oklahoma, one of a large number of beauty queens loose in the world. She had come with one of the bull riders. "I can't stand a woman that's gotta shit."

By four A.M. the party dissolved.

Anson ended with a local girl who grabbed him by the crotch and squealed, "I got mine."

Luther and Miss Rodeo America went to my room and I spent the night sleeping fitfully on the sofa outside the elevator.

The sleet was rattling against the window when I pushed open the door to my room and woke Luther. He still wore his hat and shirt. The shirt was open. Miss Rodeo America had ripped off the pearl buttons. She was asleep, her head on Luther's shoulder, her lips twisted and her jaw ajar. She drooled on his chest. It was still dark. The whole scene generally irritated the cowboy.

"Mornin'." I was cheerful. I sat in a chair by the window.

"Oh, hell," Luther moaned as he fingered the ripped shirt front. He hated to ruin his clothes. He gently manipulated his stomped ankle and wrist. They ached badly. His generally wrecked condition plus the dawning realization that he was not where good sense would have placed him made Luther's mood one of quiet anger. He was his own victim again. The next order of business was to extricate himself, quickly and blamelessly. He rolled out of bed and dumped Miss Rodeo America on the blue spread. She never murmured. While I watched Miss R. A. sleep, Luther showered and then shaved with my razor. Staring into the mirror, he worked up his rage at Nadine, contorting his lathered face as he reworked the imaginary argument, blaming her intransigence for forcing him to get drunk and not remember anything that happened after midnight. After several run-throughs he felt confident and began to relax, and soon considered the pending confrontation with Nadine as good as handled.

"My old man's gonna kill me." Miss Rodeo America was rubbing her eyes against the bathroom light.

"Husband?" Luther watched her in the mirror, a moustache of Foamy drooped around his lips.

"No, my daddy." She smiled a sleep smile. "He'll kick my ass."

"Sorry." Luther sliced the whiskers from his upper lip. "Can't blame your daddy, though." He smiled wide. "You called me daddy last night."

She gave him a blank look. "Did not."

It was getting light. Luther toweled his face and neck and limped past the rumpled Miss Rodeo America to the eleventh-floor window. Pulling the heavy blue drapes back, he stared out at the ice storm. The norther had dropped temperatures into the teens and Oklahoma City was covered with ice.

In the parking area the cowboys were attempting to get to the arena to care for their stock. Vapor billowed from idling automobiles as the cowboys scratched at inches of ice with various instruments. Anson Cross was scraping his stretch cab windshield with a short roweled spur. The local girl was asleep in the front seat.

At the fairgrounds Luther exercised his horse in the indoor practice arena behind the chutes. Other cowboys were working their horses. It was a cold morning. Horses and riders exhaled white clouds. Fresh piles of horse manure steamed.

Tonight was the last go-round and everybody was stiff and sore. This year's stock was considered the best ever assembled for a rodeo, and several cowboys were nursing severe injuries.

Miss Rodeo America was practicing her American flag carrying. Her face was wrinkled. She looked sleepily plain in Levi's and a powder-blue quilted jacket. Her long pigtails dangled from beneath her powder-blue hat. Tonight, in purple sequins with her legs clenched around that gray spotted Appaloosa and the flag gripped tightly in her hand, she would race with the spotlight around the darkened arena, a glittering, flashing, purple horseback Barbie doll and every man's Levi's would bulge uncomfortably during the national anthem.

Luther squirmed uncomfortably in his saddle as he watched the queen practice her ride.

"Goddamn." He stood up in his stirrups and clawed at his crotch, trying to seat himself more comfortably. He smiled as he watched the girl astride the gray spotted Appaloosa. "Goddamn." He broke into a broad smile and nudged his horse toward its stall. "If this ain't livin', I quit."

CHAPTER

I COULD HEAR LUTHER AND NADINE ARGUING WHEN I GOT off the elevator. I marveled at Nadine's rapierlike use of profanity.

"Who is it?" Luther yelled when I knocked.

"Your heroin dealer." The door snapped open and Luther yanked me inside.

"Christ, I ain't got enough troubles." Luther walked into the bathroom and drank a glass of water. He grimaced at the taste.

Nadine was sitting up in bed. "If you get to fuck anybody you want, I should too." Nadine was never shy in front of me.

"Choose me, choose me," I said.

"I don't fuck anybody I want to," Luther answered from the bathroom, where he was changing clothes. He frowned at himself in the mirror.

"Oh, yeah." Nadine's face was set. "Who'd you fuck last night?"

"What?" Luther was barefoot and wearing new starched Levi's. He stared at himself in the mirror, wishing he would disappear.

"You heard me, you bastard." Nadine began to cry, waiting for the answer.

"Uh." Luther opened his mouth slightly. "Jeannie Montague." It jumped out on its own and Luther braced himself.

The bedside lamp crashed into the bathroom wall. "You evil sonofabitch."

"I'm sorry, Nadine." Luther frowned as he returned from the bathroom and pulled on a clean starched shirt with snaps. "I just got drunk." Luther hadn't really gotten drunk, but he figured getting stepped on by a 1,500-pound bull was the same. It had made him feel funny, that was certain.

"Damn you, when you get a hard on, I want it. I ain't sharing you. I want a sex life too, you asshole." Nadine was in a nightshirt, sitting on the bed. Her eyes were red but she had stopped crying.

"Okay. Okay." Luther snapped up his shirt and tucked it in his pants. "We've sucked on these eggs long enough."

"I've got to go," I said, starting toward the door. "I'm doing a WBAR *Redneck Rodeo Report* on the fashion show."

"I'll see you down there." She frowned at me. "I'm in the goddamn thing."

"I'll see you after?" Luther looked at Nadine.

She almost cried, then nodded her head.

The Rodeo Wives Celebrity Fashion Show began quietly enough, with a turquoise-spangled, liver-spotted matron suggesting that everyone go ahead and eat their Jell-O since it was already there.

The luncheon crowd was almost all women. There were wives of cowboys and rodeo officials, a few local politicians, and a cowboy turned Congressman, but mostly the crowd was older women. The Anticline Dome room took on a gray-blue hue. The cowboy turned Congressman gave the invocation, praying for belly-deep grass and belly-up hippies, ending with thanks for the coming food and the already-consumed Jell-O. Then he lowered his manicured gray head and began to heave giant forkfuls of food into the maw that was his mouth. He never looked up from his food. His face hung about eight inches above the plate and a simple wrist action poked food between his jaws in perfect syncopation. He'd done a lot of luncheons.

Nadine Watt walked to the stage that was to serve for the fashion show. Her hair was pulled into loose dog ears that flowed from beneath her handmade patchwork blue denim cowboy hat. The matching patchwork denim Western jacket hugged her full breasts and the boot-cut pants outlined her firm butt and thighs.

"Ladies. Ladies." The spotted and spangled woman who had given the go-ahead on the Jell-O was now standing on the stage and clapping her hands. The dull roar of conversation and random clinking of silverware and glasses quieted. "Before we get started I'd like to introduce a very special guest, Miss Rodeo America, Jeannie Montague."

Miss Rodeo America's young body was encased in a full mink Western suit and her dark hair was crowned with a two-thousand-dollar mink hat. She stood onstage, statuesque in silver-inlaid boots and solid gold long-rowel spurs.

She thanked "Ah . . . everybody responsible for . . . ah . . . letting me win and . . . ah . . . thanks especially to the cowboys and . . . ah . . . my mom and my dad . . . even though he's mad at me. . . ." She laughed nervously and said, "I just *love* cowboys."

At that moment Nadine Watt stepped out from behind the rumpled red curtain and punched the grinning teenage rodeo queen square in the back of her mink hat.

Miss Rodeo America sailed off the stage and landed heavily on a ringside table. Nadine stepped off the stage and walked quickly but proudly out the door. Miss Rodeo America cried as she cleaned gobs of mashed potatoes and steam-table peas from her flowing dark hair.

Nadine was packing a bag when I knocked and entered. Luther was not there.

"Would you take me to the airport?" She was jamming her clothes into two leather bags open on the bed. I helped her close the bags.

She sat on the bed and cried softly, then stood and put her

arms around me. I kissed her gently on the forehead. She pushed away, smiled, and wiped her eyes.

Nadine sat down on the bed. "Luther and I have no life together. I won't share him forever. I'd rather be rid of him than go on like this. I didn't do all that work so he can run around with beauty queens and have Stormy Claridge stroke his boots. I deserve something. Hanna's going to be grown and gone in a few years. Then I'll be *all* alone." She stared at the wall. "He can't face the guilt of watching me grow old, seeing what the years with him have done. Damn him, I want a sex life too."

"I agree with you totally," I said, "especially about the sex life." I ran my fingertips under her paisley neckerchief, tickling the soft warm skin in the hollow of her throat.

"Don't do this, Mabry."

"Remember that day in your daddy's pickup at Lake Benbrook?" I asked. "You said the next time we'd do something even better. This is next time."

The pearl snaps on her silk Western shirt were as simple as the hand-tooled belt and the zipper of her slacks. The difficulty was with the handmade Lucchese boots with twelve-inch French leather uppers. But by then she was lying back with her eyes closed and didn't seem to care. When I took off my clothes she caressed me but kept her eyes closed.

She wrapped her legs around my hips and squeezed tightly when she reached her climax. She moaned deep. All I could think about was how rough and old her hands felt.

"I'm divorcing Luther." Nadine held her shirt to her breast. The skin of her neck was lined. Her breasts sagged. I'd never seen her without a bra. "I guess it's too late for us, isn't it?"

"It's too late for me," I said. "I'm an athlete, Nadine, just like Luther. When you do it long enough and hard enough, you break something. Emotions die and circuits burn out. Love and competition get all mixed up."

"What was this?" She indicated the rumpled bedclothes. "Just fucking?" Her voice rose.

I nodded. "Luther calls it a hot beef energy injection. I needed it. The pussy or the money, that's what it's all about and I'm on a comeback. Sorry."

"You weak sonofabitch." She slapped me hard across the face. "You're not as good as Luther." She pulled on her silk shirt, but left it unsnapped. "Athletes," she said, sneering at me. "You're all the same—as soon as you're on the road your dick gets hard."

"Well, Nadine," I said, "nobody likes to lose at home."

I took Nadine to the airport. We didn't speak. She cried all the way. It wasn't like I thought it would be. It's funny what you think.

I returned to my room and turned on the Dallas-Washington game. The score was tied, 17–17, and Summerall and Brookshier were babbling about "the game of the year . . . match of the titans."

My neck began to get stiff and sore. I stood on my head. It eased the pain and I watched the game upside down for a while.

I had a feeling when LD caught the Washington quarterback for a three-yard loss at the fifty and brought up a punting situation with one minute, thirty-five seconds left in the game. When it happened it made me feel weird and sort of guilty. Ezra Lyttle fielded the punt on the five.

On the fucking five! That's a hundred-dollar fine.

Ezra took two steps with that ball and Chris Hanburger took him off at the shoulders, knocking the ball thirty feet in the air. A Redskin picked it up and sauntered into the end zone. Those assholes at RFK went nuts. Washington was in the play-offs. Dallas was out. Not that it mattered to me.

That night at the final performance, Luther Watt won his second straight All-Around Cowboy title. He did it in style, taking a first in the calf roping and the bull riding. He looked great taking his victory lap. The crowd loved him.

At the Gusher Club Roy Duncan punched out Willy Roy Rogers before he was halfway through the opening lines of "Redneck Fuckers." Willy Roy was game and didn't want to stop, but his profusely bleeding nose ended production of *Willy Roy Rogers Live at the NFR.* So much for outlaw ambience.

Luther just drank steadily and around midnight slipped off to his room, where he was fellated by Miss Rodeo America while he watched the videotapes of his winning performances.

CHAPTER

THE EARLY MORNING SUN HAD PUSHED THE DALLAS SKYLINE shadows out over the Trinity flood plain. The air was cold. The sun was hot. I drove south on Stemmons Expressway along the river's west fork.

I left Luther drunk in Oklahoma City. The only time I have seen him more depressed was the time he carved up three Oklahoma cowboys and two Texas Rangers dragged him off his horse in the middle of a performance. Anson Cross had tried to bail him out with one thousand dollars but the Rangers said "for a thousand you don't even get to look at him." I had to fly in with a Fort Worth bondsman friend of Billy Bentson. That happened the last time he and Nadine split up.

I turned east on Oaklawn Avenue and wound my way into the notorious Oaklawn section. I like living there. They were my kind of queers, killers, whores, and junkies. I parked in the Lucky Duck's underground garage. There was a torn pair of pink panties lying beside a red splash on the concrete floor. The Grateful Rapist strikes again. I didn't stop to investigate. I was tired and irritable.

LD had his sign "Am working on tome—would appreciate any cooperation"—stuck on the door.

I pushed the door open anyway. LD was sitting at his desk reading his manuscript. The stereo earphones cupped his ears. Ezra Lyttle was sitting on the couch, his head in his hands.

LD looked up at me blankly. He seemed confused by my presence. He took off the earphones and set them on his desk.

Ezra looked up at me, his eyes red. He had been crying.

"You bastard," he sobbed. "Recognize these?" He held out the fake turquoise-studded gauntlets and cap gun I had lost at the Midland/Odessa Battle of the Celebrity Sexes Golf Tourney and Charity Telethon.

I nodded.

"You sonofabitch," Ezra cried. "You were supposed to be my friend." He threw the gauntlets and cap gun at me. "I can understand Hondo and LD, they can't help themselves, but you—" He lost his breath and sobbed. "You've ruined my life." He lunged toward me and hit me on the forehead with his fist. I stumbled backward and careened off the open door onto the floor.

LD walked over and looked down at me. He grabbed my feet and dragged me out into the hall.

"Damn, Mabry, you oughta be ashamed of yourself." He slammed the door.

I sat, stunned. The door behind me opened. Trey Everett stood sleepy-eyed in his NFL Celebrity pajamas. Sonny Jeeter's face was on the chest.

"What's all the racket?" He squinted down at me and rubbed at his eye. "You fall down?" He was a cute boy. He looked like his mother.

I nodded.

"Come on in, I'll fix us some coffee." The little boy padded barefoot back into the apartment still rubbing his eye. "Mom's still asleep."

Trey poured me a cup of coffee and went to his seat in front of the television. Trey made better coffee than his mother. He was watching the farm reporter talk to a brindle cow about "magnesium oxide for better butterfat production." Trey turned down the television.

"They waived LD, you know," he said. "Stormy Claridge had the story this morning on the radio."

"How can they waive him?" I asked, rubbing the sore spot on my forehead. "He's the whole right side of the defensive line."

Trey laughed. "What defensive line you been watching?" Trey fancied himself a football expert. "They've been trapping him all year. He's over the hill."

"Bullshit, he's doing that to protect the secondary," I said.

"Yeah, sure." Trey smirked. "You're the one that thinks the secondary's bad."

I heard a door slam and watched from the window as Ezra stormed across the courtyard. He was still crying.

I finished my coffee and walked back across the hall. LD was sitting with his feet up on his desk and his hand behind his head. The earphones were back in place and he was staring out the window at the mimosa on the far side of the pool.

"Thanks for the help," I said.

LD pulled off the earphones. "Nothing I could do. Stormy told him all about it—really taunted him with the cap gun. He's been here since we returned from Washington. Took some of my speed. If I hadn't dragged you into the hall he would have beat your dick flat. I'm sorry, Mabry, but I won't be around to help you out anymore. You're on your own—you've got to quit breaking down."

"People break down all the time."

"But they try and get out of the habit. You haven't got Sunday to make everything all right."

"What about you?" I said. "Sunday's just another day for you."

"It's always been that way for me. Listen, man, I have seen *real* crazy. When they scare you to death they make you a different person. I'm learning to like me and you'd better do the same. Nobody expected you to do better except you, and you're crazy. Willy Roy's right, we're all outlaws . . . grab the money and run." LD stood and looked out the window. "I hate it when I fail, but that's what it's all about." He scratched at his balls. "If things aren't bad enough, we lost our financing on the Celebrity Bar & Grill. Bankrupt and we haven't been open ten days. We went over budget on decorating by a cool $150,000. Lost our ass. Sure an expensive way to drink and watch pussy." LD stared down at the swimming pool. There was a Coors can sitting on the diving board.

"What with the bankruptcy, yesterday's fumble, and Stormy telling him about you and her at the golf tourney, Ezra's really depressed. Stormy told him no marriage until he straightened out his finances. He's taking it pretty hard. He says you've broken his heart."

"He believed her?"

LD nodded. "The gauntlets and cap gun added a certain authenticity. He woke Farah about four this morning and told her."

"Terrific." I slumped down on the couch. "I guess it won't do any good to tell them I didn't come."

"Maybe you oughta spend some time in the Coldspot."

That afternoon I went to the Northpark shopping center to get Farah a gift. I think I was trying to maintain our relationship. I'm not sure. Just inside the big department store a skinny guy with dirty hair came racing down the escalator and crashed into me. He was waving a big, ugly 9-m.m. Browning automatic. His eyes were red and terrified. He shoved the square barrel of the automatic at me.

I tried to scramble away from him, shuffling backward, afraid to take my eyes off the gun. The barrel looked the size of Wonder Cave. I stumbled and fell just as the gun bucked up with a roar. The slug hummed by my ear and blew the leg off a mannequin in an Edwardian suit. My head banged on the terrazzo floor. A security guard leaped from the escalator and knocked the crazy man to the floor. They fought for possession of the gun in front of a growing crowd of customers and floorwalkers—a junkie shoplifter and a one-hundred-dollar-a-week security guard.

"Do something," somebody said.

I crawled toward them on my hands and knees.

"Leave them alone. That's what he's paid for."

The cop wasn't too happy to hear that. The skinny man was on top and had the gun in his face, squeezing the trigger. The guard jammed his thumb between the hammer and the firing pin. I crawled up just as the guard wrenched the gun free. He handed it to me. There was a big chunk of bloody flesh stuck between the hammer and the firing pin.

The shoplifter quickly gave up as reinforcements arrived. The guard cuffed him quickly and they hustled him off.

I sat on the floor, still holding the gun.

"I'll take that." A man in a tailored suit was standing over me. His hair was gray at the temples. I handed him the gun. He held the shoplifter's loot: six pairs of Italian wraparound reflector sunglasses.

"Thanks." The man slipped the gun into his coat pocket. "In times like these it's gratifying when citizens get involved." He sounded like he had it written down.

I nodded. I was having difficulty breathing. I kept hearing a buzz in my ear. I stared at the floor and tried to get my breath.

"Let me help you." The man extended a hand and pulled me to my feet. "You're Mabry Jenkins, aren't you?"

I was still breathing hard. I nodded.

"Well, thanks again." The man inspected my clothes closely. "What happened to you? You just get too old to play football?" He walked away, his jacket whomperjawed from the weight of the big 9-m.m. automatic.

I never did get Farah anything.

I woke up frightened the next morning. The newspaper carried the story on the front page with the head:

EX-CORNERBACK STOPS END RUN . . . NABS GUNMAN

People may think that Mabry Jenkins is over the hill as a football player, but yesterday, before an appreciative holiday shopping crowd, the ex-gridder put in a stellar performance as

> a concerned citizen. When a drug-crazed shoplifter waving a loaded gun tried to escape pursuit by security guards, Jenkins, an ex-Dallas defensive back, executed a perfect flying tackle and disarmed the gunman.

The article went on to point out that I had been replaced by a younger and sturdier Bobbyday Burke but that I hadn't shown my age yesterday.

The phone rang. It was Stormy Claridge.

"Mabry. Mabry. How wonderful."

"What's wonderful, Stormy?"

"You're a hero. I read about it in the paper."

"Well, the paper didn't get it exactly right. I didn't tackle anybody. I got knocked down."

"But they said you helped get the gun. People could have been killed." Stormy was yelling. "How brave."

"I wasn't all that brave."

"I've got a crew with me right now. We're grabbing a mini-cam and coming over. I want an interview. It will get on the national news tonight."

"I'm not giving an interview, Stormy. The whole thing is out of proportion. I didn't do anything."

"The paper says . . ."

"The paper's wrong. The cop did everything. Go interview him."

"That's not news." Stormy's voice fell. "Come on, Mabry, as a favor to me."

"No, Stormy. I'm not going to be on television."

"Please. It means a lot to me."

"No, Stormy."

"Okay, asshole, just wait until you want another favor from me." She slammed the receiver down in my ear. The buzz sounded chillingly familiar.

The phone rang again. It was Hondo Higgins.

"Jace is interested in financing my porno musical," Hondo said.

"Oh, yeah," I said. "With Stormy blowing the motorcycle gang of crazed Vietnam vets to music?"

"Yeah, except the motorcycle gang is out. We changed it to a donkey. Gonna make it a political movie. Besides, everybody blows motorcycle gangs."

"You could say the same about donkeys."

"The SPCA is giving me some shit about using a real donkey and I need an extra $500,000 to construct a mechanical donkey. Have you seen Junior?"

"He's probably shooting his cannon at the Gun Club."

"That damn oil royalty check he gave me bounced. Tell him to call me. Ciao, guy." Hondo hung up.

I dressed and went to the recreation center. I humiliated a St. Mark's basketball coach in five straight games of one-on-one. After a long shower I went out to the Celebrity Bar & Grill. It was closed. A bankruptcy notice was nailed to the $15,000 handmade door. I stopped at the Sportspage.

They were showing football highlight films on the wall behind the bar. They were old films, including the shot of me knocking Paul Warfield out cold in the end zone at Texas Stadium. The guy on the screen just didn't look like me. He was too jaunty, too cocksure. He held himself too upright, walked too proud.

I watched myself strut off the field in the Philly game with the interception that sewed up the division title. I was holding the ball over my head with one hand while I held up one finger. Number one. Number one.

Titus Bean sat down next to me and pointed at the screen. "That guy is just waiting to get taken off at the knees. Can you give me a lift down to Turtle Creek? I have to meet Junior's boyfriend Stephano—he's got some information he wants to sell."

Shortly we were driving down Lemmon Avenue toward Turtle Creek.

"Did I tell you?" Titus said. "The Chemco poisoning was

no accident. It was part of a Defense Department antiterrorist program. Army Intelligence told Chemco to add PRP to shipments of livestock feed. They wanted to see how fast toxins would move through the food chain and if they would be picked up in routine gas chromatograph testing. They thought the levels were harmless."

Titus lit a cigarette. "Now they can't get it out of the food chain. It won't break down. PRP dust collected in the feed mills and cross-contaminated everything. It comes out in the animal shit, contaminates the pasture land, and is seeping into the ground water. They shipped some bags of PRP directly to farmers. Contaminated the fuck out of them and their families. That's where the dead babies are showing up. Also, the DEA sprayed the Mexican marijuana crop with Agent Blue and the PRP is absorbed right into the lung tissue. It's a pernicious compound. The cancer rate in this state will go out of sight in about ten years." Titus laughed. "I got my fucking Pulitzer now, if I live to collect it."

We turned off Lemmon onto Turtle Creek Boulevard.

"Did you know all this used to be a horse farm?" Titus watched the multistoried mansions roll by. There was a lot of money in the palaces that lined the bluffs along the gentle stream.

"There it is." Titus pointed across the creek to a granite turret that towered above the tree line. The house was obscured by trees that ran up from the creek to the top of the bluff. It was Jace Everett's house. I drove on to the next bridge, crossed to the other side, and headed back. Titus directed me past the main entrance to a smaller delivery entrance. The drive wound through several acres of manicured landscape, tennis courts, and swimming pools back to a small stone guest house. We pulled up, the door opened, and redheaded Stephano signaled.

"You better stay here," Titus said. "Stephano is a little edgy."

The thickly built journalist walked slowly up the walk and

into the house. The door closed. It started to rain. I turned on the radio and listened to WBAR, "The Country Place," the flagship station of Jace Everett's broadcasting empire. Cowboy Bob, the afternoon drive-time deejay, was jabbering, trying to give away $10,000 to the first person who would answer their telephone "WBAR All-American Music." Nobody did. He settled for giving away three Willie Nelson albums to the fourteenth person to call the station after the Jock Itch commercial.

A woman from Irving was caller number fourteen. She was overwhelmed.

"I'm caller number fourteen . . . I don't believe it . . . you're *kidding* me . . . oh, my God . . . *I'm* caller number fourteen . . ." I turned the radio off. The rain picked up and was hammering the car, making it impossible to see out the windows. I sank into the noise and made a mental note to call a scout I knew with the Toronto Argonauts.

The passenger door jerked open and Titus tumbled inside, soaking wet. His face was scratched and bleeding.

"Stephano is a petulant little devil," he said, touching his wounds with his fingertips. I gave him my handkerchief and drove us back out the winding drive.

"Amazing story." Titus began talking. "Stephano says Junior is in the importing business with Fernando and Raul, the Cuban narco traficantes. They use the *Gorilla Woman* and Jace's planes to haul cocaine from Mexico. They make their connections with a fella in Baja who smokes cigarettes through a hole in his throat."

"I know the gentleman."

"Stephano traces the Cubans all the way back to the Bay of Pigs," Titus went on. "He says now they're connected to the Mafia in Miami." He continued, "Stephano claims he and Lee Harvey Oswald were lovers and he'll sell me Oswald's diary for fifty thousand dollars. He wants to get out of town. Says Junior swindled everybody. He's desperate for money."

"It's funny I never heard this before," I said.

"Where do you get your news?" Titus sneered. "Television? You better remember, when they give somebody two hundred thousand dollars a year to read you the news, you can be damn certain whatever you're getting, it isn't the news. I mean the real news." Titus stubbed out his cigarette on the sole of his shoe. "The real news makes sense."

"You calling Walter Cronkite a liar?"

Titus laughed.

"Oh, come on," I said. "Is this how you research all your stories? It's insane that one redheaded weirdo hairdresser faggot could have history's most important pieces of information." I laughed and shook my head.

"Listen, man." Titus looked at me full face. "This is a very small town."

"I may find out more tomorrow. I'm supposed to meet Jace out at the Adobe."

I dropped Titus off at Mother Blues. The marquee read:

Willy Roy Rogers and the Blackland Farmers
Together Again

☆ ☆

COME DRINK WATCH WILLY ROY FEEL BAD

☆ ☆

$3.00 cover

NO SHOES
NO SHIRT
NO SERVICE

"I got my shot at the Dinah Show." Titus laughed and stepped out in the parking lot.

As he walked off I could hear the Blackland Farmers singing the opening strains of M. D. Shafter's "Reality So Long":

I felt the watchman's nightstick go sticky on my mind . . .

CHAPTER

THE NEXT DAY I HEADED OUT TO JACE EVERETT'S ADOBE Ranch for the Celebrity Charity Santa Gertrudis Sale & BBQ. This year John Connally was to be the Celebrity Auctioneer.

As I was leaving my apartment a tall fellow met me at the door. He showed me his identification. He was Mr. Green from American Express. He took my American Express card, ripped it up, and tossed the pieces at my feet.

The front lawn of the Adobe main house was speckled with pink and white Neiman-Marcus caterer's tents. I steered my car up to the drive and turned it over to a black man in an orange coat. There were swarms of them parking cars.

A helicopter swept low over the house to land on the tennis court, interrupting a game of mixed doubles. Several planes circled like bright-colored buzzards, waiting their turns at the airstrip. Taxiing up the runway was a DC-3 with a picture window on the side.

In the first tent I found Junior Everett talking to Barbara Walters, who was there to be "up close and personal" with John Connally.

"Barbara, honey, we still got a fifteen-thousand-dollar position open on this particular well." Junior's forehead was perspiring. "Hell, you can't lose." He was showing her photographs of drilling rigs and storage tanks.

Barbara's face kept twisting into alternate scowls and smiles. She seemed to have no control over her facial muscles.

"There's no risk here, Barbara darlin'." Junior was insistent. "Hell, I have some gas leases out in the San Juan field in New Mexico just waiting for deregulation. We call them ignored reserves. This Eastland County well is gonna hit, believe me, there's producing wells all around it, you should see the sand samples. But if it doesn't hit I'll give you a position in this San Juan lease and you'll get your money back as soon as they deregulate."

Barbara smiled, then frowned.

Junior smiled. "Well, think about it, honey. Hondo Higgins and Walter Cronkite are in on this well." He clapped her on the back and strode off.

Barbara turned to me. "Have you seen Governor Connally?"

I shook my head.

She unfolded a sheet of paper and stared at it. "He must be here somewhere, he's on my itinerary. I've got a crew coming. Where's the Mexican food tent?"

I pointed off toward the corral. She staggered the first few steps as she left.

The Santa Gertrudis sale wasn't scheduled until evening. I watched the pigeon shoot for a while and then wandered into the bunkhouse, where a television was turned on to *Network Newsbreak.* The network newsman had a map of Dallas projected behind him, with several red *X*'s clustered in the north side of town.

"Ezra Lyttle was seen earlier in the day at the Lucky Duck Apartments and later leaving the scene of the crime." The newsman read his script like he knew what he was saying. "Stormy Claridge in Dallas has the story . . ."

Cut to Stormy Claridge standing in front of an expensive two-story Highland Park white frame house.

"It was on this very spot yesterday afternoon that little Wendy Brown came outside to play with her new Sonny and Cher dolls"—Stormy held up little Wendy's Sonny and Cher dolls—"when a bright red convertible passed by and went to the end of the block." Stormy pointed up the street and the camera panned to a cul-de-sac. "The car returned and stopped in front of little Wendy's house." The camera panned to the curbside. A large *X* was chalked on the pavement. "And then what happened, little Wendy?" Stormy bent and the camera panned down to little Wendy Brown, anxious and freshly scrubbed.

"Well, I saw the red car stop right there." Wendy pointed and the camera panned back to the chalk *X*. "The man inside the car said he would trade me my Sonny doll for a Greg Allman doll. I never seen a Greg Allman doll, so I went over to the car and looked in."

Little Wendy paused.

"Yes, little Wendy," Stormy prodded. "Go on, tell all the people in television land what happened then."

"Well, he didn't have no Greg Allman doll at all." Little Wendy paused again.

"Well, what did he have, little Wendy?" Stormy was insistent. "What was it he did?"

"Nothing."

"He didn't do nothing, I mean anything, little Wendy?" Stormy was getting angry. "We *know* he did something. What did he do?"

"Nothing."

"Little Wendy"—Stormy grabbed little Wendy's arm—"if the man didn't do nothing we wouldn't be here with the television cameras and I wouldn't be asking you these questions." Stormy pointed into the lens. "You're on national news, Wendy."

Little Wendy snarled, "I think you are a Commie."

"I'm not a Commie, little Wendy, I was in the Miss Texas Pageant. Now what did that man do?"

"He didn't do nothing. He just didn't have no clothes on."

"There you have it, folks." Stormy stood and began wrapping up. "Reporting from the scene, this is Stormy Claridge." She smiled and held it, waiting for the cut. Stormy finally got national exposure, if you'll excuse the expression.

"Is there such a thing as a Greg Allman doll?" little Wendy asked. Stormy held her stiff smile. The technicians finally cut to the network newsman sitting in front of a huge picture of Ezra Lyttle. "Police arrested Lyttle at his home." They cut to film of Ezra being led into the police station. He smiled and waved. They showed him being fingerprinted and then being led down several different hallways with newsmen scurrying around and two fat plainclothes officers frowning and pushing people back to make room.

". . . late this afternoon Lyttle's bail was posted by his teammate LD Groover."

The film shown was shot over LD's shoulder through the bars, showing Ezra being led out. The barred door slid back. LD hugged Ezra, then led the way out, stopping only to punch a reporter from the *Morning News.* It was a short chopping blow that knocked the man to one knee. The last clip showed the two teammates, pursued by reporters, getting into LD's car and driving off.

Walking back toward the main house, I met Titus.

"They busted Ezra for running around naked," I said. "I just saw it on television."

"That's too bad." Titus seemed preoccupied.

"There'll be a lot of jokes about fly routes and exhibition season, I guess."

Titus nodded. He was lost in thought.

"What's the matter with you?" I asked.

"My publisher fired me last night." Titus frowned. "He says my sources aren't reliable." Titus looked toward the ranch house. "And Jace just offered me $25,000 to finish the screenplay for Hondo's porno musical." He scratched his head. "I'm taking it. Hollywood is perfect. I need a sense of outrage. It's a chance to make some money and I could have a real impact, get with the people that run things." Titus ran a hand across his face. "I'm tired of being everybody's favorite asshole."

Titus was *my* favorite asshole.

I left Titus and walked to the building where Jace kept his breeding heifers. Farah was outside.

"You bastard." She glared at me. "You just had to fuck her, didn't you?"

I wasn't sure who she meant. I kept silent.

"All I asked was that you be dependable, but you had to try and be *successful.*" She made a face like the word tasted bad. "A perpetual erection on a perpetual comeback. It's all competition to you. I was Junior's wife and Jace's daughter-in-law—that's what you want. Drove your buddy Ezra right off the deep end. You're dangerous." She looked around the ranch-house grounds at the pink-striped tents and the rich and famous guests. "You really don't ever let down, do you?"

"I told you when we first met," I said. "I'm in the game and ain't going out without a fight."

"You and Billy Bentson and Titus, a perfect threesome. A professional athlete, a petty hoodlum, and a guy who writes words for money. Looking for marks, looking for people you can use. You steal from people's lives and then stand around with your hands in your pockets."

I took my hands out of my pockets.

"You're just pathetic." She walked off toward the main ranch house.

Mr. Pathetic gets the kiss-off.

Inside the building Jace was standing by a workbench.

"Come look at this." Jace showed me a pair of praying mantises, dropping the male into the jar with the female. The male immediately began trying to mate. The female gnawed out his eye, then chewed off his head. The male kept trying to mate. She ate his legs, then stopped to rest, voluntarily spreading her parts. The union took place. Then she ate the rest of him. Jace put the jar back on the shelf.

"You notice she stopped long enough to mate with the leftovers," Jace said. "Aggression and sex—very dangerous things to get confused."

I nodded.

"I'm firing you from WBAR," Jace said, leading me into the stall area. "George says you stink and Farah doesn't want you around anymore."

George Billings was waiting in the stall area. His color was bad and he had a tooth missing. A Santa Gertrudis heifer was penned in the working stall. Jace donned a plastic glove that covered his arm to the shoulder. Billings held a syringe. The heifer looked nervous. Billings looked nervous.

"Tell me, Mabry"—Jace flexed his fingers in the plastic glove—"what did you major in at college?"

It seemed like a funny question.

"Communication Arts. I got a B.A." Until now that had never seemed like a funny answer.

Jace pursed his lips and stared at the cow's ass.

"I think you have great potential." Jace lifted up the tail and plunged his arm up to the elbow into the cow's cunt. The heifer looked around at Jace. He began a slow fucking motion.

"How would you like to coach racquetball in South America? It's a country-club sport down there. I've got contacts that will set you up. You'll be coaching the next Latin American national heroes." Jace increased the speed of his thrusting arm. "They want to build an Olympic contender. Show those South American Communists how to play." Jace continued thrusting at the cow. He was getting winded. "We're also starting a South American sports-television network and you'd be in on the ground floor."

For a time we said nothing as Jace concentrated on fucking the cow with his arm.

"This is what it's all about," Jace panted, nodding toward the ass end of the pedigreed cow. "The next generation, ensuring its quality, keeping the bloodline pure. Reproduction is more than just fucking." For a moment the only noise was Jace's labored breathing and the wet suction sound.

"Farah's real upset by your behavior," Jace said.

I didn't ask what behavior.

"Hell, I like you." He increased his arm fucking. "Look at all the things I've done for you." He was really pouring it to the cow. "I have confidence in you as a winner, but without football you've become superfluous and can't cope with civilized life." There was no malice in his voice. "I don't want you to think that's a put-down. It's just advice. When I see somebody lost, the first thing I tell them is exactly where they are. It helps calm their panic." He was up to his armpit in cow cunt. "You have to quit worrying that you aren't getting your share. Fucking other people's wives and girl friends, it's very distasteful." He waved his free hand over his head. "This little darlin's ready, George."

Billings held out the syringe. His hand shook noticeably.

Jace shoved his full arm into the cow cunt. "Athletes are savages." He fixed me with a gray-eyed stare. "Savage technicians."

I knew exactly what he meant.

EPILOGUE

BACK IN THE SADDLE AGAIN

Whiskey and pain both taste the same
during the time they go down . . .

I DON'T KNOW WHAT IT IS THAT WAKES ME AT THIS TIME every summer morning, but I've been doing it since I was a rookie. That's ten years of summers waking just before Dobie Rank makes his rounds. The first thing I see is the white plaster ceiling (I sleep on my back with my legs elevated—my right knee still swells sometimes). Then I hear the distinctive squeak of Dobie's crepe-soled Riddell trainer's shoes. I always wake before the squeaks. I don't know why. And I always wake up completely, my mind alert and functioning. It's a good feeling. I land conscious, on my toes. It's the same kind of concentration that keeps me conscious when I take a good blow. Concentration keeps me intact. I believe in the psychology of the victim. You make your breaks.

I lie in bed staring at the white plaster ceiling and listen to Dobie move down the hall on his wake-up circuit. This year Dobie has to make sure all the coaches are awake before he wakes up the players. If I were a coach I'd want to be awake first, but I never really wanted to be a coach.

It's hard to believe I have been doing this for ten years. Sleeping in the same dormitory bed, staring at the same white ceiling, listening to the same Oxnard and Port Hueneme weather forecasts. It's the sameness that I like. It's a good fantasy. Outside, I find life hard—nothing is ever resolved, and everybody's paranoid from watching each other on television. We all get too much feedback on life.

After the Washington game Buck Binder had been quoted as wanting more old guys on his team. Buck was an old guy. He called me about coming back in March. The club released Ezra for showing Little Wendy his Greg Allman doll and right after the season Bobbyday Burke strained his knee in the Superstars competition. Buck was short on secondary experience.

During team meetings Buck doesn't like to turn his back on us to write on the blackboard. Yesterday Bobbyday Burke coughed and Buck spun around in a crouch, holding his chalk like it was a knife. He thought we were coming right over the chairs after him. Buck is finally as paranoid as me. He needs a Super Bowl bad.

Beecher is my new roommate. Old "root hog or die" from the University of Michigan is still living up in the Bitterroot Mountains in the off-season. They moved him to defense and he's done a good job replacing LD. He's always showing me pictures of his kids. "Now that's power, man," he says. "I mean real immortality, my little bit of eternity."

I've never seen him jack off.

LD got his knee blown away the first day of two-a-days with the Saints. They signed him in the off-season.

"I was looking for a job when I found this one," LD told me over the phone. I knew what he meant.

LD's book *The God Squad* didn't do as well as expected, but it helped him out of the hole dug by the Celebrity Bar & Grill. At the Celebrity Bar & Grill bankruptcy hearing Junior was unable to account for $150,000 in the decorating budget. Billy Bentson got most of it across the gin table. LD's working on his second book, *The Celebrity War*. He calls it "a rollicking look at white phosphorus, antipersonnel mines, and free-fire zones." I read the first chapter. It isn't that funny; besides, public interest in Vietnam ended as soon as the last man was off the Saigon Embassy roof. Hondo's got a survey that shows it.

LD captured the "Grateful Rapist." It was funny how it happened. LD was jacking off in his Coldspot with the door open when he noticed a guy in an Air Force uniform walk into the Lucky Duck underground garage. It was two A.M. LD finished up quick and went down to investigate. The guy had a Delta stewardess up against a new Toronado. LD grabbed him. He was a full chicken colonel and he turned out to be George Billings. LD didn't recognize him right off because George was almost bald and had lost several of his teeth. Eating PRP during the telethon damn near killed him.

The judge gave George two-to-ten in Huntsville as "a warning to other people like you out there." Astronauts gone bad, I guess.

Right now Billings is trying to get into a work-release program to help with California's space program. The coast is the most.

Smoking Jim still hasn't got his grievance settled. The club leaked the rumor that he had become a junkie. Last week he was busted for grass. He lost his house, his wife left him, and his lawyer has filed suit against him for fees and reasonable expenses. Smoking Jim called out here last night. I told him I couldn't get involved.

"Hey, man," he said, "don't worry about me, I'm coming back." His tongue seemed a little thick.

Ezra came by just before I left for camp. He still spends half his time coming and the other half going. He's trying to connect with the 49ers. I told him I'd call a scout I know with Atlanta. The guy owes me a call. Ezra told me that if he could have survived his friends and loved ones he could have been an all-time great defensive back. I doubted that. Guys always think they are better than they are.

Stormy finally got her own line of cosmetics and a spot on *Good Morning America*. She and Luther Watt are dating.

Luther's ahead for the All-Around Buckle again, but he's having hard luck. Last month, rushing to Frontier Days, he had his truck up to 100 on the flat and when he pulled into Cheyenne his trailer gate was swinging open. Somewhere between Denver and Cheyenne his horse had fallen out. But, Luther's doing lots of television work and has his own line of Western clothes. He may be the great American athlete. He and Jace probably can get the East Germans.

Nadine Watt moved to Fort Worth and is dating Dub Brown, her old sprinter from Paschal. He's a beer distributor now and Nadine helps Dub do the books on the distributorship. She says she and Dub were lucky to find one another again and she and Luther were lucky they had the time they did.

I don't know if Nadine ever told Luther about us at Oklahoma City. I'm not going to say anything. As Ezra will tell you, there's a big difference between being found out and exposing yourself.

Hondo's porno musical died. They invested $500,000 in the mechanical donkey, but couldn't perfect the ejaculation mechanism.

Titus never did get Oswald's diary from Stephano, but he's chasing a rumor about a dead Secret Service agent in Kennedy's limo at Parkland Hospital. Now the FBI hangs around all the time and the IRS audited Titus's last seven years' returns, disallowing all the medical deductions he took while his wife was being squeezed to death.

The H.E.W. Secretary's law firm is defending Everett Chemco in the $100-million lawsuit for poisoning everybody in Texas. They say the cancer rate is going out of sight in ten years. I'm not going to worry about it myself. Thinking your food is poison is paranoid.

Jace and his lawyers had a big strategy meeting in Baja last spring. It was in all the papers, along with the story about Junior and Stephano.

Celebrity Swindler Dead

Dallas—The FBI today announced the breakup of a nationwide confidence scheme based on the sale of worthless oil and gas leases involving the son of a prominent Dallas oil man. Jason Everett Junior and his roommate Stephano Valentine were found dead this morning at their home by FBI agents.

In a classic Ponzi-style swindle (paying early investors with later investors' money) Everett is reported to have skimmed over two million dollars from such notables as Stormy Claridge and Hondo Higgins. None of the money has been recovered.

Valentine, a Dallas hairdresser and onetime intimate of Lee Harvey Oswald, recently appeared before the House Select Committee on Assassinations. "The deaths are not related to the Committee testimony," an FBI spokesman said. "It's just your typical homo murder-suicide."

The two men were killed by a single blast of roofing nails from a two-pound ship's cannon.

Junior finally made his big score. I wonder if Jace is proud of him. Probably not. It's not successful to be dead. It's a sign of evolutionary weakness.

That same week the *Gorilla Woman* disappeared mysteriously between New Orleans and Yucatan with Fernando and Raul aboard.

I turned down Jace's offer to coach Olympic Racquetball in South America. Jace denied that it was a CIA operation, but I figured if we lost I'd get my cock plugged into a wall socket. *That's* the big sport down there.

Farah moved out to the Adobe with Jace. It turns out that they knew each other at the World's Fair. They met the same day Sonny Jeeter lost his shoe and wristwatch in the Log Flume Ride. Jace was considering investing in the Texas Pavilion and Farah served him a corny dog and a Dr. Pepper. They ended up in his suite at the Sherry-Netherland. Farah explained the whole thing to me after Junior got killed. She said Trey was Jace's son.

She always said it was power she was after.

The Adobe now has a complete complement of fences and guard dogs. Jace is worried about kidnapping. I visit a lot. Trey and I are good friends. I asked Farah about her dream of Jace keeping Trey in a cage.

"There are ways to enjoy the cage," she said. "The real freedom is in keeping quiet and watching it all go by. It's the real power."

Before I left for camp I suggested we get together. "I'm a doer, not a watcher," I said. "High performance. I told you I'd come back."

Farah just laughed. "You're still crazy," she said, "and will shortly end up in a real cage, that house trailer on the Blanco River."

I'm not worried. I've come back. She'll come around.

Dr. Friedman stopped by the room yesterday to say hello.

"You sure fooled me," Friedman said. "I sure didn't think you'd be back. You're one hell of a ballplayer."

Everybody thinks he's a football expert.

"Jenkins, Beecher, get up." Dobie Rank, the trainer, banged open our door. "Breakfast at seven. The taping schedule is posted." He left the door open and went on to Alex Hart and Sonny Jeeter's room.

The sounds of the dormitory coming awake are comforting. I have grown used to this particular fantasy and enjoy the men I share it with. Once you're back it's like you were never gone.

Today is the last day of two-a-days. I am stiff and sore, but my knee is hardly swelling. I seem to have more headaches now, but Dr. Badd says not to worry. It's just a pinched nerve or something.

"We'll get a few more years out of that old body," he said.

I have learned about living with pain. Buck's wrong about not minding that it hurts. It has to matter. The successful competitor *becomes* his pain.

Life is a contact sport and I've got a team to make. Discipline, confidence, and imagination—that's all a man needs. Just don't let down. The old killer instinct.

There will be cuts today, but I'm not worried—I'm having my best camp ever.